DRAGON MYTHICANA

DRAGON MYTHICANA

EDITED BY
A. BALSAMO

Inkd
Publishing

CONTENTS

INTRODUCTION

There are few creatures that touch the imagination the way dragons do. I have always been fascinated by them. I am excited to present this anthology of curated stories to you which represent many types of dragons in all kinds of situations. I hope you enjoy reading them as much as I did selecting them.

A. Balsamo studied Communications, English, and Business, graduating college in 1984. Her editing journey started in the public affairs department of a major market radio station in Miami. She has been editing the spoken word in the legal arena since 1985. Currently she does freelance editing and proofreading with a focus on the genres of fantasy, horror, memoir/nonfiction. In addition to freelance work, she is a staff editor for Inkd Pub working on various anthologies. In her spare time she enjoys pursuing various artistic endeavors and playing with her cats.

You can reach A. Balsamo at ABalsamo@inkdpub.com.

PREFACE

Inkd Publishing provides an inclusive space where creatives can explore short stories and where readers can pause their busy lives to delve into a fantastical tale.

Feel free to join our newsletter to keep up to date at InkdPub.com

SIR PERCIEVAL AND THE DRAGON

MICHAEL ALLEN ROSE

Sir Percieval's muscles burned. His heroic efforts to ascend the sheer cliff face had turned to ashes in his mouth. When he'd tried to climb it, he'd only gotten a quarter of the way up before having to turn around and go back to the bottom. He was only one knight, and though the spirit was willing, the flesh was susceptible to fatigue.

Despite his expertise in scaling such obstacles, turning around had been a terrible ordeal. The cliff was devoid of any natural holds, and so he'd had to make his own indentations into its face, using only his weapons. He inspected his blades and shook his head. When he began the hunt, they were razor-sharp and strong, now the edges were duller than he'd like. Sir Percieval took pride in keeping all his equipment clean and polished, and it mortified him to wield such shoddy weapons. Hopefully, the creature up above would fall before their assault, regardless. The monster's presence would be suffered no longer.

As Sir Percieval gazed up at the heavens, he spied

movement at the very top of the cliff. A low growl left his throat as he stared skyward, and he watched as the dragon once again took flight. Its wings beat as it turned spirals far above, mocking the knight.

"Beast, enjoy your time in the sky while you may. You shall not live to see another day, I swear it."

Sir Percieval had come to this realm when he was very young. In those days, he thought little about the monsters that roamed the land, content to play childish games, kicking a ball around, or play fighting to hone his skills for adulthood. He needed not concern himself with the dangers of the world, for they rarely touched his sphere, or if they did, he did not see them. As far as young Sir Percieval was concerned, the monsters may well have been invisible.

Over time, he had grown to love this place, and its inhabitants. The people who lived here were good, and generous. They had provided him soft beds to sleep in, shared many feasts with him, and often showed him great affection. The least he could do was to keep them safe from invaders. And slowly, as he grew older, he realized that the realm's edges were not impenetrable. Creatures from forgotten lands would creep in, find cracks in the walls, slipping in under cover of darkness, stealing food, spreading filth and disease. Sir Percieval would have none of it. He had sworn an oath to protect these people, no matter what.

The dragon had arrived only recently, and was unwelcome here.

It first appeared only the day before, but to Sir Percieval, it felt like ages. Time moved strangely for him, seeming to stretch and constrict all around him. He could barely remember the time before he had come here, and yet sometimes the days felt eternal. He would go for hours without seeing another living soul, and wondered in the most hidden parts of his mind, whether they would ever return, or whether he had become the only living soul in the world, doomed to everlasting loneliness.

When he first spied it in the distance, it seemed like a trick of the light. The vile creature had moved so fast, and ascended as it arrived, silhouetted against the light beaming down from the sky. Sir Percieval had never seen such a monster. Two large gray wings flapped to carry its spiny body forward. Spikes stood out from its head, and their giant, domed eyes shone blackly down, surveying these new hunting grounds. It soared skyward, circling around the brightest point above, making it impossible to watch for long. This was surely a beast born of fire, and in its quest to return to where it came, it would burn the realm.

It had been in motion almost constantly, flying around the area, raiding food stores, spreading its plague. Sir Percieval shuddered at the thought of the monster breeding. What would become of the realm if a whole flock of these dragons rampaged through it unchecked? He could not allow that to happen, under any circumstances. The beast would wait. Now was the time for training.

LUCKILY, here at the foot of the cliff, he had made camp, with adequate food supplies and training equipment to last him some time.

"I wonder what the lifespan of that thing might be?" he thought to himself, as he prepared for his exercise. He owned a large, stuffed beast, which he would joust at and grapple with, to hone his combat skills. It sat silently on the ground before him. Sometimes, he would talk to it when nobody else was around, a subtle indicator of his solitude. He let loose a war cry and leaped upon the practice dummy, throwing it down to the ground, then coming up underneath with an uppercut, sending it flying through the air. Sometimes, it almost seemed alive. He drew his daggers and advanced on his opponent, thrusting and pivoting here and there, slicing it from head to guts in what would have been a death blow for any mortal, living being. "Well fought, my friend," Sir Percieval cried out. If he could sharpen his skills, these tactics would surely fell the flying monster above.

For a moment, he pretended to be unaware of the training dummy, focusing on his breathing. Caught unaware by a surprise attack, Sir Percival would have to be ready to fight from a position of disadvantage. With a howl of fury, he leaped up and back, twisting his body as he did so, landing beside his target and raking across it with his weapons. The figure flew upward, and Percival met it with a mighty blow that sent it skittering across camp and into his sleeping quarters.

It was time. He was ready.

VERY SOON AFTER, Sir Percieval sat at the foot of the cliff, staring upward. A flicker far above told him his target awaited him. He crouched, and then, with agility befitting only a true knight of the realm, leaped upward, sinking his blades into the soft climbing surface. For a moment, he felt as though one of his holds was about to give, nearly tearing away under his assault, but then, steadying himself, he carried on.

He was nearly a quarter of the way up when the sound of a mad scrambling dash from below broke the stillness. Before Sir Percival could turn his head, he felt something sharp sink into his hindquarters from below, a terrible hooked blade. Treachery. He knew who had attacked him even before the voice that followed bubbled up.

"Ha ha! I've got you, now, Percival! Surrender, or I shall pull you down." Mordred. Of course. He had not seen his brother in some time, but Sir Percival knew that Mordred was always just out of sight, waiting for his chance to strike. Sir Percival felt himself slip, and wriggled to free himself, but Mordred's grip was too tight.

"Let me go, Mordred!" howled the knight, kicking his legs, trying to put some distance between himself and his brother.

"You left yourself open to attack, brother. A foolish error." Mordred screeched from below.

Sir Percival turned to look at his brother. Mordred looked so much like himself, it was uncanny. The same orange hair, the same complexion, he even wore his whiskers in the same rakish manner. But, his smell was different. And of course, there was the black spot over Mordred's left eye, a mark from birth. Sir Percival had always thought that mark was an omen, and in moments like this, it was hard to deny.

The next moments seemed to happen in slow motion. Percival scrambled upward with an unnatural burst of speed and strength. Mordred followed, trying to catch his brother, but only succeeded in batting at the brave knight above him, annoyed. The dragon took flight and began to dive down across the edge of the cliff. Percieval watched, the image of the beast growing larger in his dark, widening eyes. The knight's teeth began to chatter, and he felt a rush of adrenaline, as he readied his blade, holding fast with three of his limbs. The dragon was coming, flapping his mighty wings, and peering deeply into his opponent's soul. This was to be the moment where the knight would take his shot. As the creature descended, Sir Percieval tensed, his blades fully deployed.

He could not think about the betrayal of Mordred, not now, not when his objective was this close. The moment was nigh, and here came the beast, gliding down along the surface, nearly face-to-face with Sir Percieval now, as he swung with all his might.

Before he could make impact, just moments before the killing blow might have found its mark, he felt his brother's blades once again, only somehow, Mordred had overtaken him. His brother's arms wrapped around his hips, and he felt his brother's hot breath upon his back. "You think the game over, but it has only begun, dear brother."

Percieval felt his brother's weight, as Mordred kicked free of the climbing surface. He tried to hold on, but their combined weight pulled his weapons out and then, suddenly, they were falling. Like two dancers, the pair swung their bodies together in midair, growling, spittle flying. Gravity took over and the ground was coming up fast.

"You fool!" cried Sir Percieval, "I almost had it! This was to be my moment of triumph!"

"You were too easy a target, brother!" Mordred cried back, as they continued to plummet. Just before landing, both warriors twisted their bodies, like acrobats, into landing position. They hit the ground and bent lithe limbs to minimize their impacts, then pulled themselves up to full height, staring each other down.

Percieval did a quick mental check of his condition. Despite the danger, only his pride had been wounded. The creature above, now far away once again, was probably laughing at his failure.

Mordred circled Sir Percieval, a playful gleam in his eye. "You see? Now, we must fight. There can be only one winner, brother, in our eternal struggle, and I shall be victorious this day."

"Like hell you will," said Sir Percieval, as he leaped toward his opponent and crashed into him, sending both tumbling in a tangle of limbs.

EVERYWHERE AROUND THEM, suddenly, footsteps. Gigantic and definitive. Neither could look to see what caused the cacophony, however. The two knights stared at each other, trying to make themselves look as large and intimidating as possible. Being distracted now would lead to a bad outcome for the first one to look away. Even as the thunderous steps approached, they could not take their eyes from one another.

"Percy! Morty!" a voice boomed from above. "Cut it out."

A pair of enormous hands reached beneath the two kittens and scooped them up. It was the giantess, known as Juno. She who brings food and water, she who drags the ribbon around for chasing purposes, she who snuggles on the couch, first of her name.

"What the hell, you two. You're not supposed to climb the curtains. Jesus."

Sir Percieval settled into the giant's hand, as she cuddled his body close to her chest. The giant had always been a source of kindness. He looked over at his brother, who had already forgotten their quarrel as he was attacking the strings of Juno's hoodie. Juno looked up, quizzically. "What were you looking for? Oh God, a moth? You hate those, don't you Percy?" The moth fluttered about, just above the curtain rod. "Get out of here, moth, shoo." Juno deftly moved Sir Percieval to her other arm, putting him next to his brother. She swung a mighty palm at the dragon called "moth" and it flapped off toward the great light in the center of the ceiling. It had retreated, but Percieval knew it would be back.

Mordred had calmed down and was happily dangling from the giant's forearm. "You could have helped," mumbled Percy.

"Your tail looked fun," said Morty, implacably, and began to purr, as Juno sat down on the sofa. She deposited the two brave warriors in her lap and reached for the tiny black box with the buttons, and after a moment, the window with the moving colors and sounds turned on.

RELAXING into the soft lap of the giantess, Sir Percieval licked his right paw. He would sharpen his blades, exercise his hunting instincts, and try again. As he allowed himself to settle in, he felt the magic rise in his throat, and his inner purr rumbled forth. He felt his damaged soul begin to heal, giving Mordred serious side-eye. Mordred simply blinked back, a slow blink of supplication. Sir Percieval sighed. His brother wasn't so bad, he supposed. Just reckless. Impulsive. The tiniest shadow flickered over the paw that was currently in the process of being cleaned, and Sir Percieval looked up at the sky to see the dragon, far above, so distant it might have been a trick of the light. Soon, his eyes fell shut and his purr rose into the night, as Juno's hand found his chin for scritches. The knight knew in his heart that there would be other days, and other dragons to slay.

MICHAEL ALLEN ROSE *is an award-winning writer, musician, editor and performance artist based in Chicago, Illinois. His stories have appeared in* The Magazine of Bizarro Fiction, Heavy Feather Review, *and* Tales From The Crust *among other periodicals. He has published several books including* Jurassichrist *(Perpetual Motion Machine Publishing) which won the 2021 Wonderland Award for best bizarro novel, and* The Last 5 Minutes of the Human Race *(Madness Heart Press), winner of best collection in bizarro fiction 2022. He is the host of the annual Ultimate Bizarro Showdown at Bizarro Con in Oregon. Michael also releases industrial music under the name Flood Damage. He lives with an awesome cat named Dr. Light, and enjoys good tea. You can find more at www.michaelallenrose.com*

CLAWING UP THE CORPORATE LADDER

MOLLY ANN MCDONOUGH

"Wow, even the reception area smells like smoke." Jessica, my bestie since childhood, plopped down beside me. She grabbed the latest copy of Bloomberg Businessweek to wave in front of her face. "Do you think he's just ripping cigars in there?"

I looked toward the receptionist, too far away to hear us across the cavernous space. "I don't know. He's smelled like that every time I've seen him."

Jessica leaned closer with a conspiratorial smile, the magazine now fanning us both. "Oh, you think our dear regional manager smells like that on purpose? He asked his personal perfumer to make him smell like a man for all his starched-boxer underlings? They mixed him up notes of Cuban cigar, peated scotch, and sports-car leather, and he spritzes on his "Eau de Definitely, For Sure Has an Adequately-Sized Dick" every five minutes?"

I covered my mouth to hide my laughter. After making sure we hadn't drawn the receptionist's attention yet, I asked, "What are you even doing here?" I hadn't expected Jessica to put her name in for the statewide manager role that our regional manager visited this week to fill. She privately, and sometimes openly, disdained our bosses, clients, and the work we did. Granted, moving assets around to make our rich customers even richer wasn't exactly a soul calling, but it paid the bills.

Jessica rolled her eyes. "I think James is finally about to propose. He's started talking about children. I told him there was no way I'd be having kids until we were married for a while. I figure, if I get this promotion, we could save enough for me to take a few years off when the future babies are young. What about you?"

While I didn't have the same level of resentment for this work as Jessica, she knew I was waiting for an opportunity I actually cared about to come along. "My dad's emphysema is getting worse. I've been wanting to retire my mom so she can be with him fully in his remaining years. At this salary I could."

Jessica squeezed my hand. "You and your parents should come round for dinner soon. Or maybe we could make food and go to theirs if it's hard for your dad to leave the house right now? It's been months since I've seen them."

I smiled. "I'll ask them after work."

The office door opened, and a renewed wave of Mr. Ignacio's smokey scent enveloped us. He ushered out Doug, our most sexist and simpering coworker. Jessica openly scowled at him as he walked by. The receptionist called, "Ms. Ashworth, Mr. Ignacio will see you now."

Jessica mouthed, "Good luck" as I stood.

Inside the opulent office that would be mine if I got

the promotion, I extended my hand. "Thank you for interviewing me, Mr. Ignacio."

He grabbed my palm with a professionally firm grip. His skin was so warm—hot even. If I was that heated my skin would be clammy with perspiration, but his was dry. "No need for thanks. Your qualifications got you here, not me. And please, Diane, call me Darius."

I'd already stalked him online and knew his first name. Jessica likely hadn't and I hoped she'd be able to resist making a face if Darius made the same request of her. Even I'd speculated if he had changed it from Stephen or something to sound more imposing. I also wondered whether he kept it so oppressively warm in the office as a power move. I already itched to remove my suit jacket.

The heat was incongruous with the corner office. Through the two full walls of windows looking out on the skyline and water beyond, I could see the sunny day outside. But though all the blinds were up, the office remained shaded. Perhaps the expensive glass had some invisible tempering property to make it so dark within without dimming the view. And I could hear the air conditioner running. The unexpected heat, paired with the darkness, raised some primal alarm. The hairs on the back of my neck rose as the first beads of perspiration rolled down my back. I felt like some small rodent that had come within the shadow of a hawk above.

My most expensive heels clicked across the stone floor. I sat in one of the rich leather chairs in front of the desk. It didn't contain the ashtray I expected, which was a relief. I'd rather my boss be pathetic enough to intentionally smell like cigars, than damage my lungs during the interview and early days in the office — should I get the job.

My thighs began to sweat. I tried to discreetly widen my knees on the leather surface. Darius, sensing my discomfort, said, "I apologize for the air conditioner's disappointing performance. We've called someone out to look at it, but couldn't find anyone today. Please feel free to take off your jacket." As I removed it, his eyes roved over me. Not in a sexual way, but in appraisal. He seemed like a man that noticed everything and appreciated quality—both as a personality trait and as a professional advantage.

"I like your earrings. Beautiful antiques." On the surface, his smile looked charming. It was wide and white. But too wide, and too white. As if Riding Hood's Big Bad Wolf had gotten veneers. Many of my colleagues had them, and they always gave teeth a slightly rounded, blocky look. His still appeared sharp. Very sharp.

"Thank you." I reached up for my small gold hoops with the teardrop rubies hanging from them. "They were my grandmother's. I almost never wear anything else."

After we went through the expected interview questions, Darius asked me why I wanted the position. I gave the answer I'd recorded over and over in my phone and practiced in front of my mirror. I was "honored to assist our esteemed clientele... natural progression of all the impactful work I'd done the last six years... excellent quarterly reviews and uniformly solid reputation among my clients, superiors, and peers.... etc..... etc."

The entire time he'd nodded along and kept his eyes trained on my face. Now he leaned back and steepled his hands in front of his mouth. "That all may be true, but it's not the reason you want this job. What's your motivation?"

I calculated rapidly in my head. He seemed to want honesty rather than corporate swill. A risk to give him the truth, but also a risk to withhold it. "And of course, the increased salary would really benefit my family. My dad's health isn't the best."

He bit his lip, narrowed his eyes, and tilted his head. "That's not a reason for you though. I'm not sensing where you want this for yourself. But once you experience the perks of the job, I believe we might change that." He smiled his too wide smile, and then stood abruptly. "It's been a pleasure, Diane Ashworth."

I HADN'T EXPECTED to hear back about the promotion for weeks. I don't think it takes that long for companies to pick someone. They could decide the same day they finished the final interview. The candidates' qualifications and performances wouldn't change, and the interviewers' impressions would only fade. The reason it took so long to hear back was because the company wanted us to hope and wait awhile. If they finally extended an offer, it would feel like a rare blessing barely won.

So when Darius called me in for a meeting that Friday morning, I wasn't sure why. "Did you know, a few promotions ago, this used to be my office?" I nodded. He walked to the shelves that covered the wall to his right. On the shelf at his waist, rested a gold dragon statue with star sapphire eyes. He tilted it and the shelves swung open to reveal an expensively equipped bar. "I inherited this, though I did add the dragon mechanism. How do you take your martinis?"

"It's beautiful. And dry, gin, with a lemon twist please." This seemed like a promising, if unsettling, 9 a.m. drink.

He filled a gold shaker with ice. An undoubtedly expensive gin I'd never seen before followed. A towel insulated his hand from the cold metal as he shook our drinks. He took two gold-stemmed coup glasses from a freezer, poured into them, and placed garnishes. "I also added this glassware and the stone floor." He set a drink in front of me and sat on the corner of his desk. "I've gotten approval to extend the statewide manager role to you, Diane. Congratulations, I look forward to seeing how you make the office your own." I looked up into his enormous smile and felt my own grin split wider than natural to try to match his enthusiasm.

"Thank you so much, Darius! I assure you our clients will be thrilled with your decision." We clinked glasses and each took a sip of our drink.

"I trust you like the martini." He moved around his, now my, desk.

"It is the most perfect martini I've ever had." I took another sip. "I would've taken you for a scotch drinker, though."

He smiled his sharp smile, and I shook off the trepidation that cut through me. We'd be working together more closely now, and I needed to get used to the intimidating front he presented. "I enjoy scotch as well, but I prefer drinks from a stemmed glass. You may have noticed, I run hot, and it's best for my business meetings that I don't have to race to finish drinks before they warm."

"That makes sense."

He leaned forward. "Now, let's go over some details. I'll announce your promotion this afternoon at the corporate lunch. You'll have a week to transition your current workload to your replacement. Then two weeks with me learning the secrets of your new office." Despite what he said about not hurrying, he downed his martini. As I tried to balance pacing my drinking to his and not letting the booze go to my head, I thought of the cappuccino unfinished on my desk. I didn't normally go straight from coffee to cocktails. I pressed my shoulders back and refocused on his words, before my thoughts drifted to hoping the air conditioner would be fixed by the time I moved into the space.

I TOLD Jessica about my promotion before the lunch meeting. She let out a subdued squeal and quickly pulled me into a hug. I asked, "You're not mad I got it instead of you?"

She scoffed. "Even if you didn't deserve it more, which you do, what kind of shit friend do you think I am? I will *always* celebrate your wins, and I will *shamelessly* abuse being besties with the most high-powered suit in the office!"

After the meeting, and the less sincere congratulations from the rest of my colleagues, Jessica waited in my office. She wore a headband with a cutout of a llama piñata. She pressed one with a margarita cutout into my hands. "It's time for Tres Amigas Margaritas!!"

I looked at my watch. "Jessica, it is 2:30. I can't leave in the middle of the afternoon to get drunk at margarita happy hours with you. Especially not on the day they announced my promotion." Tres Amigas Margaritas was a tradition we started as broke college students when we'd heard of two bars with Friday afternoon margarita happy hours on the same street — Uno Momento Perfecto and Dos Amigos. When we'd stumbled out of Dos Amigos, already drunk at 5 p.m., a few blocks over to Third Avenue, and found a dive bar called Sloppy Joe's offering $4 well margaritas, Jessica had cheered "Uno, dos, tres! Marga, margarit, margarita!" and our Friday tradition had been born.

"Of course you can. If anyone questions you on it, pretend you're a man. Puff out your chest. Flex your hairy forearms." Jessica demonstrated the posture. She looked down her nose at me, which she had to tilt her chin ridiculously far back to achieve since I'm taller. "I am promoting office morale and strengthening bonds with my new underlings. Perhaps that's difficult for someone in *your* position to understand. Any other questions?" Jessica pressed her palms together and said in her normal voice, "Please! We haven't done Tres Amigas Margaritas in over a year!"

I gave an over dramatic sigh. "Fine." I smiled. "But don't invite anyone from the office until we get to Dos Amigos."

While we proudly waited for our first margaritas in our sparkly cardboard headbands and designer suits at Uno Momento Perfecto, I said, "I'm going to wait three months to tell my parents about the promotion, I think. That should be long enough for me to make sure the job is stable."

Jessica nodded. "They'd be crazy to fire you, babes. But it would be awful to retire your mom just to have to take it back if you lost your job. Don't be too cautious, though."

By the time a few of our college friends and trusted coworkers joined us at the second happy hour, we were on our third margaritas. One of our college friends ordered tequila shots for the table. "To Diane's shiny new job!"

We all licked our salt, tossed back the shot, and bit our limes. By the time we entered Sloppy Joe's, the college crew had taught the work friends the traditional happy hour chant. We all shouted "Uno, dos, tres! Marga, margarit, margarita!"

The bartender, Earl, who'd been there since the first time we stumbled in, grumbled, "I'd hoped I'd seen the last of yous."

"We know you love us, Earl." I blew him a kiss.

He looked at the new drunk faces. "We're cash only. ATM's near the ladies room. Margarita for everyone?"

I led us in another chant of "Marga, margarit, margarita!" in response.

I STARED in awe at what Darius had revealed behind another section of the bookcase — an entire hidden office, nearly as big as the one we'd left. It was as modern as the unhidden office was classic. A massive, electric standing desk had five monitors spread across it. Each showed a different chart, spreadsheet, or news source, all updated in real time.

He pointed at the large tower computer under the desk. "That's the most advanced computer in the building, probably in the city. These models are all proprietary." He waved his hand, palm up, toward the screens. "The ones we didn't develop in-house, we bought entire companies to maintain exclusivity. They gather information on climate, geological events, politics, technological trends and research, religious shifts, etc. Information that, in some cases, no other financial firm in the world has access to. Then it organizes it into associations, trends, and financial recommendations, which we use to magnify the wealth, and thus maintain the loyalty, of our already successful clients. In our world, hoarding information is how you consolidate capital."

As Darius put a hand on the middle of my back to steer me toward the models, a chill went through me. Were riches of this magnitude meant to be consolidated? There were decent people like my parents struggling to work until they died, while we helped people add more zeros than they could ever use to their accounts. At our society's level of advancement, when we could have enough resources for everyone, it seemed unconscionably cruel to hoard it all in financial models to benefit so few. Once we stepped up to the screens, with Darius close at my side, heat replaced the chill. Perhaps this high-powered computer and all these electronics were partially responsible for the swelter.

AT THE END of my training weeks with Darius, he took me to La Petite Chance, the nicest French restaurant in the city. I had to reschedule the dinner with Jessica and my parents for a second time, but they understood when I told them where my boss was taking me. Jessica and I had planned to go when we got our first jobs, then found

19

out they required a $300 deposit from each patron and balked. Instead, we'd given ourselves no limit on how many drunk eats and cocktails we'd allow ourselves and had a fabulous, and more affordable, day out sampling dive bars and restaurants.

We followed the maître d' to our table, and he pulled out my chair. I tried not to ogle the perfect silverware or the three votive candles floating in water-filled vases of tapering height in the center of the white tablecloth. Darius nodded toward the thick wine menu placed between us. "Do you have any preferences?"

"I prefer dry wines. I drink reds more, but I also like whites when it's hot or I'm having seafood."

Darius smiled. "Not prohibitively picky. Do you mind if I choose something for the table then?"

"Please do."

When the waiter returned, he ordered two bottles in what sounded like flawless French. He had me taste the white, and he sampled the red. Naturally, it was the best chardonnay I'd ever had. Darius placed a small blue velvet box in front of me. I looked at him in confusion.

"To celebrate your promotion."

I raised my eyebrows. "Isn't that what this dinner is for?"

"When handling this level of wealth, you should be rewarded with temporary sensory pleasures, as well as with beauty you can savor for years." When I still hesitated, he added. "Enjoy it. The company can afford it. I promise."

I smiled. He was right. If I traded my brilliance and most of my waking hours for this role, I should at least enjoy it. I opened the box to find a pair of stud earrings.

They had small round diamonds, and below that, larger star sapphires. They were exquisite.

"I thought they would complement your grand-mother's rubies nicely."

"I only have the one piercing, but they are truly gorgeous. Thank you." I tried to smile as wide as he always did.

"Aw, I'm sorry. I could've sworn you had two piercings."

My face flushed in discomfort. My reservations, which had almost entirely receded over our weeks working together, returned. I didn't expect most men to notice earrings, but Darius clearly did. I had a hard time believing he had imagined another piercing.

"Well, you could always get a second. I'm sure you have other earrings beyond these gorgeous rubies and sapphires to wear." He gave his sharp grin.

Why would he lie? To try to get me to not wear my grandmother's earrings occasionally? I was being silly. I tilted my head and adopted an overly dramatic, thoughtful expression. "There's an idea."

By the time we'd worked our way through foie gras, oysters, and escargot, I was tipsy. While we waited for our mains, and a third bottle of wine, I asked, "Doesn't it ever seem like too much to you? I don't want to ruin this." I waved at the table in front of us. "Because it's phenomenal and I'm enjoying it immensely… but all the excess. All the mountains of gold we help our clients hoard in their offshore accounts and on the shore beach estates. Isn't there something better we could do with it?"

"We're not stealing wealth from the peasants like some medieval land baron. We're creating it from thin air. Plus, the economy and our industry are how they are, whether or not we participate and profit. Why shouldn't you, as a decent person who wants to use that cut of the pie to help her family, take it?" He leaned back and swirled the remainder of his wine by the stem of his glass.

I nodded and noticed my skin had flushed again. This time from the wine and pleasure of the occasion. "That makes perfect sense."

THREE MONTHS INTO THE JOB, I was comfortable. I had replaced the sitting area furniture with a set in the softest Italian suede. The couch was not only of imported quality you could spot from the doorway, but surprisingly comfortable. I'd taken plenty of naps on it after late nights in the office or too many drinks with clients.

I wasn't only comfortable in the space, but confident in the job. My clients were thrilled, I was actually enjoying the work, and my bank account had grown fat enough for me to sign on a two-bedroom apartment in a building with all the amenities within walking distance to work. I scheduled my new furniture to be delivered and assembled this Friday, and all my stuff to be moved Saturday.

This afternoon I had my first review with Darius, and I wasn't even worried. I looked at my phone screen to check the time as it lit up with a call from my dad. I'd put all non-work calls on "do not disturb," and it'd been weeks since I'd talked to my parents. I still had an hour before my meeting, but it'd be better to find some time to call my dad later.

When Darius arrived, I led him over to the new furniture and prepared our martinis. I held the bottle of gin, black with smokey gray details that didn't hint at the ostentatious price, out to him. "Have you had it?"

"Only once, and it's been years. From what I remember, it's very good."

I pouted. "They only produce fifty bottles a year. I had to trade a client three free hours of consulting for this and I waited for you to try it."

He laughed. "I'm honored. It's not your fault I'm a lush. I got something for you too." He placed a green velvet box on the Italian marble coffee table. "To celebrate all your new clients. You've exceeded even my three-month mark when I started this office. It may be a record."

"Thank you, Darius. It's easy to bring on clients when what we're offering is so enticing." I smiled so wide my mouth cracked in the corner. I dabbed at the blood with a linen napkin. "Sorry, that keeps happening. My lips have been so chapped."

"I found the air in this office arid at first, too." As I added our lemon twists, he asked, "Did they ever fix the air conditioner?"

"They said nothing was wrong with it." I shrugged as I walked our drinks over. I set one in front of Darius and sat on the couch next to him. "It cooled down for a while after you left, but now it's as hot as ever. I've completely acclimatized, but my clients often seem overheated."

We clinked glasses and sipped. The gin was worth the three hours of labor at our top-tier rates. Then I reached for the jewelry box. I admired how the green velvet looked against my sharp gold manicure for a second before opening it. Inside, I found another set of earrings. A round sapphire, a small diamond, and an enormous emerald connected by gold links. "They're perfect. They'll complement the pair you got me first so well." I gestured to them, beautifully occupying the second piercing I'd gotten. I felt a small twinge of guilt as I removed my grandmother's earrings and replaced them with the new ones. It was only polite to show I appreciated the gift, and they were too large for the second piercing.

"I'm glad you're enjoying them." Darius leaned forward to hold my hair out of the way. I felt a breeze on my face and the shadows in the room fluttered as he angled his broad shoulders toward me. I remembered how Darius's presence initially made me feel like a rodent in sight of a hawk. Now I was in the skies with him, poised to prey on those below. It was superior.

We were superior.

I ONLY REMOVED my sunglasses once I was in my private elevator. It had been the kind of weekend where I drank and ate more than most people's annual salary. I hadn't paid for it, of course. The client who had invited me and a guest onto his superyacht to celebrate his investment portfolio outperforming in five months what it had done in the last five years with his previous firm paid for everything. At first, I'd considered inviting Jessica, as we were supposed to celebrate her engagement this weekend. But she didn't really understand these sorts of events. And it made better career sense to fold Darius, as my superior and the one who hired me, into my wins.

To make up for bailing, and how little time I'd had around work lately, I'd made her and James a reservation at La Petite Chance on Friday and told them to use my card on file. I'd also gotten them a gift card for a couple's massage at my favorite spa.

When I stepped into my office, Jessica was waiting. She and my other work friends had stopped dropping by unscheduled months ago, but perhaps she couldn't wait to gush about La Petite Chance. She sat in my desk chair with her arms crossed and a scowl on her face. This definitely wasn't a "thank you so much" visit, then. But there wasn't any way she could know I had the option of bringing her this weekend. I didn't even tell her where I'd been.

She sniffed their air when I entered. "Did you start smoking?" she nearly yelled.

"Of course not." I tossed my purse and sunglasses onto the desk.

"Did you start using Darius's Small Dick Perfume?"

"No. Too many peated scotches last night," I lied. I found that Darius had been right about stemmed glasses being preferable. "Did you come to interrogate me about my perfume choices?"

"Why is your mom still working in that shitty pharmacy?"

"Ah. So that's what this is about." I gestured to her surly posture. "Hanging out with my mom when I don't have time for you now?"

Jessica interlaced her fingers on my desk. Took a deep breath and then looked up at the ceiling before pinning me with her gaze. "No. I was with James this Saturday on the way to his mother's. We went in to get a card, after 7 p.m., and your mom was still working. That part of town isn't safe at night, Di. James wouldn't even let me walk into the store alone."

I gave my longest suffering sigh. "I've asked her repeatedly not to take the late shifts. I'll speak to her again."

Jessica opened her mouth and just blinked at me a few times. She closed it and opened it again. "What happened to fucking retiring her after three months, Di? Remember your *entire* reason for taking this soul sucking job? It's been six months!"

"I know." I moved to the bar. This conversation required alcohol. "Want a drink?"

She looked at the gold clock on my desk. "It's barely 9 a.m."

"It's 9:12 and when has that ever stopped you?" I smiled my largest smile. My mouth no longer split in the corners. I just had to be careful not to let my lips catch on my sharp canines, which I'd gotten pretty good at.

"I want you to explain yourself."

I made a pitcher of agua de valencia, grabbed two wine glasses and moved to the couch. Jessica rolled her eyes but accepted the cocktail I poured her, and then sat in a chair rather than next to me. "I've just been so busy with work —"

"Bullshit. This is the reason for your work. Make time."

I took a sip of my drink without cheering Jessica. "And moving."

She scoffed. "Into your expensive-ass high-rise that you paid expensive-ass movers to do everything?"

Jessica had offered to help me move. I'd laughed and told her I was paying people for that. "So that's what this is about? You think I'm spending the new salary frivolously?" I reached forward and saw the shadows of wings over my shoulders. I clutched her knee. "I have an account set up for them. With our investment strategies, I can get so much more return rather than giving them a modest amount to live on now."

Jessica looked down at my hand and then up at me. "They're not going to care about your impressive ROI in twenty years. Your dad is dying now."

"He's not dying. People can live for a long time with emphysema, and I can pay for the best doctors now." I removed my hand from her knee. Her skin had begun to perspire under mine.

"You're entirely missing the fucking point." She held her glass against her flushed cheek. "This job has changed you."

I laughed. My hot breath raced up my throat and nearly sizzled in the air. "I haven't changed." I sat up straight and flexed my invisible wings behind me. I ran my tongue over the tip of my fang. "Perhaps, I'm myself…but more."

Jessica frowned and shook her head. She moved to the edge of her seat to leave.

I held out a hand. "But you're right! I'll tell my parents about the promotion and sit down with them this week to make a sensible savings plan with my mom."

"That's a start. When will you retire your mom?" She took a long drink, and then glared at her glass, clearly annoyed it was delicious.

"I need to look at the financials."

Jessica stood up.

"Oh, don't be like that." I looked at the tiny diamond on her ring finger. It couldn't be worth half the second earrings Darius had gifted me. Luckily for James, Jessica didn't really care about things like jewels. But perhaps I could change that. "You know, I'm likely to get promoted again within the next six months. I'll get to choose my replacement."

Jessica looked toward the door. But she didn't leave.

MOLLY ANN MCDONOUGH is a fiction author, poet, and multidisciplinary engineer. When Molly isn't reading, writing, or coding, she enjoys being an enthusiastic amateur in her many neurodivergent hobbies. These include learning and forgetting Spanish, petting cats, and volunteering in regions affected by natural disasters. In her life and writing, Molly is on a quest to spread magic, mirth, and meaning.

A FOOLHARDY RESCUE

KEVIN A DAVIS

I sighed as a small human crawled under the back of the tent housing my cramped iron cage. It wasn't unheard of for some penniless sod to sneak a peek at me without paying the dues required of this traveling shit-show they called a circus.

"Might as well crawl right back out. No show tonight." I expected a squeal of fright from the little critter since the interior would be pitch black to their pitiful excuse for eyes. Instead, I smelled determination from the leather-clad intruder.

"My name is La'akeanonalani, or La'akea for short, and I'm here to rescue you," said a young female of the species. She wore a tight-fitting black outfit consisting of trousers and jacket with a loose cowl. Coils of stanch rope wrapped diagonally from her shoulder to waist. A pair of grappling hooks dangled at her hips. The blade at her belt might just pierce through one of the rats infesting the tents – might.

I coughed out a laugh with a puff of smoke. "What makes you think I wish to be rescued?"

KEVIN A DAVIS

The human named La'akea bowed formally in front of the iron bars of my cage. "You are Nedgaroth, prince of the Tadashi dragon clan, rightful ruler to all of the Vendin Heights."

If my handlers hadn't fed me Toothrot by the handfuls, I would have lit the tent aflame with my bellowing laughter. "Didn't you read the sign outside? Neddy – the world's smallest dragon?" It was an exaggeration, I had a few inches on Wenkinban out of the Ladx clan, mostly tail, but it counted. My brother had insisted on the petty title when he'd tossed me to these louts. "Besides, if I escape, I die."

"You speak of your brother, the usurper." La'akea used an annoyingly pompous tone.

"Yeah. Whatever the circumstances, he's five times the size of little ole me – and has control of the clan. You're wasting your time. I ain't leaving." I scratched at itchy scales with a claw, then pointed to the edge of the tent hoping she'd take the hint.

She straightened her back and continued to speak like a character from one of the popular fantasy rags. Not that I don't enjoy a good tale and would dance on a tentpole to have a decent library, but I could endure the mind-numbing captivity of this dump. La'akea even gestured as she spoke. "It has been seen and foretold that you will defeat the usurper, rising to your proper glory. The Tadashi clan will once again be revered by the Three Kingdoms and feared by the west as is their due."

"Wait, what?" Getting news outside the circus wasn't easy. "What's happened to the clan?"

"The usurper –"

"Daxagroth, my brother's name is Daxagroth. What

did he do?" My neck craned and my snout neared the edge of the iron bars, but she didn't retreat.

"As you wish. *Daxagroth* increased the tax to all the holds until some could not pay." She spoke my brother's name as if with venom. "They are left unprotected. He stole what he claimed as 'his tithe' from Adel and they have raised Dragon Daggers to protect their land."

I winced at the mention of the weapons. The massive, barbed arrows thrown from a ballista could pierce dragon scale. Dax had always been arrogant, but I hadn't expected him to snub the Concords. "Why?"

"Greed, my Prince."

Nothing I can do about it. I waved my claws at the ninny-headed human. "Don't even start. I'm perfectly happy here in my tent."

"Cage."

Leaning back, I glowered at the impudent critter. Humans, smarter ones, could be quite engaging – or annoying.

She pulled a vial from a pouch in her jacket. Her eyes had adjusted to the darkness as she strode unafraid to the two swinging gates at the front of my cage. When she plucked out the stopper with a pop, the sharp scent of acid wafted in the air.

"Stop." I slammed four claws into the iron bands that formed the door. If the greasy owner of the circus found me freed, I'd be punished. This impossible human couldn't make me leave, but I'd not see another slumber in the sun for weeks when they saw my gate open.

La'akea, frail in comparison, with round eyes that lacked concern, smiled and placed her free hand on top of one of my black claws. "Your place upon the Vendin

Heights will be restored; I know this. You will not harm me."

I snorted at the audacity of the creature. Her expression and scent were fearless. She deserved the truth. "I cannot best Dax. There is a reason I sit here. He offered me death as an option. I am a coward."

Her laugh threatened to bring someone, even at this dark time of the morning. "Tell me this story when we are done, Prince." In a smooth motion, she poured the acid inside the keyhole of the iron lock.

I removed my claws from the bars slowly as her hand lifted free, and watched wisps rise from the sizzling metal. My days ahead would be spent in the darkness of the tent, not seeing the sun or feeling its warmth on my hide. Frustrated, I wound my tail around my front claws and settled into a tight mass, glaring at the disturbed human who thought she could make me leave. I had no intention of dying under my brother's flames.

"Why do you care?" I asked.

She produced a thick leather piece from a jacket pouch and a mallet from her belt. "Oak Waters Hold is one of the places where your Tadashi no longer protect us from the western riders. My uncle and brother are all that have survived the raids, so I traveled to Adel to beseech aid. I found none, but learned what I must do." At the mention of her family, I smelled the pain of terrible loss. She forced a smile. "As I am your savior, you are my uncle and brother's."

How could Dax have let his greed override his duty?

She wrapped the leather of the lock and tapped experimentally with the mallet.

"I'm not leaving. You'll do nothing but cause me punishment."

"It has been foreseen." La'akea cocked her head at the lock, shifting the blow of the mallet.

"So you've said." I focused on her strikes, dulled by the leather. "You are asking me to escape to my death. A sacrifice that will mean nothing."

"You will restore your rightful place." Her blow snapped the lock open, and she swiveled it. Tossing her mallet to the side, she pulled open one of the gates.

A coward, I couldn't leave. I'd made this decision when Dax had given me the opportunity. "This is my rightful place."

La'akea opened the second gate. "You belong in the skies protecting your domain, or sunning with your clan upon the Vendin Heights. The holds need you. Your dragons need you. Centrax needs you to return so that she might as well. Alone – "

I rose. "Wait. What happened to Centrax?"

The small human strode into my cage, fearless. "Your brother exiled her soon after you were sent here. She has been seen riding the winds of the barrens to the west."

"Why would he do that?"

"Why did he exile you here?"

I stared at the open gates to my demise and fought the stifled anger attempting to reignite. This foolish woman would lead me to death, unless her prophecy held any merit. Archaic witches were known to glimpse the future, and many human tomes abounded with ancient predictions. Did it matter? Could I let my clan sour in disgrace without at least trying? My mother had nurtured us to prominence and strength for forty years, thinking she left it to my administration. I had failed her.

Shame in the light of my mother's memory stirred

me to my decision. I would certainly die, but not as a craven circus freak.

As I stepped a claw toward the open gates, La'akea smiled, turned to lead, and drew her blade as she approached the tall canvas of the tent. I crouched, snaking my neck so that my horns did not scrape the opening of the cage, and held my wings tight against my sides to squeeze through.

With deft cuts, she sliced the thongs that tied the outer flaps. Stretching from the toes of her boots, she managed to reach the uppermost one. Her march out, pulling one length aside, seemed stately and proud as the light of the twin moons bathed the circus grounds.

My scales scraped against canvas as I exited. The drab wagons and striped tents surrounding us sat quiet in the dark of morning. Horses whinnied far to the right. Torches flickered at the outer borders of the field used by the circus. The tall, lamplit stone buildings of the local town rose over the short wall surrounding it. The Serrin mountains to the northwest cut into the stars of the night horizon where the distant Vendin Heights awaited unseen. I loosened my wings and stretched.

La'akea had a coil of rope loosed from her shoulder. "Lean down."

I scoffed. "You think to ride me?"

"I have to be there when you meet the usurper – your brother, Daxagroth."

Some element of the prophecy, no doubt. I rolled my eyes to the twin moons, halfway to their setting on the western horizon. "Have you ridden the patrol dragons?" Clans often allocated lesser dragons to the cities that requested them. How humiliated could I be after the circus?

"No. But I've studied them. I have prepared for this."

My head snapped to her. "Most humans faint at their first attempt. Those who don't, take years to gain any expertise."

"And yet, I must." La'akea gestured brusquely for me to comply while she tugged on black leather gloves.

Sighing, I dropped my chin horn to the dirt, sending dust swirling with my breath. "I'm a bit small for riders, even puny ones."

"I have faith, Prince." She tugged at one of the large horns curving from my skull to pull herself up, and her weight settled on my neck.

As she tied loops about my jaw horns, I lifted my head slowly. Rope lashed under my throat and I swallowed at the pressure as she tied herself to me as if to a common pack animal. *Dax is going to die laughing. Perhaps according to prophecy.*

My eyes drifted to the sign on my tent. "Neddy The World's Smallest Dragon!" I'd resigned myself to a life in this abominable circus with only a small hope that my brother might see reason. When he'd announced himself as prince of our clan after our mother's passing, I'd argued, then acquiesced. He'd not been placated and had offered me a choice; humiliation or death.

"Spit and spittle. We've got to go."

I jerked out of my musing, and La'akea grabbed one of my skull horns to steady herself. My nose caught her alarm, and that of another human farther away.

A young man rounding the side of a tent squeaked, then ran out of sight yelling, "The dragon! The dragon is loose!"

The circus guards armed themselves with swords, an

occasional halberd, and a rare crossbow. I preferred to avoid the latter at close quarters, especially with my fire glands emptied from sweet Toothrot.

"Go," La'akea urged. Her legs tightened on my neck, heels digging in uncomfortably.

She still smelled of alarm, and now of growing anticipation. If she fainted, I hoped she'd tied herself in tight so that I could land her far from any threat the guards may pose with a mounted chase, but close enough that she didn't slap around on the back of my head like a loose tarp on a wagon.

Loping on all four legs, I raced westward between my abandoned tent and the taller one reserved for acrobats. My wings stretched wide, and stiff shoulder muscles woke with actual use. I heard louder, gruffer yells coming from the grounds. A well-placed halberd on a grounded dragon could cause damage.

Pumping down and slightly forward to gain lift, my wings billowed dust and loose grass ahead of me. La'akea's weight on my neck forced me to shift my position and balance as my claws tore through sod and sand indifferently. At the first hint of pressure pushing back, I tucked my forelegs and altered the angle of my beating wings, launching with one final thrust of my hind legs. My tail whipped to balance an unaccustomed load, then I flew over the circus grounds.

A night guard appeared at the edge, rising from where he'd been sitting. His expression almost indifferent as he could do nothing to stop us now.

"La'akea?" I wouldn't be able to smell her emotions, not in flight.

Her grip loosened, indicating she hadn't fainted, yet. "Yes?"

"Just checking." My neck ached as much as my shoulder muscles. Topping the height of the tallest tents I aligned toward the closer mountains, rather than directly for Vendin Heights. The circus had traveled far to the east, nearly to the coastal towns of the Three Kingdoms. Even muscles used to flying would have needed multiple stops to get home.

Home. I hadn't considered that a place anymore.

La'akea puked.

I glided. My belly scales a dark blue, I'd be little more than a silhouette against the stars. "La'akea?"

She coughed. "Sorry, Prince."

Yes, Dax's demise would be unstoppable laughter.

Less than an hour later, I spun down to land us at the shore of woodland lake. The farms had long since dwindled to thick green trees dotted with water and occasional grassy hills. Morning would lighten the skies soon. It felt more wonderful to be flying again than I would admit to my tiny rescuer. I still might die, but I'd flown free again.

La'akea's voice ragged, she smelled grateful. "Should we stop so soon? I'm okay." Her body trembled as I rested chin horn into the wet sand.

"Get off. I'm hungry. I'm going to eat something moist for a change." My own muscles quivered. "After a quick rinse."

"Sorry." She shifted as she untied herself.

The cool air smelled rich with deer, pigs, and wild sheep. I salivated at the opportunity, staring at the dark woods. The wildlife had fled at my arrival to their water-hole, but I'd passed a knoll that promised an easy hunt, even without fire.

La'akea stumbled as she slid off, but remained

upright to remove the ropes. "I'm getting used to it – flying."

"Wonderful. I'm glad you're having fun." My tone came more from humility at being ridden. "I am glad you're doing better. Riders, I am told, are trained in much shorter increments."

She pulled away the loose ropes. "I don't believe we are meant to spend time training, but it will unfold the way it must."

As I lifted my head and stretched my neck, she watched me. "Tell me of this prophecy. Did it come from the Song of Two Lands? Maybe the Winds of Salt and Snow?"

Her eyes focused on the rope she coiled. "Neither."

I rolled my aching shoulders. "Which of the great tomes then?"

She straightened, no longer shaking, and locked eyes with mine. "None of them. I pleaded with the city lords, but they wouldn't even give me audience. Everyone spoke of the troubles with the usurper, but none would consider a solution."

"Daxagroth," I corrected with a grumble. Had she lied? Made all this up to get me to kill myself trying to save her family?

"Daxagroth. Yes, Prince. I found a soothsayer and went to her with my question. She prophesied your return."

"A soothsayer?" I bellowed and shoved my snout nearly to her face. Some charlatan in a run-down shack preying on the desperate. "For coin?" The foolish human had paid for a tale and then dragged me with her to dooms end. I should have her tell the story to Dax once he stops laughing over seeing her perched on my head. That should put him over the edge.

La'akea didn't back down. Most humans couldn't help themselves but flee when anger took a dragon, but she didn't budge an inch. "I believe it. After all, you didn't harm me – and escaped with me, so the prophecy has to be true."

Smoke leaked out my nose as I huffed. "Don't call it a prophecy. It's a tale told for coin." My teeth snapped at the last word and I whipped away from her. She was a fool. *As much as me for listening to her.* I sloshed into the lake, watching silver flashes of fish scamper away.

I could go back to the circus and accept the punishment. As cool water streamed across my scales, I considered a better idea, at least until Dax learned of my whereabouts. I could join Centrax and hunt with her. Not that much more than a rabbit lived in the western barrens. Plunging my head under water I shook sore muscles and swallowed water through gritted teeth.

When I returned to the shore. La'akea had curled into a ball to sleep. Even as I flapped wings to dry them, she remained still. Foolish human.

I took off in search of food.

The twin moons had set and a dawn promised the day with a gray horizon. The fresh air contrasted the stale waste in my cage or that of the humans and their animals. For the first time in months, I feasted on a fresh sheep. Even sated, anger bubbled inside, but I brought the daft human back a hind quarter. She'd make herself prey sleeping alone on the shore in the open.

I curled up, tail to nose, as the sun rose. Luxurious warmth began to settle on my hide, lulling me into a false sense of contentment. How could I feel at ease, with everything so badly scrambled? After a rest, I'd consider the problem with a level head and decide where to go and whether La'akea would be flying, or walking out of this forest.

La'akea woke me with a rap on my forehead; rope hanging from her hand. A doused fire reeked nearby. "Ready to go?"

The afternoon sun shone in my eye as I studied her. "What makes you think you're coming with me?"

Nonplussed, she patted my nose as if I were some tail-wagging mutt. "Prophecy, remember?" Her snarky tone grated on my waking nerves.

I snorted smoke and jerked up, hoping to startle her. "Fish tales, not a true divination."

She stood in place, shaking off some of the beach sand I'd sprayed on her. "True enough. It got us this far."

"Your lie got us this far."

"Never lied. Let's go." La'akea swung the rope. "Thanks for the food, by the way."

"You're welcome." Stretching wings, I paused to frown. I had no reason to be polite to her. *Should have let her forage snails, or something.* Passing her a little closely, I headed to drink from the lake. She'd been ignorant, not deceptive. My assumptions caused as much of the misunderstanding as her lack of details.

The cool water refreshed while I peered west. Even at full health, it would have taken me a couple days to reach the Vendin Heights, more for Centrax if she still flew over the barrens. I returned, aiming for a commanding voice. "No more talk of this stupid prophecy – and you can accompany me. If Dax catches me in the air, it's your fate as well."

La'akea shrugged with an impudent cock of her head. "If that's what it takes to fulfill it, so be it. Who am I to question the fates or the prince?"

It's not fates, you puny, foolish human. "Get on." I lowered my neck for her humiliating harness.

My shoulder muscles ached a short bit into the flight, but I kept going into the night, not willing to stop until hunger got the best of me. The moons rose as I took down a bull moose with the audacity to stand its ground. Again, I returned some to La'akea, but she already slept. After an initially rocky start the first day, and the puking, she'd taken to riding well. Not that I had any experience in the process.

We woke the next morning with the black stone of Varnoth's Tooth barely visible on the western horizon, and I knew we'd be in sight of my home by sunset, if I could fly that long. La'akea had eaten while I slept, dousing a cooking fire before she woke me.

I flew with an apprehensive vigor through the first half of the day. Her prophecy nothing more than spun words of a charlatan, I failed to see a reasonable course that wouldn't end up with me roasted under Dax's breath.

La'akea yelled from her seat behind my head, she hadn't figured out that I could hear her just fine. "I need to land."

The forest below gave way to farms to our right where a large hold had grown up beside one of the many rivers here. Beyond those fields, I saw few options for a treeless stretch where I could take off from once on the ground. "Why?" I asked.

She paused for minute before answering. "I've got to pee."

I grimaced, considering the options, and glided to the left, away from the hold. My clan, the Tadashi, didn't protect this far east, but I'd rather not have someone mention my presence to Dax. "I'll find something."

"What?" she yelled.

"Okay." My predicament wouldn't go away by avoiding it, but I did exactly that.

The best option I found to land was a wide stream with a questionable depth. It appeared shallow. I circled down to the opening in the trees, tucking my wings awkwardly at the last few feet before spinning sideways to drop into the slow-moving water. Muck swallowed my legs while La'akea hastily began untying herself.

"Thank you, thank you."

With her loose on my head, I remained sunk up to my belly and slowly stretching my neck to the shore. When she climbed off and ran into the woods for privacy, I searched for better footing and found none.

Takeoff proved a disaster. The first attempt planted my face in the muck and the second left me coated so heavily that I clipped a wingtip on the trees, but I flew. Dried mud flaked off me for hours before I spotted a lake in the afternoon to bathe, eat, and rest at, in that order. Chilly rains came with nightfall, but ended quickly.

We rose in darkness with the twin moons deep in the west. "When will we arrive?" La'akea asked before I'd even got a chance to rise for water.

"Today." I was in no shape for any fight, let alone one with my brother. "I plan to skirt around Vendin Heights and meet up with Centrax."

La'akea skittered between me and the lake. "But the prophecy —"

I steadied a glare upon her without words. My fire glands had swelled slightly; I might have one good ball of flame available with the Toothrot out of my system.

She stepped out of my way stiffly, without another word.

With the sun rising at our backs, we flew. My home, the Vendin Heights, rose in the northeast. A massive, golden plateau, pockmarked with sleeping caves in the cliff walls, stretched for leagues into the north, but I would not be heading there.

Below us grew one of the last of the forests before the barrens and plains of the west. La'akea's family would be near here, if they'd previously been under the protection of the Tadashi dragons. I didn't ask, and she didn't mention it.

We flew lower than I would have when my mother reigned this territory. My eyes constantly flicked about the wide expanse of sky and checked the horizon. The sun had nearly risen overhead, when I caught movement in the blue sky to my left.

Black with red scales highlighting his shoulders and streaking down his side, my enormous brother cruised with two smaller dragons, orange Peritx and green Egrath. Coming from the north, they appeared aimed to cross our path. They had not seen me, based on the easy beats of their wings.

Going still and silent, I pulled in my wings, tilting them to drop me down toward the green expanse below.

Wind began to whistle as I sped. I kept a single eye locked on the trio. If I could land or crash into the trees below without them spotting me, I'd at least be alive. We'd be alive.

Despite my discrete plummet toward the forest, Dax saw me.

He bugled out my name and snorted fire. "Nedgaroth, you defy me?" His massive wings tucked in to drop toward my targeted destination.

This wasn't happening. My nostrils flared and I pivoted, turning under his present trajectory before pounding my too small wings to regain altitude. La'akea distracted me when she grabbed my horns, but I couldn't blame her.

The other two dragons glided in a wide circle, leaving Dax to his vengeance.

My brother spread his wings, stalling his descent, but took a couple beats to turn. I would have a precious moment where my more agile size played any benefit, then he would catch up with me.

"Die Usurper!" La'akea screamed from my back.

"Please shut up." I glanced at the Vendin Heights, but they would offer no place to hide. *Doomed. Poor foolish human.* La'akea would die with me.

Dax's cough signaled me that his fire glands poured the thick oil into the back of his throat.

When I spun nearly upside down to change direction, La'akea silently flailed on my neck before she grasped my horns firmer. Panic disappeared from my chest, and I closed my eyes.

The roaring fireball skimmed past us, heading for the forest below. In truth, fire had negligible effect on a dragon unless it could be sustained, or they were foolish enough to keep their eyes open. I peeked cautiously and began beating the air for altitude. My rider would not have the scales and thick hide to protect her from my brother's fire.

Teeth and claws offered the true threat in a battle between dragons, and my jaw could not clamp on his throat, while his maw could snap off my head without effort. We were going to die. *Stupid prophecy*. I could be sunning outside my circus tent if she hadn't brought her foolish notions. *Or if I'd simply stayed.*

As fire blossomed red in the verdant green below, I flew higher while Dax repositioned to chase. I rose above his altitude, and he flapped to regain momentum. My life forfeit, could there be some way to save hers?

"Get ready to cut your ropes. I'm going to dive back behind him. When I get into the treetops you'll have to jump." A fragile human might break a few bones in the fall, but it would be far worse from this height.

"I'm not sure that will work. 'You will aid the prince in restoring his rightful place, though it might require a leap of faith as though a sacrifice,' were her exact words. If I'm on the ground –"

Anger boiled in me. "You are a fool – quoting a charlatan who spins words for coin." This foolishness had brought me to my death, and the human wanted to keep spouting this nonsense.

La'akea didn't respond, perhaps finally seeing the reality of the situation. Looping and tucking wings to my side, I dropped directly at my brother.

He paused his wings to determine my maneuver. His vengeful eyes watched as I approached, before he rolled himself, readying to chase my descent.

My muscles were sore and weakened, but on a good

day I would not have been able to out fly him. The best I could do was to save one of us.

La'akea jumped off.

It took seconds for me to process what the foolish human had done. She'd dug her heels into the top of my neck and launched off me. When had she loosened herself from the harness? It still looped about my horns and scales like an ornament.

Like a falling rock, I passed Dax before throwing out my wings in a faltering attempt to stop my descent. He curved gracefully above, belly to the sun as he rolled into position to follow me. Meanwhile I spun awkwardly, catching air in my wings while I searched for La'akea.

A pebble compared to his massive bulk, she fell past his head, finally catching his attention. I thought for a moment she flailed in panic, but the brave, stupid human threw her grappling hook and line at Dax's neck.

As I regained control and began beating wings to gain altitude, La'akea lurched to a stop, tied to the line. The grappling hook, or the pitiful weight she added would do nothing to hamper Dax. *What were you thinking?*

My brother rolled with an angry snort, his wings extending and foreclaws flicking at the rope with razor claws. La'akea's body whipped upward like a child's doll on a cut string. If she survived the snapping about, the fall would kill her.

However, she'd angered Dax. He dug out the barbed grappling hook and beat monstrous wings to reach her body that toppled loosely end over end in a slowing arc.

I raced behind him. Imagining a fool plan of beating my brother to the rope that hung from her and scooping in to save her. *Futile.*

His monstrous form spread out ahead of me in

beautiful elegance. A hunter supreme. Wings beating efficiently and neck outstretched; his mouth open and ready to snatch her from the air. His black eyes were crescent orbs, locked on their helpless prey.

I squeezed my fireglands of every drop of fuel I could muster into the back of my throat, targeted for the distance, and blasted a fireball at my brother.

He couldn't see it coming. I'd aimed carefully for the time it would take to travel and his speed; all to hit his head. My pitiful ball off fire trailed toward him, closing the distance.

Flames splashed orange and red about his massive skull horns, and I could not be sure of my success.

Dax roared and whipped his head from side to side, dripping fire. Only his disorientation gave me hope that I'd blinded him.

Altering the angle of my wings, but keeping up the pounding rhythm on aching muscles, I dove to intercept La'akea. I still might have to deal with the others in my clan, faithful to Dax, but one disaster at a time.

Dax continued to roar, erratically flapping, and losing altitude. The onlookers had gained another so that three dragons circled high overhead.

La'akea didn't move as she plummeted. Any conscious creature would flail in this situation. Survive little fool. Had this actually been her damnable prophecy?

I aimed for the short bit of rope whipping over her. The forest rushed toward us. There would be one chance. Tilting slightly, I appeared to fly toward a direct collision with her, but my timing proved perfect. Catching the rope in two claws, I spun slightly and beat wings to slow our descent.

To the east, fire ate into the forest. Above, Dax had eased into an aimless flight westward. I curved gently toward a grassy hill where sheep scattered for the woods.

Wings beating wind onto flattening grass, I lowered La'akea's limp body to the slope before dropping down beside her. She smelled alive, but soft-shelled humans were fragile. "La'akea?"

The rope about her hips did not appear too tight, and she breathed.

A shadow passed over us and I considered moving away from her if the others decided to attack me for what I'd done to Dax. I couldn't be sure of the alliances within the clan.

Peritx and Egrath didn't position to swoop in for a grounded attack, but circled to land. I still could not know their intentions, and the third had left the skies. My muscles ached. Some small part of me dared to hope, but I buried that emotion where I'd tucked it long ago. Exile seemed more likely.

Both settled downslope from where I stood over La'akea. Stepping around to the front of her, I placed myself defensively, not that I could do much against them if they attacked.

After she stretched her iridescent green wings to the grass, Egrath spoke first. "I greet you, Prince of Tadashi. Welcome home."

Shocked, I didn't respond.

Peritx's burnished-orange wings pressed to the grass and he lifted his neck. "I greet you, Prince of the Tadashi. You have returned victorious. Your mother would be proud."

My mother would be sad that her children fought. "Thank you for the greetings, Egrath, Peritx." I studied them, thoughts reeling. "You believe the clan will accept my return?"

Peritx snorted a smoky cloud. "We have discussed the possibility for quite some time, quietly in these grim times." He carefully did not disparage Dax.

"The method of your arrival was – most interesting," Egrath shifted her eyes behind me, causing me to turn.

La'akea had risen to her elbows, both wincing and smiling. "Prophecy." She poked at her hips, grimacing.

I spun carefully. "Are you okay?"

She shrugged one shoulder. "Hips are sore. I'm bruised, but no broken bones and I'm alive. For that alone I'm pleased. I hadn't been sure. The prophecy wasn't clear about that part, if you noticed."

"I'm not sure about your soothsayer, but I can speak to your bravery." *Foolish human.*

"Prophecy, Prince." La'akea asserted with an almost exasperated tone.

She'd brought me home. "Prophecy then. I'm grateful and indebted to you, La'akeanonalani – for the rescue."

Kevin A Davis is a fantasy author with sixteen published books in three series; the episodic, award-winning DRC Files with Kristen, the Khimmer Chronicles featuring the lively assassin Ahnjii, and the AngelSong series centering around the indominable Haddie. In 2024, he published his first middle-grade novel. A multitude of his short stories of have been published in anthologies in fantasy, science fiction, and romance genres.

He publishes a wide variety of anthologies under Inkd

Publishing and their first non-fiction book about paranormal investigations.

Residing in north Florida, he attends conventions throughout the year either as staff, vendor, speaker, or a fan with a wide interest in speculative fiction from epic fantasy to science fiction. Considering his in-depth interest in the works of Robert Jordan and Brandon Sanderson, and passion for writing, he is the Director of the Authors Workshop Track at JordanCon.

www.kevinarthurdavis.com

www.facebook.com/KevinArthurDavis

DRAGON SEEKING ACCOUNTANT

JENNIFER M ROBERTS

A crack of lightning illuminated the source of Jordan's greatest pride and deepest shame. Like a movie frame caught in a strobe light, it was there one moment and lost in the gloom of the encroaching storm the next. Ribbed columns lined the theater's facade, interspersed with a series of banners proclaiming upcoming productions, all part of the contest series *Make Me Cry*. An oversized Greek tragedy mask presided over the doors, frozen in a fierce frown.

"I shouldn't be here." Jordan turned off the ignition and leaned into the steering wheel, squinting up at the scowling mask and the dark clouds. It seemed like a bad omen. He looked down at the invitation in his hand. A narrow slip of paper printed with a single line of text, clear, concise, and completely confusing. "I would like to engage your services in a private matter. If interested, arrive at 8 p.m., Tuesday, Main Theater."

That was it, nothing more. Jordan had spent the afternoon searching the scrap of paper for a hidden message or a clue about the reason for the meeting, but he hadn't found one. He had double checked the name and address on the envelope because he was certain it couldn't have been meant for someone like him. There had to be a mistake.

Lightning strobed through the sky again, making the golden orb nestled in the cupholder glow for a second. Jordan ran his hand over the smooth surface. It fit comfortably in his palm, a living memory of the best day of his life. According to the contest lore, the trophy was a dragon tear. It was part of the lore of the theater, the fiction that the contest had molded itself around. Mr. Henshaw had bought this theater and found a large egg tucked in a pile of props. The egg hatched into a baby dragon who cried golden tears. The point of the contest was to write a play that would make the dragon cry, and the play that produced the most tears won.

It was a gimmick that helped brand and sell the contest. As much as Jordan loved dragons, he still found the dragon story to be cheesy. Perhaps because there was a part of him that still longed to see a real dragon. At ten, Jordan had held out hope that it might happen; at forty, he knew better. No, the magic of this place was not in the fake dragon tears, it was in the stories it brought to life and the opportunities the contest granted to aspiring writers. Jordan could still close his eyes and remember the jolt of surprise as Mr. Henshaw called his name, the applause and congratulations, the hope he had for a bright career as the egg had been placed in his hands. A promise for a future that had never been fulfilled.

What would they think, whoever was waiting inside that theater, when they realized that he had never completed another play? Jordan did not want to find out. But the possibility that they wanted him, that they wanted a play only he could write, was what had brought him here tonight. That granule of hope, smaller than a grain of flour but glowing brighter than the golden trophy, pushed him to get out of the car. Fat raindrops began to fall from the sky. Jordan pulled the collar of his trench coat up around his neck, scurried across the empty parking lot, and pushed through the wide glass doors.

The foyer stretched around him, a yawning mouth ready to swallow up whoever entered. There was no one waiting for him; only one open door to the main theater beyond and the glow of dim red lights beckoning. Jordan shook his arms and legs. The fabric rattled and water splattered on the floor. In the empty space, the sound felt massive. Jordan stopped and looked around, but there was still no one to meet him. He brushed the last bits of moisture off his arms quietly, smoothed his hair, and marched through the open door.

Red surrounded him. Red curtains, red seats, red carpet. Jordan remembered this space from the few months he had spent working with the director and crew to turn his play into a reality. It had not changed, but the effect was still startling. Jordan looked up and around at the empty seats and the closed curtains across the stage. Where was the person who had invited him here?

"Hello?" Jordan queried the empty space. The theater acoustics picked up Jordan's voice and amplified it, making his greeting sound louder than he had intended. There was no answer. Jordan turned to walk backward down the aisle; there was no one in the sound booth, no one anywhere.

Was this a trick? A joke? He shouldn't have come.

Jordan knew there was no reason that a theater would call someone who hadn't written anything of note.

"Hello." The voice was warm and deep, and the acoustics of the room made it difficult for Jordan to tell where it had come from. Jordan looked up and around, but he still did not see anyone. "Please have a seat."

A spotlight flicked on, illuminating a desk that sat stage left, on the narrow strip of stage in front of the curtain. A laptop sat on the desk, the green power light glowing dimly, a folding chair in front of it.

"This is the reason I invited you here," the voice said. "Would you like to take a look?"

Jordan walked up the steps to the stage and let his fingers brush across the laptop surface. Did they want him to write a new play? Or was he here to provide input on a work in progress? Either possibility made Jordan hungry to reconnect with the world of fiction and fantasy that had slipped away from him as he studied spreadsheets and tax law. It paid the bills, but it didn't give him the deep satisfaction that he had felt the day he won his golden tear.

Jordan sat down in the folding chair and lifted the lid. The screen went from black to glowing white. A program was already open, lines of numbers, charts, and dollar signs. These were the theater's accounting ledgers.

"You don't want me to write anything." Jordan slumped in his seat, deflated.

"Of course not. You're an accountant, aren't you?" This time, the voice was accompanied by a faint rustling, and Jordan thought it was coming from behind the curtain.

"I am. But I thought—" Jordan glared at the ledger

on the computer screen. "Did Mr. Henshaw know that I never wrote another play?"

Jordan remembered the kind elderly man who had called to tell him his play was selected for the contest, who had fed him cake and encouragement, and had ultimately handed him his prize trophy. Jordan had been sad to see his obituary in the paper a few months ago.

The theater sat silent for a moment. Finally, the voice spoke again.

"I miss him." The three words were said in the tone of voice of someone who had lost their entire world. "I should hate him. He was my jailer, but he was also my father."

Jordan raised an eyebrow at the cryptic response, and he could feel his curiosity turning to irritation. Mr. Henshaw had no children. Jordan remembered that fact from the obituary. There had been no mention of who would inherit the theater and carry on the work of launching new authors to promising careers.

"Who are you?"

"I am the judge."

"Well, that tells me nothing," Jordan muttered. The contest judges had never been named.

"Please look at the accounts. Do you think you can manage them?"

Jordan rolled his eyes at the insulting question. This guy invited him here, and then questioned his ability to do the job? Of course Jordan could handle a theater's accounts. Jordan flipped the laptop lid open, answering before he even looked at the spreadsheets again. "Yes. I can handle—wait a minute." Half a glance turned into a sharp search through the rows of numbers, and Jordan felt the heat of his anger rise. "You're using the theater to launder money."

"What? No, I'm not." The voice sounded genuinely surprised.

"Yes, you are. There is more income here than is possible from your ticket sales. I'm not going to help you scam people."

"Oh. That. It's not money laundering. I need a way to convert my gold to dollars. You know the story. You have my tear."

Jordan stared at the curtain. Had the voice behind it just claimed to be the dragon from the story? Jordan felt the room grow hot with his anger. Did they really think he was foolish enough to believe the gimmick? Yes, his play had been about a dragon, but Jordan knew that dragons weren't real no matter how much his inner six-year-old wanted them to be.

"A story printed on a playbill doesn't justify crime. Wherever that extra money is coming from, I don't want any part of it."

Jordan was ready to storm out of the theater, but the sound of the curtain rolling back made him turn to the stage. In the widening gap, he could see scales. A clawed paw. Yellow eyes. A snout. Jordan gasped and stepped back. His heel hit empty air and he threw himself forward to avoid falling off the stage. He landed on his knees and stared up at something impossible. Red scales the same color as the theater, sharp white teeth each as long as a finger, a head the size of a laundry basket and a body the size of a small car with wings tucked in close to its back. This was a dragon. Not a prop, not a set piece. A living, breathing dragon.

Jordan had never seen anything so wonderful.

"I am not trying to trick you, Mr. Dawes."

"You're a dragon." Jordan knew that he was stating the obvious, but he had to say it out loud. The dragon watched him patiently. Jordan reached forward and touched one scaly red paw. It was warm and smooth and the muscles flexed under his fingers. Definitely not a prop. Jordan realized that he had stopped breathing for a moment. Two dreams, both come true on this stage. *Was it possible?* "You're real."

"My name is Isufio."

"Hi Isufio." Jordan lifted his hand in a hesitant wave as his brain caught up with this new development and a few bits of their previous conversation became clearer. "You—that story—Mr. Henshaw—" The dragon's earlier words hit him hard. Mr. Henshaw, the kind old man who had given Jordan the best three months of his life, had found a dragon, hidden it from the world, and set up a theater contest to make money off its tears. "What happened to Mr. Henshaw?"

"He died of a stroke," Isufio said. "I am grateful to him. He could have tortured me to get my tears, but he set up a contest and let me watch plays instead. In the end, he left me this theater, but—if I hire the wrong person, I will just wind up locked in the basement again. I need someone to be my helper and keep my secret. Someone who can handle the accounts. I hoped, as a former contest winner, you would be willing to help me."

"Me. You—" Jordan stared at the dragon, the real, live dragon, and realized the risk the creature was taking. "You trust me?"

"You have the most noble job. You handle other

people's funds and don't steal or cheat them. You know how to act with honor."

Jordan had never thought that his eight hours a day in a gray cubicle doing math could be summed up in a way that sounded so enticing. "Keeping the books and keeping a secret like this are two different things. How do you know I won't steal your gold or lock you up again?"

"I watched you for three months while you cast and rehearsed your play. I saw you stand up for that little boy who was being bullied. I saw Mr. Henshaw give you a hundred-dollar bill instead of a ten when you went to fetch him a coffee, and you gave him all his change back. I know you were a good man. I hope you still are."

Jordan wasn't sure whether he should feel concerned that he had been watched, or proud of the dragon's observations. "I spent three months in this theater and I never saw you. There aren't any rumors. Any sightings." Jordan was beginning to realize that the cubicle that trapped him for eight hours a day was nothing compared to Isufio's life. "Have you ever been outside?"

"No." The word was sad and filled with longing.

"You've never flown," Jordan said. Somewhere inside Jordan, the six-year-old that had always wanted dragons to be real was screaming with outrage at the thought of a dragon trapped away from the sky.

Isufio shook his head. "No. No, I don't fly."

"You have wings. Dragons fly. In every story every-where dragons can fly." Jordan's inner six-year-old was stomping his feet now. This was a deep injustice, and it needed to be put to right.

"Those dragons didn't grow up in a basement." Isufio narrowed his eyes, his tone irritated. "This doesn't have anything to do with my finances. I need an accountant, Jordan. Do you want the job?"

"Do you want to fly?" Jordan knew it was rude, but he couldn't let the thought go.

"I just need someone to make sure the taxes get paid and the utilities stay on. You can do that, and I can pay." Isufio reached into the wings and pushed forward a bucket filled with golden eggs identical to the one Jordan had in his car.

Jordan stared at the gold. He suddenly felt sick at the idea of taking something from someone who had already had so much taken from him.

"I don't want money."

Isufio bent his head down to look Jordan in the eye. "What do you want?"

Jordan looked past Isufio's shoulder to the wings folded tight to the dragon's back. "The same thing you do. Freedom."

Isufio pulled his wings closer to his body. "I don't fly. It's not safe."

Jordan knew that tone of voice well. It was the one he used every time someone asked him if he ever wanted to write again, if he liked his current career. If he missed the dreams that had fed his youth. So, Jordan could say with absolute certainty, "You want to."

Isufio closed his eyes and sighed. He looked small, not in size, but in the wilted way that comes with age, when skin sags and youthful energy fades. "Someday."

"Someday usually means never." Jordan had waited twenty years for the "someday" when he would write again, but he never had. "Why not today?"

"People would see me," Isufio said.

"There's a storm tonight. Nobody would see you."

"The airplanes."

"This isn't like Chicago or New York. We don't have that many planes." Jordan wasn't sure what had gotten into him. "I don't know if I can work for a dragon who can't fly. Do you plan to die in this theater, having never, ever seen what is outside?"

"No." Isufio's wings unfolded from his back, stretching across the length of the stage. The dragon looked over his shoulder at them and moved them up and down as if experimenting. "The back door, in the alley. There is a loading bay there with big doors."

Because the dragon would not fit through a regular door, Jordan realized, he led the way through the back of the theater. He pushed the handle on the double doors to the alley, wedged the doorstop underneath, and stepped to one side. Isufio paused at the threshold, staring out at the brick walls of neighboring buildings and the rainy night beyond. Jordan waited in silence, giving the dragon his moment. This was the first time Isufio had ever been outside. Isufio stepped into the rain, letting the water flow over him, and lifted his head to the sky. The lighting had passed, only a steady downpour remained. Isufio laughed, like a child getting ready to do something they knew they should not, and looked down at Jordan. Rain dripped from his horns and down his scales. It was beautiful.

For the first time tonight, Jordan felt worried. What if someone saw them, and Isufio wound up trapped in his basement again? What if another human tried to steal his gold?

"You're sure about this?"

"More than anything." Isufio lowered his shoulder to the ground. "Are you coming?"

"Me?" Jordan looked up at Isufio's back. He had never wanted anything more. Jordan reached up carefully to find a handhold where Isufio's wing joined up with his shoulder and climbed onto his back. The scaly skin was rough under his hands. Jordan settled between Isufio's shoulder blades and patted his neck.

What if he fell? This was either going to be the worst or best moment of his life.

"Ready."

Isufio crouched like a cat ready to pounce and pumped his wings hard, stirring up a wind and scattering rain in all directions. He jumped, hovered, and dropped back to the ground. Jordan felt his stomach in free fall like the middle of a drop on a roller coaster. He gasped. Was that it? Isufio flapped his wings again, launched, and went up, up and then fell. This time, the dragon caught the edge of the theater roof with his claw and pushed himself higher. His wings caught the wind and man and dragon rose toward the clouds.

Jordan felt the wind rush past him, the persistent patter of rain on his face, and the elation that he had only felt once before on the day he won his golden tear. Jordan let the moment hold him and stayed in that feeling for as long as he could. It felt like a small eternity, but it only lasted a minute. Isufio's wings slowed and he fluttered back down to land on the theater roof. After a moment of rest, the dragon stepped off the edge and dropped into the alley again. Jordan slipped off his back and staggered, like a tourist back on land after a cruise. Like a tourist, he didn't want the trip to end yet. Jordan was still caught up in the rush of euphoria. He had witnessed a dragon's first flight. It had been the most amazing moment of his life.

"I never thought I would do that." Isufio was breathless, as if he had just run a marathon. He looked down at Jordan. "This is a problem."

"What problem?" Jordan stared at Isufio. Had the dragon not enjoyed the flight as much as he had? "That was amazing!"

"Yes, and I want to do it again." Isufio looked up at the sky, determined. "That can't happen here. I have to practice. Get stronger. I'll need someone to arrange a truck big enough to take me out of town. A place where I can go out and no one will see me. I need a very, very good accountant."

Accountant. Jordan looked up at the dragon in front of him. If he had become the writer he had wanted to be, he would have never ridden on a dragon's back. The path to his current career was one Jordan had regretted for decades, but without that career, he would never have found his way here. For the first time in his life, "accountant" sounded better than "playwright."

Jordan smiled. "I'll just have to give my two weeks' notice."

Jennifer M Roberts earned her BA in history, but she prefers to dream of how things might have been rather than focusing on how things really were. She hails from the Midwest and enjoys sweet corn, contra dancing, and historical re-enactment. To learn more about upcoming and future projects, visit www.jmroberts.com.

DRAGON EYES: AN UNCONVENTIONAL FAIRYTALE

DANIELLE DAVIS

O*nce upon a time, there was a princess whose parents locked her in a tower.*

Once upon a time, there was a dragon that guarded a tower rumored to house a beautiful princess.

Once upon a time, these were different stories.

KING PRINCE and his wife Mylena loved their daughter, who was born after a long period of doubt whether an heir would even be possible. From the start, she was like something from a fairytale. Her hair curved in long, silken waves the color of ripe chestnuts. Her figure was slight, her skin fair. Such were the luminous nature of her eyes, people several kingdoms away heard of the clearness of their hazel depths and how they sparkled with intelligence and wit.

What they didn't know was that she could turn into a dragon.

Well, that's mostly true. She couldn't change at will,

but rather was forced, by whatever element of nature caused the transformation, into her dragon form for three consecutive months out of the year. Usually, this took place in the winter months, when her warm dragon's hide favored the brittle kiss of ice and snow. But it meant that for every nine months of dancing and fostering and treatise counseling the kingdom enjoyed, there were three months of solitude. Visitors to the gate were turned away regardless of their standing. All but essential personnel were granted winter leave of their duties at the castle, to resume at the beginning of the new year. It was a tidy solution to a rather awkward problem.

However, it only worked for a few years. At first, keeping a dragon child secreted away in the castle, playing games and learning lessons from only a handful of personal servants and tutors, was easy. But as the child grew, so did her dragon form. So it was, on the eve of her ninth birthday, that she was sent to another area of the kingdom: an isolated, abandoned castle that had once housed a minor duke before his family fell ill to a plague. There she and her contingent of servants stayed for the winter months, until the spring buds showed their naked tips to the world and they were able to travel back to her parents' castle.

So it went, for a little over a decade. Princess Sheena grew from a smiling, observant child into a beautiful, witty young woman.

Well, a beautiful, witty young woman and a fantastically large dragon who learned to breathe fire. But more on that later.

What's important to know now is that this... peculiarity... affected how her parents raised her. There were no lessons on proper harp playing, a common practice when it came to beguiling potential suitors. No embroidery, to sew favors to give to knights at tourneys. Her parents were careful to ensure there was no expectation on her part, as was instilled in the other princesses she knew, of snaring a likely Prince Charming of her own.

Their intent was benevolent—to save her from the disappointment she surely would face later. They could not, in good conscience, give her hand away to a man who would shortly discover exactly what he'd married come their first winter together. What that gave to Sheena, however, was a freedom of study unknown to the other princesses she knew.

Instead of learning the harp, Sheena decided she preferred the jingling johnny, a clashingly raucous percussion instrument she'd once seen a minstrel play at the Summer Fair. She built one herself using a sturdy staff and fixing all manner of tin items to it: small bells, rocks trapped between two tin plates... you get the idea. Instead of embroidery, she learned darning instead—an ironic joke considering her likelihood of becoming the Spinster Princess. She spat when she coughed up snot during cold season. She played chess better than her father's military general and argued politics with his councillors. She wore men's riding pants when she charged out on the fat warhorse she'd begged off her parents because she loved his dapples.

And when suitors arrived, she behaved as she normally would. Over dinner, she asked their opinions on the likelihood of a peace treaty with the barbarian tribes of the south. She asked after their kingdom's imports and offered suggestions for improving their economic leverage. Most got the hint before dessert.

Those that didn't got to enjoy her warbling rendition of "happy birthday" with jingling johnny accompaniment.

Then, with the last leaves of fall making their sad descent to the ground, she and her attendants bade her parents a tearful goodbye and left for the Iron Tower, so named for the iron bars that fortified the doors and lower windows.

WHAT NOBODY COUNTED ON WAS how, well, *tedious* this whole procession began to be for Sheena. Year after year, it was always the same: come home, pretend to be a normal girl, then hide away in her tower. Transform, rinse, repeat.

And though she appeared to take great delight in besting suitor after suitor, it wore on her. Her parents were thrilled—it seemed their diffidence to the idea of finding a man had worked to everyone's advantage. But she had a longing in her that she couldn't quite name, a desire to actually find a like personality, to be able to debate about topics of interest with one who matched her enthusiasm for them. To find someone who accepted her as she was rather than what she pretended to be.

She also noticed, as she moved from teenager into young woman, certain changes in her dragon form that her human one didn't share. Not the obvious ones, mind you. The internal ones. As a dragon, she retained the power of speech and intellectual reason—that remained about the same regardless of her form. But most of the emotions she felt with raw acuity as a girl—love, fear, sadness, hatred, and (most especially) boredom—were dulled to the merest afterthought when she was a dragon. All her dragon form cared for, foremost, were those emotions attributed to lesser creatures: hunger, territorialism, mating instinct. She could still feel the "human" emotions as a dragon, but their importance was minimal.

Inevitably, she learned the one major downside to being a dragon: knights. One injudicious outing on her part—a brief foray into a nearby farm for a midnight snack of raw lamb chops—resulted in accidental discovery by the farmer's son, who had gone out to make sure the cows had enough hay for the night.

Rumor being what it was, word spread about the dragon scourge that had taken up residence in the abandoned Iron Tower. And, since rumors reproduced like bunnies, there were soon others. The dragon guarded a princess trapped in the tower. There wasn't one dragon, but five! That the dragon had slain three members of someone's uncle's second cousin's daughter's family.

The average number of knights she had to dispatch every winter was about five. The first one or two were usually rookies, newly knighted youths whose shiny armor reflected the sun from two counties away. These she usually ate before they even knew she was nearby. With a carefully angled aerial attack, she found she could eat both knight and horse in a single gulp, if the horse was smallish.

The third, and sometimes fourth, knights were usually more seasoned. Their armor had nicks and dings from a few significant battles, maybe they'd led a war party or two for their king. These knights put up more of a fight on account of being handier with a sword. Sheena learned that a few fireballs distracted them enough for her to unhorse them with her tail and then swallow them whole.

The last few knights of the season were the worst. These were the battle-hardened warriors. Those whose armor had faded to a dull glint from the countless battles they'd fought. After nearly losing her head (literally) to a fellow calling himself Sir Thomas the Bold, she learned to blast them with fire before they got close enough to use their swords. Under a steady stream of flame, they usually cooked within their metal boxes in under two minutes. She *did* always like her meat well-done.

The year Princess Sheena turned twenty, though, everything changed.

"REGINA, can you bring me another of those memoirs from the library? I've finished the one on King Balgus the Huge last night." Sheena's voice rumbled through the room like the sound of distant thunder, making Regina flinch. "Sorry," Sheena grimaced. Well, she grimaced as much as her sinuous neck would allow.

Regina gave her a dark look but put down the tray of smoked meat she'd brought and turned to leave. "Mistress, you read faster than I would have given you credit for, given how small those pages are."

Sheena grinned, revealing her double set of needle-like teeth. Her long, black tongue lolled from the side of her mouth. "I learned a new trick for turning the pages. If I just hold the covers with my claws and blow gently to one side, I can turn the page. It helps me read much faster than before."

With a laugh, Regina's dark look turned to an affectionate glare. "At this rate, you'll run through the entire library before December!"

"Ugh." Regina sent a disappointed puff of dark smoke from her nostrils. "That would make for a tedious winter."

Regina grinned and left the room. Aside from her, Sheena only took two other attendants these days: a cook and a tutor. Since both of them were out on errands for the afternoon, Sheena was surprised to turn toward the rock slab that served as her bed to find a young knight standing in the middle of her room.

Sheena reared back. The movement brought her head several feet off the ground—and out of reach of the knight's sword, though it remained sheathed at his hip—and close to the ceiling. Her neck coiled into a curving S shape as she flexed the muscles along her back to flair the sharp scales at the base of her neck and shoulders. Though most of her was covered in tiny, fine scales as soft as hide, her protective scales were thicker and more rounded, able to deflect a sharper blow that might otherwise break the skin elsewhere on her body. She flexed her scythe-like claws and fixed the knight with her best glare.

"Who are you?" she demanded. When she didn't try to soften it, the natural volume of her voice made the furniture in the room tremble.

The knight remained in place, silently regarding her as he leaned slightly back to take in her full height.

"Answer me!" She stomped one foot and rattled the protective scales threateningly. The knight didn't move, even as small pebbles rained down on his armor with small pings.

Sheena rolled her eyes and snorted, which sent the frills at the back of her jaw fluttering. "This is the part where you draw your sword, genius," she said in a stage-whisper.

The knight slowly reached up and slid his helmet off his head. He stared at her with wide, wonder-filled eyes. An unruly lock of dark hair fell over his forehead and he brushed it back as if it barely registered. "I had heard tales of you, you know. How fearsome your teeth. How hot your fire. How querulous your temper—"

"Querulous, me?" she interrupted. She snaked her head down so that it was at eye level with him. "Are you sure you heard that right?"

The knight paused. Even with that cow-like expression of confusion on his face, she had to admit he was good-looking. Not that it mattered.

"I'm pretty sure that's what I heard." He lowered his gaze and frowned, thinking. "I mean, it sounded similar…" He looked up and met her gaze directly. She marveled at the lack of fear and guile she saw there. "What sounds like 'querulous' but means 'dangerous?'"

For a moment, she wasn't sure how to respond. Was he mad? Didn't he realize he was staring down a dragon that had not only spoken to him, but which had killed several men before him? But he continued to stare at her with a little frowny line between his eyes that she found endearing.

"Perilous?" she suggested.

He clapped his gloves together and pointed at her. "That's it! For some reason, I always confuse those two."

She stared at him for a long moment. "Right… Well, let's rewind this a bit and get back to my original question. Who are you?"

"Gareth." He said the name in an offhanded tone, as if it were unimportant. He was still staring at her with a mixture of awe and fascination.

Sheena rose to her full height and fixed him with her most menacing glare. She prepared to launch into her speech, the one she used for the more experienced knights in the hopes she could dissuade them from a fight. So far, it had worked on two of them. "Well, Gareth, I will give you one chance to leave without issue. If you choose not to heed my warning, I can guarantee your death will be most... Why are you looking at me like that?"

He shrugged and grinned at her. "Are you sure the rumor I'd heard wasn't actually 'garrulous'?"

She lowered her head again to his level. "You have got to be the rudest knight I've ever met. How did you ever make it to knighthood?"

His grin didn't falter. "I kept my mouth shut mostly." She noticed his eyes were blue as a summer lake and sparkling with mischief.

"I doubt that's an ability you possess," she muttered and huffed a dark cloud of smoke into his face.

He twisted away, hacking and waving to clear the air around his face. "You surprised me. I expected you to ask why I was here."

Sheena gave the best approximation to a shrug her dragon form allowed. "Why would I ask that? Past experience would tell me you're here to kill me."

"That would be a most unwise thing to do, I think." He turned away from her and strolled around the room, pulling his armored gloves off as he spoke. It was the first time a knight had ever—knowingly—turned his back to her. "I imagine you could kill me faster than if I jumped from this tower." His fingers grazed over the periwinkle tulle that formed the canopy of her bed. He made an appreciative noise and turned his attention to a painting on the wall.

"Care to get to the point anytime soon? I have a Latin lesson in a half hour." Sheena let him hear the irritation in her voice, but inwardly she was intrigued. This had gone like no other meeting she'd ever had.

Instead of answering, he pointed to the picture. "This you?" He looked over his shoulder at her with raised eyebrows, waiting.

The painting showed her, sitting demurely on a chair with her body turned away from the viewer. But her face curled back over her shoulder to return the look. The painter had captured her eyes almost perfectly so they dominated the entire image with a piercing gaze.

She gave him a suspicious look, then nodded.

He looked back to the picture, then turned and fixed her with an appraising look. "I think I like you this way better, if you don't mind my saying so."

Her eyes widened in shock. For a moment all she could do was stare at him. Then she moved with the liquid grace of a predator to stalk a circle around him. "Explain yourself."

"You're certainly a beautiful woman, don't get me wrong. But the eyes. In that picture. They don't look any different on you as a dragon. But they suit you better this way. At least as a dragon, you don't have to hide what you are."

Despite herself, she was curious. "And what is that?"

In a soft voice so low she had to ease closer to hear, he said, "Wild. Fierce. Maybe a little bit feral around the edges. But smart. And brave. And…" He looked down again, struggling to find the words. "Oh, I can't define it. It's just... as a girl, those eyes make me think someone's hiding on the inside, that there's more to her than I see on the surface. As a dragon, your appearance personifies what I feel like might be hiding there."

She gave him a long look and saw something similar within his eyes. There was a look of wildness there, too. Something unconventional. Something searching. Something exotic, but at the same time familiar. Something that beckoned her. Something waiting for the right person to unlock the secrets there.

"Tell me," she said in a coy voice. "What are your views on the prospect of the local kingdoms expanding their trade options with the southern nomads?"

Gareth thought for a moment. She watched the ideas flicker within his eyes as he formed his answer. After several long moments, he met her gaze. "I think it would be a wise move if we could get their guarantee of safe passage through their territories. They have a textiles reach to the east that we haven't been able to extend, no matter how hard we've tried, and we have an agricultural advantage they might appreciate given their nomadic culture."

Sheena bared her teeth in a wide smile. Gareth returned it. "I don't know how you got up here, Gareth Silvertongue, but I hope you've given some thought as to how you're going to get back down. If you'll excuse me, I have a Latin lesson to prepare for." Still smiling, she turned to leave.

"Wait!" Gareth called. "Can I come see you again?" The naked hope in his voice made her heart turn over.

"I won't be here. My transformation ends in a few days. Then I'll return to my human form and my parent's castle. Since you prefer my dragon form, I'm sorry to say I won't be in it for quite some time. Much longer than a knight like you cares to wait."

In a gentle voice heavy with emotions she didn't dare name, she heard him say, "My cares are my own business." When she reached the doorway and glanced back over her shoulder, he was already gone.

The disappointment she felt surprised her, but she knew it was for the best.

THE NEXT DAY, she woke to find a white rose lying on the windowsill. Around the middle, a silk ribbon attached the rose to a note. In a simple, unadorned hand she read: *You aren't the only one who isn't what they seem on the surface. See you in a few days.*

DANIELLE DAVIS (SHE/HER) is a liar, a cheater at cards, and a misrememberer of song lyrics: only two of these are true. Her horror and dark fantasy have appeared in The Santa Barbara Literary Journal, Andromeda Spaceways Magazine, *and 50+ anthologies. She is also the author of* Bone on Bone: A Collection of Short Stories. *An active contributor to* Writer Unboxed, *she is also a member of Horror Writers of America (HWA). You can find her on most social media platforms under the handle "LiteraryEllyMay" and at www.literaryellymay.com.*

THE LAST WILD HUNT OF QUEEN MORGANA

SHARMON GAZAWAY

Queen Morgana arched her wings, clawed toes curling. Her hunger was all-consuming, blocking thought, shaping desire.

Pacing the turret, she returned again to the balcony, claws clicking across volcanic glass pavers mounted in carved bone. She squinted hard eyes up at the night sky partially shrouded by a volcanic plume. There, a faint glowing speck shot across the cosmos, growing larger as it approached Lo-Dibar's atmosphere. A shiver of anticipation rippled down her scale-armored spine.

More male dragons on the way at last. Would this lot be as paltry and weak-willed as the last? She hoped not. She relished a rigorous chase—and struggle. She licked her snout. It had been an especially long bi-solar year, and her stomach growled with the ferocity of a hatchling. Salivating, she snatched up a femur and banged the iron gong.

The air still vibrated as Chidra flapped onto the balcony, her fleshy wings brushing the window's bone arches. "Your Highness?"

"They're almost here. Prepare the Valkyrie horde."

Chidra flashed fangs in a smile, bowed her mottled bald head, and swooped back out into darkness.

———

HE WASN'T PARTICULARLY LARGER or stronger looking than the other males who followed behind him. From her vantage point in the darkened turret, Morgana watched how he bore himself—almost princely, but without arrogance. Too bad. She liked taking down the arrogant ones.

When he stepped down from the spacecraft, three other dragons flanked him, providing an undivided front. The ship's door closed like a jaw, then lifted off. The last for another bi-solar year.

The leader—for clearly he was a leader—sniffed warily, his lip curling back as he caught her scent. She knew from experience it was near irresistible—though tainted with an ancient warning for her prey. It was only fair.

Not that she was very interested in fair. She was interested in dominating. Putting more heads on her wall. And feeding.

The leader snorted, rejecting her scent. He cautiously approached the glistening Stranger's Pool. One of his comrades—a burly one, scarred and brown —put out a clawed hand to prevent him drinking, then knelt and lapped at the pool, testing it first himself.

What bizarre conduct! One male dragon protecting another? Were they defective? Morgana tapped a claw on the ivory balcony.

Her rumbling stomach shook her out of her reverie.

What did it matter, after all? They were criminals sentenced to be executed by her. More importantly they were food, the only food she'd have for another year. But any curious behavior of her prey intrigued her. She'd seen so many, all so monotonously the same…and she was fatally bored.

She shifted her weight impatiently from foot to foot as the four dragons drank deeply. Chidra and her horde would allow them to drink. It would provide stamina for the hunt. Morgana trained her attention on the leader— the others were nothing, chattel. The luminescent pool lit up his deep green scale-armor, green as the hills among which she once lived and ruled. Hills of home she would never see again.

Almost as if he sensed her thought, he peered up through the lightly sifting ash with pale green eyes.

Like peridot, she thought. A favorite stone of hers since a hatchling. She sat back on her haunches. He couldn't see her. Could he?

She chuckled silently. He couldn't see her, but he sensed her. He knew she waited above them, tensed to pounce.

Chidra swept into the room. "My Lady, the horde is ready."

Morgana salivated at the words. "Very good. Let them loose." She flexed her golden webbed wings and sharpened her claws on the volcanic whetstone at the foot of her throne. She gazed down from the heights of the balcony, the distance shrinking the green leader. He's just food, she reminded herself.

Chidra dove and darted above the heads of the male dragons, taunting with her fanged smile. "Let the hunt begin!" she screeched.

"Lady Dragon! Here I am, yours for the taking," the leader roared, arching the remnants of his prison-clipped wings.

How dare he mock her. She glimpsed the slight turned up corner of his snout before he charged away from the pool's circle of light into the cover of the shadowy petrified forest. The airborne Valkyrie horde bunched into a tightly whorled vortex surrounding the remaining males, then exploded into a screeching fury, scattering the dragons.

Morgana churned her ponderous wings, seething with anticipation as she took to the air. She caught sight of the leader skulking between the stony trees. She already knew his scent—sulfurous, rank, titillating. She ignored the other dragons. They would serve when her appetite was blunted with their leader.

He could not fly, but he was fast on foot. She alighted on the ground and folded her wings tight against her blood-red scales. A foot race it would be. She found the pull of her claws through ashen bramble and the strain of her thigh muscles exhilarating. She thrashed into spiky brush he had just torn through. She tasted his scent, hot on his trail.

Then, abruptly, it ended. She skidded to a halt. How had he doubled back? Impossible. She wheeled about, sussing out the thick darkness. Usually her poor night vision wasn't a problem. She could ignite the forest with a breath. She hesitated, reluctant to end the hunt so soon.

But she had no choice—use fire or lose her quarry. She inhaled deeply, her lungs like leather bellows. She blew flame and incinerated a blaze through the forest, illuminating the dark. Nothing.

She heard a faint *whoosh* from the treetop above a split second before he landed on her back. He leveraged a stone branch across her windpipe.

"What an honor to make your acquaintance, witch," he rumbled, his snout pressed to her ear.

She shook with fury, unfurling her wings as best she could. She pumped hard but couldn't rise with his weight bearing her down.

"No fun when the wings don't work, eh?" His breath was hot against her cheek scales.

She dropped her weight, catching him off guard, tucked and tumbled, rolling her weight over his. Using the advantage of surprise, she flipped over on top of him, pinning him against a charred tree trunk. In the glow of the smoldering embers surrounding them she saw his green eyes shift from round with surprise, to slits of laughter.

Then she did something she had never before done. She rolled off him and backed away. Shaken, she took to the wing, refusing to think about what she was doing. She caught sight of one of his three comrades, swooped down, and sank her claws deep into his chest. One of the others—the loyal water tester—screamed, "Vega! No!" and clawed at her back. She flung him off, and tore into her victim.

She swallowed, sated for the moment, as the leader's howl of outrage echoed through the rock forest and shivered down her spine.

"Unfair! Cheat!" He bellowed, running into the clearing where his comrade lay eviscerated. His burly scarred friend caught him and held him back.

"It's only cheating if there are rules," she roared back, licking her lips.

Growling, she retreated and soared back to her turret. His cries followed her. "Foul! Dishonor!"

THE VALKYRIES SWARMED HER. "How could you let the leader escape?" Chidra screeched. "You had him! Have you grown weak and infirm with age?"

They all screamed accusations at her, circling the vaulted turret room with dizzying vehemence.

How dared they berate her! She placed a clawed hand over the ruby amulet on her breastplate. "Have you forgotten who I am?" Morgana demanded. "Your very breath is in my hand."

Chidra reluctantly bowed her head and, trembling, led the horde from her presence.

Her energy spent, Morgana crawled into her emerald-studded ivory bed and pulled a white ermine fur up to her chin. She was disgusted with the horde, and disgusted with the strange dragon leader who defied her —and mostly disgusted with her own weakness. Unfair witch, he'd called her. Dishonorable. Both true. She'd been called much worse. Why did his words sting?

She thought back over the millennia, remembering past mates—the strong, the fierce, the cruel. She had devoured them all. Their strength became hers, they were a part of her still. But so also was their callousness, their cold, calculating minds. Their utter selfishness and disregard for any, strong or weak.

She missed herself, at times. The young dragoness who had dreamed of power, yes, and of wealth, of course, but with a mate. One who would share it all with her.

But in the end, it had been dominate or be dominated. And to be dominated was not in her DNA.

She stared into a winking emerald couched in the ivory of her bedstead. Green. His plated armor green as the moss on the runed stones of her homeland where the rivers ran clear and green as peridot. She would give every emerald in her cache to fly over those hills just once more, to walk carefree through those waving fields of tall grass.

But that world, the tender green world of her hatching and lush youth, was gone, and nothing could bring it back.

Why didn't you slaughter him while you had the chance? The horde had demanded.

Why hadn't she, indeed?

She rose from her bed, dragging the white fur with her. She stood on the balcony staring into the Stranger's Pool. She felt a stranger here herself, despite the millennia she'd lived here. *Existed* here.

She unfurled the white fur over the balcony, its limpid length brushing the outer wall. She held it there and shivered till daybreak.

When night gave way to the blue and pink dawn of twinned suns, the leader called out, "Witch! Is that a signal of truce, or just another scurvy trick?"

Morgana's heart jumped oddly. She squared her shoulders. "You address your queen in that way?"

Ash spewed from a distant volcano mount.

"Queen! Queen of what? You're not in a palace, Lady, you are in a prison—tossed meat once per year."

His crew laughed. "A queen rules. What do you rule over?" he shouted, beating his armored chest.

She felt her pupils contract with outrage, fire glutted her throat. She swallowed it back. "I wish to discuss terms with you."

"There is only one term I will agree to. Prove yourself honorable, spare my men, and set your sights on me."

The fierce protests of his crew reached her ears.

"I'm afraid you have spent too much time among human knights. Honor won't fill an empty belly."

He clenched his fists. "What are these terms you propose?"

She ran her claws through the soft fur. "For amusement, I will play this game of honor with you. I will meet with you by the pool."

Chidra waited for her in the Hall, her agitated wings churning the air. Her tone however was subdued. "My Lady, how can you make terms with such a perversely weak creature? Or treat him as an equal?"

Morgana shuddered to think. She couldn't even explain it to herself. Then she caressed the amulet on her breastplate. "Remember your place, Valkyrie."

THE SMALL POOL SEPARATED THEM. His scent filled her nostrils. "I've always...been rather fond of green," she admitted, drawing him in, moving toward him around the pool.

He circled slowly in the opposite direction. "You're quite handsome—for a treacherous wyrm," he admitted grudgingly. "Now, state your terms."

She hesitated, then drew in her breath. "Sacrifice yourself to me and I'll spare your comrades."

His eyes did not waver. "And how could I be sure you'd keep your word, since I wouldn't be around to hold you to it? After all, 'honor won't fill an empty belly.' " He inched toward her crouching on all fours, a stance of power and attack.

"Oh, but you would be around." She smiled deliciously, showing all her fangs. "As my mate."

His jaw dropped in a way that tickled deep in her belly.

"Your mate?"

They circled each other in a wary waltz. "I realize your options are limited—be eaten, see your men eaten —or accept my proposal." She detected his nostrils quivering with her scent. "But come now, I'm not completely repulsive to you, clearly."

He didn't deny the attraction.

"Captain, you can't trust a word she breathes!" his men pleaded. "Don't do this!"

They continued their mate-circling, his eyes probing hers. The surface tremored beneath them as tectonic plates grated across one another far below. His men grew silent. Chidra and the horde hovered nearby, listening, their gray mottled skin rippling with disapproval. Silence hung thick in the air like ash.

The scarred brown dragon quietly stepped forward. "If my lord the captain agrees to this, this *proposal*, that leaves one problem." He crossed his arms over his chest.

All eyes turned to him.

"What is your name?" Morgana asked, reluctantly admiring his gumption.

"Wulff, First Mate to Captain Rommul."

"Captain?" She turned to the green leader.

"Yes. I fly—flew—both ways. Wings and spacecraft."

This did intrigue her. "And what is the remaining problem, Wulff?" she asked.

"What will you eat until the next ship arrives—a year from now?"

Temporarily sated from the meal of their unfortunate comrade, she'd forgotten about food for the moment. She eyed the captain's crew with a measured gaze.

The captain glared through narrowed eyes. "I'll thank you not to look at my men as food, if you expect me to keep to our bargain."

There was not enough wild game on the wasteland planet of Lo-Dibar to sustain herself, let alone three other dragons. The captain turned his eyes to Chidra and the horde of Valkyries.

Morgana chuckled. "They are bloodless creatures who feed on cinders and petrified bark. They taste of ash—horrid—and provide little sustenance."

Chidra rankled at the insult.

"I believe I can solve this conundrum," Wulff said. "I offer myself."

They all stared, dumbstruck.

Captain Rommul was the first to recover. "Wulff, are you mad? I won't let you—"

"Pardon me, Captain, but we're not onboard the *Defiant* anymore. I make my own decisions. You will need sustenance till the next ship arrives. I would have happily given my life for you in any battle, at any time. I see this as no different."

Captain Rommul drew him away from the pool.

Their voices erupted heatedly, the captain gesticulated wildly. Then their voices softened, and they embraced.

THEY FEASTED at Morgana's grand table that had never seated more than herself. Wulff's head hung in a place of honor, high above his comrade's and the heads of all the other dragons that came before. Morgana and the captain divided Wulff's heart between themselves.

They became mellow with full stomachs, and the youngest dragon, Sear, began to tell of past glories. Morgana listened intently as he told of the captain's exploits, how his ship had been in constant threat as he saved dragons on other planets from the dragon genocide. But he had run out of luck at last, and his crew of eight had been captured, four killed in the fight. Then they, the remaining four, had had their wings clipped, their ability to breathe fire chemically altered, and were sent here to be executed, by her.

"What was your homeland like?" She couldn't resist asking. She'd been on this skeletal planet for so long, she found it hard to imagine other worlds. Her innards roiled like a magma chamber with shame that she hadn't even known there was an assault on their kind. But then, she'd rarely dallied in conversation with her past victims, intent as she was on vanquishing and feeding.

"It is a newly terraformed planet. Viridis. Rich fertile fields, cool blue lakes and deep, mist-covered valleys."

"And green?"

"As emeralds."

The captain—Rommul, as she had begun to think of him—looked at her, then around at the barren room. "How would you like to be Queen of something? An actual realm?"

He proposed that when the next ship came, they might be able to overcome the crew—and feast on them of course—and take command of the vessel. His eyes shone, his voice husky with daring. Perhaps they could persuade the dragon inmates to join them, come with them to Viridis and repopulate their homeland.

Entranced, Morgana allowed her heart to hope for just a moment—or perhaps it was Wulff's heart already having an effect on her psyche. She had hesitated before biting into it, knowing full well that some of Wulff's attributes of selflessness, bravery, deep affection and loyalty would pass to her—in the way of dragons.

Chidra spoke up softly. "You would abandon us to this cruel planet?"

Morgana stood. Rommul and his brave band had fought for others to be free. She removed the amulet from her breastplate. She lifted it high for Chidra and the horde to see and smashed it to shards on the petri-fied wood tabletop.

Chidra looked from the shattered bondage of the amulet back to the horde. They nodded bald heads in unison. "We would like to join you in your new world," Chidra said.

Morgana nodded her assent. She reseated herself beside Rommul, the promise of a green world in his hard green scales. It would be a long, barren year of hunger and suffering ahead to endure. Could they survive that long without devouring one another? Fear shimmered in the back of her mind. Would the captain

—her enemy, her prey, her spouse—turn on her? Would she turn on him, her ravening hunger mastering her?

He cocked his head, eyeing her with a side glance. Clearly, he was thinking the same.

She licked her claws clean of innocent blood, a smile curling her lip. She decided to risk it.

SHARMON GAZAWAY IS a Dwarf Stars Award finalist. Her fiction is included NewMyths' Best Of anthologies Cosmic Muse, and The Growers, and in The Best of MetaStellar Year Two. Her work appears or is forthcoming in The Fairy Tale Magazine *(The Best of Enchanted Conversation),* Abyss & Apex, Cosmic Roots & Eldritch Shores, Solarpunk Magazine, The Forge Literary Magazine, *and elsewhere. Her work is included in anthologies from Air and Nothingness Press, Blackspot Books, Brigids Gate Press, and others. Sharmon writes from the Deep South of the US where she lives beside a historic cemetery haunted by the wild cries of pileated woodpeckers. Instagram @sharmongazaway.*

HOARD TALES

A.R.R. ASH

"It's almost time! In only five years, *Lairs Magazine* is going to release its centenary Hordes 400 list." A gold dragon, the size of a small hill, swished his tail about in enthusiasm, sending a jangling wave through the mounds of coins and gems that would shame an avaricious dwarven king. Within the hollowed-out mountain, the light from the setting sun streamed through the cave opening and glinted off gold coins and aurous scales alike.

Three smaller dragons scrambled to avoid the avalanche of crashing, clinking platinum and gold and silver, rubies and sapphires and diamonds.

"I'm sure you'll be at the top of the list again, Uncle Skinflint," one of the smaller dragons said. His scales were a vibrant green, and dozens of small, conical spikes protruded from about his head and face.

"I don't know, Toothy," a small, deep-red-scaled dragon said. A line of bony spikes started just behind his eyes and ran along his neck and back, to the tip of his tail. "I hear Hardheart Hidehoard might win this time."

"WHAAAT!" Uncle Skinflint shouted, and a puff of fire and smoke, along with the smell of brimstone, escaped his maw. Atop his skull was an upward sweeping plate, from which extended an array of horns, which shrunk in size the farther they were from the top of the head. "Who told you that, Scaly?"

Scaly, the red dragon, slunk away to put a small pile —still the size of a respectable mansion—of coins between him and his uncle. "It's—well—everyone is saying it, Uncle."

"I haven't lost in a thousand years," Skinflint said, "and I'll be a snake's sibling if that sneaky silver out hoards me!"

"What are you going to do, Uncle Skinflint?" a small dragon with vivid blue scales said. Two large, forward-sweeping horns projected from either side of his face.

"I don't know," Skinflint said, his rumbling voice downcast like a sad rockslide. "Breathy, Scaly, Toothy, I need to think."

"Okay, Uncle," the three small dragons said in unison and left the mountainous cavern for the tunnels leading to their smaller grottos.

Behind them, Uncle Skinflint gave a powerful beat of his wings and dove into his ocean of coins and treasure, basking in the comforting feel of precious metal. A sensual "Ahh" followed the three dragons.

"I GOT IT! I GOT IT!" Skinflint's deep voice boomed to every corner of his lair.

"What are you going to do, Uncle?" Breathy, Scaly,

and Toothy asked together when they arrived in the cavernous treasure chamber.

"I'm going to start a business." The enormous gold dragon extended his long neck proudly.

His nephews fell into stunned silence for some time, their wide jaws slack. "A...a business?"

"Dragons...dragons don't work, Uncle," Breathy said, looking back and forth to his brothers, as if searching for confirmation. "We raze, we pillage."

"That's true," Scaly said, a bit more firmly. "No self-respecting dragon *earns* money."

Toothy nodded along.

"If that's what it takes to be number one, then that's what I'll do," Skinflint declared. "The Skinflint Bank and Trust. You'll see. I'll be at the top of the list again."

Later that year...

"Ok, class, now watch. This is the correct way to strafe a castle," a black dragon said as she dove toward a high, gray-walled fortress surrounded by a wide moat. Hundreds of minuscule forms screamed and shouted and ran pell-mell around the grounds.

Breathy, Scaly, and Toothy, along with three other small dragons—a pink, a purple, and a silver—looked on, circling high above.

"You know my dad's going to be at the top of the Hordes 400," the silver said over the sound of the wind and the crumbling and crashing of rock from the castle wall below. The screams from the panicking forms intensified.

"No way, Scaleheart!" Breathy said, completing an

agitated loop in the air. "Uncle Skinflint has a trick in his claws."

"Yeah!" agreed Toothy. "Uncle Skinflint is a genius, and he's making a fortune with his new business."

"Business?!" Scaleheart shouted, and he snorted out a spurt of flame as he burst into laughter.

The pink and purple dragons joined in the raucous cachinnation.

"Shut up, Scaleheart!" Scaly said, baring fangs as long as a dwarf is tall.

"Yeah, you'll see," Breathy said, narrowing his slitted eyes.

"What's going on here?" the black dragon said as she returned from her sorties against the castle. "Were you even paying attention?"

Scaleheart breathed in deeply, forcing his body to relax from the convulsive laughter. "Teacher Widewing, Teacher Widewing, I'm sorry, but Toothy said his uncle started a *business*."

A new bout of guffawing erupted among Scaleheart and the pink and purple.

Widewing hiccupped as she tried to hold in her own snicker, and a puff of smoke leaked between her teeth. "Now, Scaleheart, this is not the time for that. Right now, you need to be learning the proper way to assault a castle."

Casting his gaze toward the fortress, Scaleheart said, "Yes, Teacher Widewing."

"Very good," Widewing said. "Now, observe how to deal with their catapults."

"FATHER! FATHER!" Scaleheart shouted as he flew into the wide cave entrance of Hardheart's lair.

Upon the mounds of coins, gems, and trinkets worth a hundred kingdoms, a silver dragon slept curled in such peaceful repose—reminiscent of a puppy or kitten in the comfort and safety of its favorite nook—one could forget that, if disturbed, the beast would awaken with such ravenous hunger and conflagrant rage that half the continent would lie in waste before its ire and voracity were sated.

"What is it, Scaleheart?" The massive dragon opened his eyes, loosed a rumbling growl, and gave a wide-mawed yawn. A bony plate swept backward atop his head. Nearby lay the wooden remains of a treasure galleon. "My newest acquisitions will surely put me over Miser Skinflint."

"That's what I wanted to tell you about," Scaleheart said, his voice between excitement and a whine. "I just heard that he started a *business*."

Hardheart's tail twitched and splintered the wooden remnants. "A...business?" He paused for several moments while Scaleheart nodded energetically.

"Are you going to do anything, Father?"

Hardheart released a burst of triumphant laughter. "I don't need to do anything. He must really be desperate. I'll be at the top of the Hordes 400 for certain."

A YEAR LATER...

"How's *business*?" the pink dragon asked with a snicker as Breathy, Scaly, and Toothy passed upon the shore after taking their turns learning the proper way to dive toward a vessel on the open water so as to not accidently sink it.

Toothy put his head down, refusing to meet her gaze. Scaly growled, allowing a puff of sulfuric smoke to emerge from his nostrils. The pink emitted an unusual noise, somehow the combination of a snarl and a squeak, and hopped backward.

Breathy just kept his gaze forward. "This is horrible." His voice held a quality of resigned sadness. "Uncle Skinflint's obsession with winning this stupid competition is making us laughing stocks."

Toothy nodded in agreement.

"They're just envious," Scaly said with a deep growl. "Uncle Skinflint was the first dragon to make the lesser races pay tribute over many years, instead of taking everything they have all at once. That became a steady stream of income over decades, for generations of their short lives, accumulating so much more than he would have gotten from a single raid. Now, every dragon in the top 400 forces the lesser races to pay tribute."

Toothy nodded in agreement.

Scaly concluded, "Mark my words: All other dragons will be emulating him and starting businesses when he wins again."

HARDHEART'S TAIL smashed against the interior rock wall of his lair and sent stone and dust tumbling upon the previously shining gold coins. "What do you mean he's making a dragon's ransom?"

Scaleheart cowered from the older silver dragon's outburst. "That's what I've heard from our spies among the lesser races. Miser Skinflint started a bank, and he's loaning money to elves and dwarves and even humans. And he's even *paying* them interest on their deposits!"

Hardheart unleashed such a roar that the mountain itself shook in sympathetic rage. "He's paying *them* and still making a fortune!? This is…is…unnatural!"

"What are you going to do, Father?" Scaleheart asked timidly, still refusing to look directly at the irate silver.

Hardheart was quiet for some time, his chest heaving in heavy breaths, and his tail twitching in anxiety. Finally, his head shot up to the top of the high cavern, shattering a stalactite against his bony plate, and his powerful tail slammed down upon a mound of jingling coins. Hardheart's labial scales drew back in a smile. "I got it! If he wants to run a business, I'll start my own."

Scaleheart wiggled his nose and drew down his brow ridges in confusion. "A business?" At Hardheart's narrow-eyed gaze, he cleared his throat and said, "Um…what sort of business?"

"That which concerns what is most dear to every dragon, of course." Hardheart moved toward a cage that held four humans in the far corner. Each was a paragon of his or her chosen profession: a female warrior in a steel cuirass; a male wizard in a loose robe of midnight blue and a conical hat; a female rogue with a black cloak, vest, pants, and boots; and a male templar in a white tabard over chain mesh and wearing a red cape.

His warm, smoky breath washing over the four, the silver said, "Even though you hoped to rob me, I'm glad I saved you for later. You might be useful after all."

The humans looked at one another fearfully,

sweating profusely and their bodies trembling, but they otherwise did not move.

"You will work for me," Hardheart stated flatly.

Finally, the robed male stepped forward within the cage, his voice quivering. "I don't understand, Mr. Dragon, sir."

"My name is Hardheart Hidehoard," the silver declared with pride.

"Yes sir, Mr. Hidehoard, sir" the same human said, and the others echoed him.

"You will become traveling hoard security specialists. You'll offer the latest in hoard protection: magical alarms and passwords, illusions, traps, the works." When the humans remained frozen and silent, Hardheart's head descended to just outside the cage. "*Or* I could just eat you now."

The humans shook their heads so vigorously that their noggins seemed only loosely attached to their necks.

"Whatever you want, Mr. Dragon—er, Mr. Hardheart, sir," the wizard said.

Hardheart continued, his large head mere feet from the cage. "You'll go to the lairs of other dragons and offer to protect their hoards at a price they can't refuse, then you'll come back here and report to me about what treasures they possess. I'll lure them away and send Scaleheart to bypass their security and relieve them of their treasure."

The humans nodded mutely.

"But, Mr. Hardheart," the templar said, a sheen of sweat coating his forehead, "what if they… um…eat us?"

Hardheart's eyes narrowed, and his rumbling voice

fell even lower. "Would you prefer the view inside *my* belly?"

"Ah…no sir, Mr. Hardheart sir."

"Good." With a flick of his talon, the silver dragon removed the magical lock on their cage. "Now, go!"

The humans tripped over themselves to leave Hardheart Hidehoard's lair.

———

A YEAR LATER…

"Um, Uncle," Breathy said, peeking his head into the main chamber that held the bulk of Skinflint's hoard. "There are some humans here to see you."

Skinflint turned from the stack of silver coins he polished, his eyes narrowed in annoyance. "Just eat them."

As Skinflint turned away, Breathy said, "But, Uncle, um, they say they're here with a business proposition."

"Hmm," was all Skinflint said before falling into silent thought. "Very well." With a grunt, he shifted his great bulk on the pile of coins on which he sat and moved toward the entrance of his lair.

There stood four humans, each an exemplar of adventuring distinction.

"I'm very busy," Skinflint said, rising up to tower over the humans. "What do you want? If you're here to rob me, can we just skip to the part where I eat you?"

"Hello, Mr. Skinflint, sir," the conical-hat-adorned human said. "I am the wizard—"

"I don't care!" A puff of sulfurous smoke erupted from his nostrils.

"Yes, um, well, Mr. Skinflint, we represent Hoard &

Home Security, Inc., the premier name in hoard protection." He gave a wide, brimming smile. "We provide the latest security measures to safeguard your lair and hoard from unwanted intrusion." Under his breath, he mumbled, "HIC insured."

Skinflint stared at the four until they began shifting from foot to foot. "Yes, I have heard of you."

The wizard took that as an invitation to continue. "Yes, sir, we offer state of the magic protections for all your hoard needs. And we are so confident of your lair's security that we offer, at no additional cost to you, your weight in gold in coverage from the Hoard Insurance Corporation."

Skinflint made a thoughtful sound and tapped a long claw against a sword-like tooth as if considering the offer. "I do have significantly more than my weight in gold. Is it possible to increase the insurance coverage?"

The cuirassed warrior spoke up, nodding agreeably, "Oh yes, Mr. Skinflint. For a nominal premium, we can increase the coverage to any multiple of your weight."

Behind Skinflint, Breathy, Scaly, and Toothy jostled one another for a better view of the interaction.

"He's going to eat them," Scaly said, showing his teeth.

"No way," Breathy said, shaking his head.

"Maybe he'll eat only some of them," Toothy offered, flicking his tongue across his teeth.

"We can see you're a dragon of discerning judgment," the wizard said. "How about this: we'll give you a one-month free trial. If you're not completely satisfied, you can cancel with no obligation."

At the word *free*, Skinflint's eyes gained an avaricious

glint. "That sounds reasonable. No hidden charges?" He asked the question in a rumbling, reverberating growl.

"Absolutely not!" The wizard looked appropriately put out by the suggestion.

"Very well, you have yourself a deal."

Behind Skinflint, Scaly made a disappointed grumble, and Breathy said, "I knew it!"

Almost one month later...

"Father, I just saw Skinflint leave his lair," Scaleheart said breathlessly after a hard flight back to Hardheart's lair. "He must have taken the bait of the rumor you started about a buried dwarven treasure. Even his nephews went with him."

Hardheart clacked his long claws together. "This is it! I'm going with you this time to dispossess my old nemesis of enough treasure to ensure that I will be at the top of the Hordes 400 list."

The two dragons took to wing and flew with all haste to cover the distance to Skinflint's lair. They alighted outside the entrance, and Hardheart uttered the override password to disable all the magical protections. A brief flash of light and a whoosh of air indicated that the safeguards were deactivated, then Hardheart barged into the cavern, with Scaleheart following closely.

When the two reached the hoard chamber, Hardheart loosed such a roar that the walls shook and Scaleheart cowered away.

"Where is his hoard?!" Hardheart bellowed.

The chamber was empty. Not a coin or gem was to be found in any nook or cranny.

"Maybe…um…maybe..." Scaleheart shrugged his wings.

"Go! Look everywhere," Hardheart ordered, and Scaleheart moved immediately to enter one of the smaller side passages.

Hardheart investigated the remainder of the lair and sniffed about, his powerful nostrils able to detect one part in a million of precious metals. His frustrated rumbling echoed through the tunnels.

Finally, the two silver dragons returned to the hoard chamber. The younger dragon looked away in embarrassment, and the older dragon bared his teeth an anger.

"I…I don't understand, Father," Scaleheart offered in quiet, tentative tones.

In sudden movement, Hardheart's tail swept to the side, struck the wall, and shook the mountain. "We have to go back!" He did not wait for his son as he exited, leaped into the air, and surged upward.

Upon returning to his own lair, Hardheart found his own collection of treasure significantly reduced. Atop the much-diminished pile was a note: "Might I suggest contacting the Hoard Insurance Corporation."

For generations afterward, the towns and villages of the region still told stories about the roar heard around the world.

THREE YEARS LATER…

Skinflint lounged atop his much-increased hoard and read a copy of the newest Hordes 400 list. He beamed at the name he saw at the top. "I'll have to send Hardheart a consolation prize for second place," he said to his nephews, who lay contentedly, partially submerged in the piles of treasure.

"That was smart thinking, Uncle Skinflint, to move your hoard to the neighboring mountain," Breathy said, taking a clawful of coins and pouring them over his head.

"But, Uncle, how did you know that the humans worked for Hardheart?" Toothy asked, dipping his head beneath the surface of coins.

"Because, Nephews, Hardheart was apparently too cheap to give them even seed money for their enterprise, and they had to borrow funds from my bank. On the loan documents, they listed Hardheart Hidehoard as their CEO."

A.R.R. Ash is a lifelong fan of both science fiction and fantasy, though he typically focuses his talents on writing grimdark. His first independently published novel is The Moroi Hunters. *He has had short stories appear in several anthologies—including* Behind the Shadows; Behind the Shadows II; Detectives, Sleuths, and Nosy Neighbors; Hidden Villains; Hidden Villains: Arise; and Noncorporeal II *by Inkd Publishing, as well as* Socially Distant: The Quarantales *by Impulsive Walrus Books—and he has received a Silver Honorable Mention and six Honorable Mentions from the L. Ron Hubbard's Writers of the Future Contest.* Xy: Descent, *the first book of his* The First Godling *trilogy, as well as* The Tribe of Fangs, *the prequel to* The Moroi Hunters, *are undergoing editing. He is currently working on* Xy: Ascent, *the sequel to* Xy: Descent, *as well as other short stories that pique his interest.*

. . .

In other trivia, his favorite dishes are burgers and sushi (but not together), and his favorite series is Dune, *though* The Expanse *by James S. A. Corey is making a run for the title. His sense of humor is decidedly an acquired taste. You can contact A.R.R. Ash and watch his interview with Cursed Dragon Ship Publishing through LMPBooks.com.*

ON THE PATH TO ST. EDMUND'S CAVE

BEVERLE GRAVES MYERS

A lys's head was finally bare. With a muttered blessing to the Goddess, she turned her face up to the star-pricked sky and shook out thick white hair. When she'd passed the last of the village's clustered huts sleeping beneath the waning moon, she'd tossed her linen cap and its tight chin strap into a manure trench. A handful of bone hairpins followed. Now the small freedom of unbound hair set her feet dancing along the familiar hard dirt track—but only for a few yards before the gnawing ache behind her ribs slowed her worn sheepskin shoes and forced her to lean on her stick for support.

Don't waste your strength, old fool.

Alys squared her shoulders and trudged on. Her presence at a cave in St. Edmund's Wood was required. The cave had been a sacred meeting place in the misty depths of time—and still was to those few who kept to the old ways. No matter how rocky and root-bound the path or how fierce the wild beasts roaming the green-wood, Alys must persevere. Even youthful memories of hunting parties sent up the mountain after Old Stinker, a fearsome half-man half-dragon said to make off with wandering maidens, wouldn't stop her.

She'd been summoned to a death watch, and she meant to be there.

Just after sunrise, Alys left the trackway for a barely perceptible path where she was unlikely to meet any fellow humans foraging for nuts or firewood. At first, she made good time, but as the way steepened, she paused a few times to break off flowers and leafy vines that would soon be braided with a length of red wool she'd dyed for the purpose. Eventually the morning grew warm, and the patchwork bag she'd slung over her dusty surcoat seemed to grow heavier with each turn of the path. When she spied a fallen tree trunk on the verge, Alys gave a grateful sigh.

Truly the Goddess is watching over me. She will not let me fail.

Using her stick for support, Alys slowly sank her backside to the tree's lichen-covered bark. Her throat was parched and her legs trembled. After a few deep breaths, she retrieved the water pouch dangling from a leather cord around her waist and drank deeply. Then she pulled the white kerchief from her neck, dampened the cloth, and cooled her brow and wrinkled cheeks.

Better.

Pinned to the inside of her linen shift was a small bag filled with rue, vervain, and other energizing herbs. Sitting absolutely still with eyes closed, Alys concentrated on the herbs' reviving power and drank in the forest sounds with a thirst far greater than the one she had just slaked. A blackbird sang—its musical call was unmistakable. Other, softer sounds caressed her ears.

Leaves rustling in the light breeze, the distant cry of a curlew, small animals moving cautiously as they foraged in the underbrush.

Then the crack of a broken branch, sharp and loud. Her eyes flew open. Something bigger than a hedgehog or squirrel must be lurking nearby.

Holding her breath, Alys slowly turned her head to survey the encroaching wood. No one—no man. A man's designs worried her more than a beast's. A bear or boar would have no use for her and go its way. A desperate man living outside the law might wring her neck for a few pitiful possessions and leave her body for scavengers to strip the flesh and ravens to peck out her eyes.

All was quiet, but the sensation of being watched hung in the air with the flitting dragonflies. Alys sat stiffly alert until she felt safe enough to let her muscles relax. She blew out a relieved breath and gave an inward chuckle. At least it wouldn't be Old Stinker.

Not that she didn't believe in dragons. Many tales had reached the village, told by tinkers, gypsies, and wandering players. In the east, they said, in lands bounded by a massive, winding wall, dragons still roamed. With long, snake-like bodies that nearly dragged the ground, these eastern dragons walked on four clawed feet and dwelled near bodies of water. But English dragons? No honest hunter or woodsman had spotted a scaly, winged, fire-breathing creature since the Great Pestilence had scoured their lands. Alys shook her head. Old Stinker nabbing pretty maidens was just a cautionary tale, a lie meant to frighten girls into keeping near the village.

Alys rubbed her aching side. Despite the pain, her

stomach rumbled. She searched her patchwork bag for a slice of parkin, a ginger cake Yorkshire women baked with oatmeal and black treacle. A few bites and another swig of water quieted her hunger. To allow her legs a bit more rest, she pulled out her red yarn and began twisting it with the supple vines and long-stemmed wild-flowers she'd collected.

By now the village would have noticed her absence. They'd probably assume the rumors of Witch Finders roaming the Yorkshire Dales had scared her into doing a runner, though if she meant to flee the god-soldiers' torments, she would have run a good twelve-month ago. That's when visions of black wagons carrying men in black hats and cloaks adorned with crosses had invaded her dreams. Many nights she'd awakened in a sweat knowing these men were determined to use all available tortures to make others conform to their god's supposed will.

Alys winced when a vine's hidden thorn pricked her finger. Before she could jerk her wounded fingertip to her mouth, several drops of blood fell to her straw-colored surcoat. They spread in scarlet blotches, the color of death and despair. An omen? Were the Witch Finders spreading farther up from the south, like a mortal stain carrying a pestilence that tricked neighbor into fearing neighbor? She shuddered violently, startling a pair of wood pigeons from their hiding place.

Time to get your feet moving. You can't sit here all day.

Alys deftly tucked the last flowers into the wreath of greenery and red wool she'd fashioned. Running her fingers over the circlet, she allowed herself a moment to admire her work. It should be worn by a bride, not an old woman. *Ah, well.* She tightened her lips and banished regret—sternly. She clasped the wreath, stretched her arms high, and slowly floated her prize down to her head. The moment it touched her brow, a lovely feeling of peace descended, infusing every aching bone and muscle. Alys's lips stretched in a wide smile.

Yes.

She would proudly wear this wreath. It would be a crown to honor the coming death watch. Her own death watch. By nightfall she would surrender the weary sigh of her last breath to the greenwood.

Without a backward glance, Alys grabbed her stick and bag and continued her climb. The village tugged at her mind as the brambles and thistles tugged at her hem. She knew the sharp-eyed, sharp-tongued goodwife who lived next door would have already invaded her cottage on the lookout for anything worth carrying away. Alys snorted. Let Goody Benson have her tattered quilt, her dented cooking pots, her one pewter candle-stick. Everything of true value had already been attended to.

Quill, her broken-winged jackdaw, would be safely perching in the cottage of a trusted friend. To that same friend, Alys had gifted her distaff and spindle as well as the dried herbs she'd have no more use for. The patch-work bag contained everything she required now.

She'd been loath to leave. Despite the new king who raved of devils and demons and ordered his scholars to produce an updated version of his church book, many neighbors still valued her ancient skills. They came to her cottage for rituals and potions crafted to ensure the health of their lambs, the yield of their apple orchard, the fruitfulness of their own bellies. She'd been discreet in her dealings, but people talked and their talk echoed round the hills. Anxiety festered.

Some who followed the old ways began to make a grand show of attending the god-botherers' church—just in case. Alys had never stooped to that. She respected her craft and could have used it to repel the Witch Finders when they showed up. Except…

Last Yule, she'd noticed a swelling on her breast. None of her poultices had stopped its spread. The lump grew and deepened and drove its evil fingers into the crevices between her ribs. She'd seen this before. There would be no cure, no respite. If she collapsed in the village, her body would be left to the god-botherers. They'd throw her carcass in a public pit with unbaptized infants and criminals who'd died on the gallows. Alys made other plans. She wouldn't put her friends in the dangerous position of giving her remains a proper burial. No. She would climb to St. Edmund's Cave alone.

The sun had climbed to midday and started along its downward arc when Alys was startled by the sounds of a wild chase through the wood. Beyond her sight, bird-wings whirred in panicked flight, unknown creatures panted and growled, branches broke and snapped. As quickly as the forest chaos had begun, it ceased.

Alys stood as if paralyzed. The rugged slope was eerily quiet except for the keening, pitiful cry of an injured animal. That wordless plea squeezed her heart. Tears joined the sweat running down her cheeks. She must do something.

Suddenly energized, Alys bolted toward the sound, hacking at the underbrush with her stick. Branches whipped her arms and the buckthorns tore at her skirt.

Her white hair streamed behind her. She was barely aware of the beautifully wreathed crown flying off into the scrub.

She stumbled to a halt at the edge of a small, shaded clearing. A red deer, a doe, lay against the gnarled roots of an ancient oak, wheezing, exhausted. Red-streaked froth issued from her mouth. Creeping closer, Alys cringed at the sight of the animal's ripped hindquarters. The doe's back legs were broken and still. Blood and sinew oozed from a gash in her side.

Alys reached the poor beast and sank to her knees. The deer was dying in agony, and Alys must put an end to it. She shot her gaze around the clearing. A row of mossy stones lined the oak's humped roots, boulders someone had rolled there to sit on around a cooking fire. Too heavy! She'd never manage to lift one and crush the doe's skull.

With a groan, Alys realized her bag held the only key. She wiped the tears from her face and slid her hand between the layers of faded patchwork. Her fist closed on what had become her most precious possession—a corked vial filled with tincture of poppy juice and oleander and other poisons. She'd prepared it to be her last quaff—the blessing that would send her quickly and painlessly to the arms of Mother Earth as she lay deep in the cave, the belly of the Goddess herself.

Dithering, Alys stared at the shimmering, red-gold liquid. If she helped the deer, would there be enough of the precious substance left to accomplish her own end? The doe's pleading brown eyes made her mind up.

Alys opened the vial and tipped half its contents into the doe's mouth. With fingers fluttering like a hummingbird, she resealed the vial and propped it up against a nearby root. Then she used both hands to squeeze the doe's mouth shut. The animal's neck muscles strained against her grasp, but Alys held on with all her might. When her arms had nearly lost their strength, a tremor traveled the length of the doe's red-furred body, and the light left her eyes.

Heart pounding and shoulders sinking, Alys closed the deer's eyes and pressed her lips to its brow. Her forest sister was now free of pain and at peace. Alys knew she'd made the right choice, but at what cost? The sun had moved behind the treetops. Honeyed light slanted through oak branches. To reach the cave by nightfall, she must make haste.

Alys bent a knee and tried to rise. Her legs refused to cooperate. She pushed trembling arms against the ground. Positioned her stick for leverage. No matter how hard she tried, she couldn't force her body up.

Near panic, breathing in short pants, Alys put her hand to her throat and grasped the bag of energizing herbs.

Goddess, come to your daughter's aid.

Again Alys attempted to rise—time after time—but she remained a pile of lank hair, shivering flesh, and sweat-drenched clothing beside the dead deer. The calm, ritualized death she had envisioned for herself was shredding away like a cloud in a windstorm.

A rage shot through Alys's veins. So close to her goal, yet her magic had deserted her. Her blood was too thin. Her bones too brittle. Her intention too weak. By virtue of pride or false hope, she'd miscalculated her powers and left this journey too late. Rocking back and forth, she stabbed fingers through her hair and dug fingernails into her scalp. She howled into the unheeding wilderness until her throat was raw.

As twilight faded into night, her fierce anger turned to despair. Utterly spent, Alys lowered her forehead to the doe's furred side. Her long white tresses would make a death shroud for both of them.

Pull yourself together, old fool. One more task awaits you.

Alys turned her gaze to the poison vial sitting in the crook of a tree root. She stared for a long time, until the forest dark crept over the clearing and the vial's contents began to whisper the temptation of sweet release. She inched her hand through leaf litter and matted twigs. Reaching, reaching, stretching almost prone. Her fingernails clicked against the slick glass.

"I wouldn't do that," a male voice rumbled.

Alys's heart leaped. She pushed up on one thin arm and whirled her head around.

A vision stood in a knee-high patch of gorse at the clearing's edge, surrounded by a mist that glowed with an inner light. The man—dare she call him a man?—stood on two legs. So yes, more man than beast. He spread his hands, palms up, as if to say, "Behold me. I am a friend."

Perhaps. Painfully aware of the dead animal by her side, Alys narrowed her eyes to take in his every detail.

He was tall, eight feet at least. Though his elongated jaw stretched beyond human proportion and horns curved from his bony brow, his chiseled features combined into a handsome whole. He stared at her with green eyes. *Goddess, those eyes.* Even across the clearing, they burned like green flames. An untamed mane of black hair surrounded his face like a thundercloud and fell to the shoulders of an antiquated doublet the color of a ripe persimmon. His muscular arms were bare and covered with smooth golden scales shimmering in the glow that surrounded him.

Alys rubbed her eyes with her free hand.

Could this more man than beast creature be real? No sound had announced his approach through the underbrush. Perhaps her weakened state was deceiving her with a phantasm.

His voice rumbled again, "I believe you dropped something."

He crossed the clearing in long strides. Despite her shivers, Alys noticed his knee-high boots crushed the dried leaves and grasses in his path. That was real enough. And there, from his right hand, a curved claw dangled the death watch wreath she'd lost in her rush to find the deer.

No illusion. This was Old Stinker. In the flesh.

He towered above her, looking down. Bright ribbons of steam curled from both prominent nostrils and joined the enveloping mist. Ah, he made his own light. When he pulled his lips away from his teeth in a smile, Alys had a glimpse of bright white fangs, just long enough to fit within his jaws and sharp enough to tear through skin and bone.

"This is a lovely thing you worked quite hard to create." He extended the wreath. "By rights, it belongs here."

He bent to place the circlet gently on her trembling head, then stepped back and placed hands on his belted waist. The sturdy leather belt held no woodsman's knife or chisel. He clearly had no need of such things.

"Now, will you allow me to help you up?" His glowing gaze ignored the deer's body, and everything else in the clearing besides Alys stretched at his feet. Her gaze was just as intent.

"I'm done for. I...I haven't the strength." It was all she could do to keep her voice steady.

"I have strength enough to share. Don't be afraid." He hesitated. Trying to assess the best way to gain her trust? Finally, he gestured to a large pearl hanging from a chain around his neck and whispered, "Please? By this treasured amulet, I swear I am not here to harm you."

The back of her neck tingled in trepidation, but she nodded her assent. *Why not? What do I have to lose?* She expected him to reach for the hand she offered. Instead, he crouched down beside her, slid his arms under hers and lifted. For a moment, she was floating, a downy feather in the breeze. When he stood her on her feet, she felt tipsy and euphoric, like she'd drunk too much May wine.

Why do they call him Old Stinker, Alys wondered. He exuded earthy forest smells. Old trees, damp moss, pine needles and...maleness. She raised a hand to her wreath and said, "You must have been watching me earlier while I rested on the fallen tree."

"I've been watching you for many years, my dear. Virtually every time you made a foraging expedition or held a ritual in what your people call St. Edmund's Cave. I've even visited your cottage."

"Impossible!" Astonishment cleared Alys's head. She stamped her feet to regain the assurance of solid ground. He may be real, but so was she. "I would certainly remember if I'd encountered the likes of you."

"Not necessarily. Like most of my kind, I'm well versed in the craft of forgetting." He cocked his head, clearly reading the disbelieving look on her face. "I first saw you when your mother brought you up the mountain looking for herbs. I can picture it still. You knelt beside her with a serious frown on your little face while she explained the uses of the plants she was cutting. She gathered her harvest into the same patchwork bag you now carry."

It was true. When her mother could no longer make it up the mountain, she'd passed her bag on to her daughter. Alys's brain was whirling. Mother had started her tutelage in herbs over fifty years ago. How could this creature have been watching her all that time without giving her some clue? And how could he display the strength and virility of youth while she was a failing bag of bones. She asked, "How old are you?"

"I stopped counting my years at three of your centuries, but there's really no comparison." He snorted out a particularly bright ball of steam. "Dragon time flows more slowly than yours, and our interest in the affairs of men waxes and wanes. Still, there are those who may speak of me. Have hunters never stumbled back to your village saying they might have caught a glimpse of a golden-scaled creature but can't clearly recall?"

Alys nodded. "They call you—" She quickly clamped her lips together. Perhaps he would take offense at his nickname.

But no. He showed his fangs in a chuckle. "Old Stinker," he finished.

They stood in silence for a few breaths. An owl hooted nearby. Crickets hummed in the background. To Alys everything about Old Stinker seemed strange and unreal, but also somehow comfortingly familiar. Curious questions competed to be voiced. "When did you visit my cottage?" she asked breathlessly, "And why?"

"At first, because I saw something special in you. As the years went by I came to enjoy your company more and more. It's lonely on the mountain, you know." He sighed deeply.

"Perhaps you remember special nights when your fire flared more brightly than usual, when your iron pot seemed to bubble with a mind of its own, when your boiling potion swirled with colors you'd never seen before in your life."

"I thought it was the Goddess blessing my work."

"Possibly. Or perhaps I added a pinch of powdered dragon scale when your back was turned. Or blew a spark of my own onto your fire. You didn't seem to mind mixing your magic with mine."

"And then you made me forget." It was a statement, not a question.

He nodded his long jaw.

"Why didn't you make yourself known?"

"Our time had not yet come." He turned away abruptly and took several steps toward a break in the underbrush. He tilted his chin up to sniff the air. Was he checking for the scent of lurking danger? Then, "Walk to the cave with me, Alys, and I'll explain."

"To St. Edmund's Cave?"

"That's your name for it."

"What do you call it?"

"Home."

Alys raised her eyebrows, considering. Before she set off with him, there was something she had to know. Alys jutted her chin toward the doe's carcass. "Is she your work?"

He grunted roughly, then replied, "No. Dragons eat the whole of our prey. And, unlike humans, we do not hunt for sport. Waste is shameful to us."

Though Alys had many more questions, her strange companion was clearly determined to get to the cave, and she knew her words would be wasted. She abandoned her stick, the gnarled piece of wood that had supported her steps for many moons, but snatched up the vial of poison and returned it to her bag without comment.

They started up the overgrown, winding path. Night had overtaken the day, and the moon wouldn't rise for several hours. Outside of their bubble of luminous mist, the dark of the dense forest closed in. Old Stinker stepped out with confidence, seemingly lost in his own dreams or preoccupations. As Alys carefully picked her way, her own thoughts distracted her more than rocks or roots.

This dragon-man spoke like the lord of the manor, full of politeness and graceful gestures, but Alys sensed he possessed a loud, wild, dangerous side. She'd once seen two young stags fighting in a mountain glen. With thundering bellows, they'd smashed and clanked their antlers together in a show of male energy that reverberated through the hills. She was picturing her companion running along a forest ridge with that same virile power when she failed to mind a low hanging branch. The crash made her see stars. She fell to the path like a bag of wet sand.

Alys returned to consciousness with a warm breath snuffling against her neck. Slowly, she opened her eyes. And gasped.

There he was. The same, yet different. Bigger and

now more beast than man. Now both reptile and bird. As the dragon drew back, she pushed herself up on shaky legs.

Coppery scales covered his entire body, which seemed more at home on four feet than two. Leathery wings of a purplish hue extended from his shoulder joints and were folded gracefully along his sides. The mop of black hair had shrunk to a small topknot between elongated horns. His eyes, still iridescent green, but now with black slits for pupils, stared at her with anxious concern.

Alys felt her ribs rising and falling with agitated breaths. This majestic figure was simply the most glorious thing she'd ever seen.

"Are you all right?" he asked in a voice raspier than before.

Her dry tongue cleaved to the top of her mouth.

"You are in no danger, my dear. I carried you up the mountain. I am still me."

"Is this your real self?" she finally asked.

He ruffled his wings, lifting his long body a few inches off the ground. "I have two guises. One is no more authentic than the other."

She nodded, looking around. He'd laid her on a bed of evergreen fronds near the overhanging rock ledge that sheltered the entrance to St. Edmund's cave. Her wreath and bag hung on the branch of a nearby tree, and a small bonfire burned brightly.

"I must be fully dragon to breath flame and start fires," he explained.

She'd meant to choose her next words carefully but ended up blurting out, "What do you want of me?"

His response was equally direct. "I want you for my bride."

Impossible! A human woman whose legs can barely hold her up and whose blood runs as thin as birch sap in the spring?

"A female dragon would surely make you a more fitting wife," Alys stated in a rising voice.

Cocking his angular head, he fixed her with one luminous eye. "Have you ever seen or heard of one? A female dragon?"

No, she realized. Her knowledge of dragon lore was sparse, but all the English dragons she'd ever heard of were males who terrorized villagers for livestock and fair virgins. They were said to be greedy and have a propensity for hoarded treasure. Especially gold and gemstones. The most powerful of their lot possessed a pearl which they wore around their necks on a chain. Representing the moon at its full, the dragon's cunning and magic resided in the pearl. Old Stinker displayed a particularly large one.

"All right. But why me? Why an old woman with a worn-out body?"

The dragon paced back and forth before the fire. Alys caught sight of his sharply barbed, forked tail and couldn't stop staring. At last he stopped, stretched his long neck, and aimed a flaring column of fire at the night sky. Turning to Alys with ferocious attention, he said, "Long ago, I had a beloved wife, the joy of my life. We lived here. This cave runs deeper than any of your people know. Its halls and passages are well warded with dragon magic."

"What happened to your wife?"

"One of your saints was determined to prove his

courage by killing a monster—something alien and feared, something everyone agreed was evil. One day when I was out hunting, he used his guile to lure my wife into devouring a deer he'd filled with poison. She fought him when he attacked her with his lance, but in her weakened state, she could not prevail. His lance pierced her heart and he cut off her head." He shuddered, copper scales dimming in color and barbed tail thumping the ground. "When I returned with our dinner, I found what was left of her bleeding crimson onto the dusty floor of the cave."

"I'm so sorry," Alys whispered, deeply moved by his tale. She stepped to his side and placed a tentative hand on the scales near his shoulder. She was surprised at their satiny softness. "Please don't think your wife's killer was one of my saints, though. I have no love for the god-botherers' church.

"I know. I opened the cave's vestibule to you and your friends because you reminded me of her."

"Truly?"

"Yes, when I first encountered my wife as a human. She was kind. Like you, she took the entire village in her care, though she was most at home in the greenwood. She felt a kinship with all the plants and creatures in it, and took us under her care, as well."

The dragon drew close. He laid his chin on her head. Without thinking, she ran her fingertips along the curves of his horns. They were the soft velvet of a young stag's antlers, not the hardness she expected. Then, he slid a claw between her thighs and stroked upward with the back of one smooth talon.

Alys moaned as unreckoned for sensations washed over her. She was hardly a stranger to the bliss of phys-ical coupling, but it had been a long time.

She'd once met a wool merchant from Ghent at the Skipton market. He'd come to buy raw wool from English sheep to feed the foreign looms. Laureys had blond hair dusting blue eyes and broad shoulders that embraced her like no one else's ever had. Over two summers they explored every sort of pleasure in each other's arms. She was actually considering whether she might make Laureys a satisfactory wife when she learned he already had a wife and four little ones back home. Alys had taken no man to her bed since.

She pulled back and turned to contemplate the mouth of the cave. She'd thought it would be a fitting place to die and begged the Goddess to give her strength to reach it. Was this the destiny the Goddess had foreseen for her all along?

A bride not a corpse.

He reached out again. This time to stroke her cheek. "Will you join with me, Alys?"

"How? How could you make me your bride?"

"This pearl." He pulled at his neck chain and gently pinched the sea gem between two claws. "Far more powerful than any stone dug from the earth. By its magic, you will no longer be human. You will have a new body. You will be a different creature altogether. A dragon."

She trembled. Unable to speak from the strangeness of it all.

He continued, "But you must wish it so. If that is not your desire, you are free to take your bag with its poison vial into the cave and end your earthly existence as you planned."

"I must ask," Alys pushed out the question that had been haunting her since she'd first laid eyes on Old

Stinker in the clearing. "Do you hunt humans?" It was hard enough to imagine herself chasing down a forest creature, ripping its flesh, licking its blood off her talons. But…a human?"

"Not as a rule, but I do make exceptions." Her companion puffed out a perfect ring of steam and flicked his forked pink tongue over his fangs. His gleaming eyes became the darkest of green as they drilled right through her. "I imagine Witch Finders would make an especially tasty dish. I could roast them in their death wagons with one breath. We could both roast them."

Alys's gaze followed the misty ring upward. Before it disappeared on the night breeze, her mind was made up. She went to the tree that held her bag and wreath. She buried her face in the worn patchwork her mother had sewn together so many years ago, breathed deeply, then pushed it away. The flowered wreath she settled on her flowing hair. With assured steps, she approached the dragon and cupped his pearl in her hand. His breath was warm on her neck. The gem pulsated in her palm.

"Will this really work?" she asked, suddenly dubious about the depth of magic required for such a fantastic transformation.

"It will if you wish it so. But remember, my darling," he said in a guttural but caressing whisper. "If you accept my proposal, there is no going back."

Alys met his green gaze. Smiling, she squeezed the pearl and wished with all her heart.

BEVERLE GRAVES MYERS is a gifted storyteller based in a historic Victorian neighborhood of Louisville, Kentucky. Her studies in history have given her the ability to make earlier eras come alive, and her sensitive insight into the human psyche developed by years of practice as a psychiatrist allows her to remain keyed to the desires of today's readers searching for meaning in their lives. Her work includes the Tito Amato Mystery Series set in baroque Venice; Face of the Enemy, *a World War II mystery cowritten with Joanne Dobson; and numerous mystery and paranormal short stories and writing-related articles. Her work has been nominated for the Derringer, Macavity and Kentucky Book awards. More info at readbeverlemyers.com.*

THE EMOTIONAL SUPPORT DRAGON

ANGELIQUE FAWNS

Harold's pink wings quivered as he coughed and teetered on the branch. The flames were devouring the forest like an insatiable, starving monster. Smoke billowed in huge puffs, obscuring the sky. He curled his talons tight into the pine tree as his transparent third lids flipped up, protecting his eyes.

If only he was a member of the dragon firefighting squad, he could help put the fire out.

Harold cast an anxious glance at the town of Lostmere nestled in the valley below as his breakfast of insects tossed in his stomach. Lostmere was thirty miles behind him and safe for now, but if the fire grew and picked up speed...

Elsa, his best human friend, lived in Lostmere. Her thatched cottage would burn like a dry match if the blaze reached town. Harold shuddered. An unbearable thought. Humans needed houses just like dragons needed dens.

He snorted at the acrid smell of burning leaves and took a deep breath. Breathing exercises helped him overcome his paralyzing fear, like when he was pulling Elsa in her chariot and they had to make the final goal of a tied runeball game. Where was his confidence? Most dragons didn't struggle with feelings of unworthiness. But most dragons were twice his size.

The bang and crackle of a falling tree shot sparks into the air and Harold shook off his descent into self-pity. This fire had to be stopped. The flames roared and danced, consuming more trees.

He scanned the horizon, wishing he could fight the inferno himself. Elsa played runeball, despite being told it was impossible. She never let her wheelchair slow her down.

Harold looked to the sky again. Where was the fire brigade?

If he'd heard the town's warning siren and was able to fly here, the fittest dragons in the area should have beat him easily. He hunched his shoulders and tried to come up with a plan to save Elsa if—

He pricked his ears when he heard the whoosh-whoop of many wings. A V formation of twelve flying creatures filled the sky. Their bright colors were a stark contrast to the gray smoke. Excitement tickled his nerves.

Bruno, a muscular crimson dragon, led the charge, his wingspan fully ten feet wide. Harold's chest swelled with pride as the formation dipped to the side of the mountain. The team simultaneously unleashed a stream of flame at the edge of the forest. The backfire flared as it consumed the grass.

Harold puffed out a thin stream of smoke in unison with the team. He flexed his muscles in sync with their flight. His imagination placed him on the line, battling danger and saving his town. Saving Elsa!

Each dragon dropped a bag of water tied to their tails, and the burn line was established. A twisty black snake of dead land. Harold grinned, his tongue lapping at bits of ash as the fire met the burn line and was extinguished.

No fuel. No fire. Bruno and his team were heroes.

He shivered with hope. The annual career ceremony was scheduled for this evening, and maybe — just maybe — he would become the newest member of the Lostmere Dragon Fire Platoon.

Harold wagged his pink tail triumphantly as the forest fire fizzled out completely. The smoke cleared and the sun emerged directly overhead. He frowned. The sun was already directly overhead? How did the morning get away from him?

Harold unfurled his wings reluctantly. He'd wanted to stay and watch as Bruno led a final flyover. That was his favorite part. The bow after the performance.

He had to get moving, the junior fire squad's final practice started at noon AND Elsa had a runeball game at the same time. Harold pinned his ears, thinking so hard smoke trickled out from his opaque lobes. Attending the final fire practice wasn't mandatory. But if he didn't show up for Elsa's game, she couldn't play. How could he disappoint his best friend? His heart swelled thinking of her toothy grin and warm hugs. She'd pretend it didn't matter, but he knew she'd be disappointed.

He flung himself out of the tree and flapped with all his might. He fell a couple of feet until he managed to get some momentum. Harold practiced flying every day and even lifted rocks, knowing he had to get stronger if he wanted to be a useful member of the fire platoon. He concentrated as his wings made the 'flap, flap' sound of a duck struggling to gain altitude.

A postal service dragon whizzed by him, sending him into a spin. Her wings had a deep sonic throb, like well-greased pistons. Three times his size, the green female had several large packages strapped to her back.

She spat at him. "Stay out of my air space pip-squeak, I've got an important delivery for Cesterfield."

He was shocked to see it was Martha. She normally flew like a tortoise. Slow and steady. "Don't rush because tomorrow will get here anyway," was her motto.

He pumped with renewed vigor and managed to catch up. "Martha, are you okay?"

"This wasn't the only fire burning today," The middle-aged dragon puffed, panic edging her eyes. "There's an enormous forest fire cutting off Cesterfield's supplies. I've got some food and basics to help until their fire platoon can get things under control. I don't want the kiddies to go hungry."

Martha slowed down to catch her breath. Harold wrinkled his nose; she was so sweaty she smelled like hamburger gone bad. Her chest heaved and her eyes bulged. Harold feared the normally placid postal worker was going to have a heart attack.

He remembered how his mom talked him through panic attacks. He managed to sync his flight speed with hers. "I hear you, Martha, it sure is frightening when a big fire threatens a town."

Martha nodded, gulping air, the whites of her eyes growing smaller.

Harold kept his voice low and soothing, "It makes

perfect sense that you want to get the supplies to them as fast as possible. But if they need to wait another hour, nobody will die, will they?"

Martha shook her big head and the throbbing of her breast slowed.

"You are the most reliable postal dragon this town has. Rain, sleet, or snow, you always deliver."

Martha took a shuddering breath and nodded. "You're right Harold. I will get these packages to them safely. If I give myself a heart attack, I'm not helping anyone. Thank you!"

Harold saluted with one pink wing as Martha picked up the pace, but not the frantic flapping she was doing before. She drew away, and he dropped closer to the rooftops in case there were more postal carriers, or worse yet, warrior dragons, using the main flight channel. He didn't like to get in anyone's way. Harold's lips curled as he narrowly avoided colliding with chimneys. Would he make it before the game started?

HAROLD GRINNED SEEING Elsa waiting for him at the sports field, her golden hair pulled into a ponytail. She wheeled her chair back and forth and chewed on the inside of her cheek. Her eyes lit up when she saw him.

She tightened her ponytail. "Harold, you came! I thought you might go to fire training. Wasn't it your last lesson?"

"Bruno told me not to worry, it didn't matter if I went to the last class. Have I ever let you down?" Harold laughed and screwed his features into a funny expression.

Elsa winked. "Never. I don't know what I'd do without you."

He crouched beside her as she strapped him into his harness. Her father had fashioned two long bars to hook into metal cups. They were sewn onto a leather strap that encircled Harold's belly. Her wheelchair was attached like a chariot, and Elsa had a mallet she could swing at the runeball stone.

"Let's go!" Harold flapped his wings.

Her smile faltered. "What if I embarrass myself out there and all the other kids laugh?"

Harold stretched his neck back so he was nearly eye-to-eye with his friend. "What's bothering you, Elsa? You've been playing all summer. What's changed?" He cocked his ear and listened.

Elsa's voice got tight and small, "Judy took me behind the bleachers and said, 'If you didn't have Harold, you'd never score a goal.'"

Harold's throat burned with outrage. He wanted to find this Judy and scorch her. Right down to her nasty skeleton. But he knew that wouldn't help Elsa. Harold let some smoke billow out his nose to cool down.

When he was calm, he said, "I hear what you are saying and I understand. I think Judy is just jealous she doesn't have a dragon of her own. Anyone can run around and kick a rune stone. I don't see anyone else with a dragon chariot." His long tongue flickered out and caught the teardrops falling off her chin.

Elsa hiccupped and gripped her mallet to her chest. "I never thought of it that way."

"You did a great job in the game last week. Didn't you hit the winning goal?"

"I did. That's right." She wiped the tears off her face. "Let's show them how it's done!"

Harold trotted onto the playing fields. Elsa whooped as he dodged in and out of the other kids. He might be slower than other dragons, but he could run faster than her two-footed teammates.

Harold knocked over any player who tried to check Elsa and they scored two goals. She whooped like a warrior dragon each time a stone entered the net. Harold's cheeks hurt from grinning.

When the game was over Elsa threw her arms around him. "I'll see you at the job ceremony tonight. Good luck Harold. I know you will become a firefighter!"

HAROLD DIDN'T HAVE the same confidence as his friend, but he always loved visiting the outdoor amphitheater. The venue was gorgeous, created with dragon-mined marble and carved wood. Harold's chest swelled as he stood in a row with the three other graduating dragons. Elsa waved from the front row of the bleachers and blew him a kiss.

The mayor, a rotund man with cherry cheeks and a wiry red beard, picked up a megaphone. "Hear ye! Hear ye! We are gathered today for the annual job ceremony. Four more fine young individuals will join the historical alliance of Lostmere and our region's dragons."

The crowd cheered, and the overhead dragons — having chewed copper earlier — spewed green and blue flames. Harold's wings quivered in anticipation.

The mayor said, "Congratulations Cletus! You are our newest teacher."

Harold puffed smoke and clapped as a green dragon with iridescent wings and horn-rimmed glasses flew up to join the group overhead. The townsfolk tossed confetti into the air.

The mayor hollered over the noise, "Bertha will join the fire platoon."

An orange dragon, twice Harold's size, spouted celebratory fire and followed Cletus into the sky. The townspeople were on their feet, doubling the confetti falling into the arena.

Harold tried to look happy for Bertha and pounded his leg on the turf, but his stomach soured. He had hoped Bertha would join the warriors. It was rare for the fire platoon to take on more than one new trainee.

His heart sank as he watched Bruno smack tails with Bertha, but he tried to stay hopeful.

The dragon beside him, a round male tanned to a toasty brown, fought to keep his eyes open. Harold poked him when the spotlight fell on him.

"Alvin, I am pleased to offer you the job of a postal worker." The mayor grinned, and the crowd roared with laughter.

Alvin was known for spending his days sunning on the big rocks by the beach. The soft dragon shrugged and lazily flew into the sky.

Harold shivered with anticipation. He was the last dragon left, alone on the marble floor. He caught Elsa's eye and she made the heart sign with her hands. The crowd quieted as the mayor held his hands over his head.

"Last but not least we have Harold. The committee

thought long and hard about this one. In the past, our dragon friends have only helped us in five professions. Warrior, mining, firefighter, teacher, and postal worker. But Harold is a special case and we have decided that he deserves his very own job."

Harold held his breath and tucked his tail under his belly, wishing fervently he'd skipped breakfast. The butterflies were rioting again. He wanted to be a firefighter. He didn't want his own designation.

The mayor bowed. "Harold you will be our very first emotional support dragon."

He staggered with disappointment and his ears drooped. He couldn't have heard that correctly. A silence fell over the amphitheater. Even the dragons overhead stopped cawing and spouting fire.

Then a few townsfolk clapped, but most were murmuring. Harold heard a few of the comments.

"Emotional support dragon? That's ridiculous."

"Have you ever heard of such a thing?"

"What would he do, exactly?"

Harold whimpered and fluttered his third eyelid. Dragons aren't supposed to cry, but he was seconds from dropping onto his belly and sobbing.

Elsa yelled from the bleachers. "He will make a wonderful emotional support dragon. Congratulations Harold!"

Applause rippled through the stadium and the last bit of confetti rained onto Harold and the mayor.

Harold drew himself to his full height, front talons pleading as he addressed the mayor, "I'd much rather be a firefighter. Maybe there's room for two?" He perked his ears hopefully.

The mayor shook his head. "I'm sorry Harold. Only

the biggest and most powerful dragons join the fire platoon. You do such a nice job helping Elsa. You should focus on that."

"But—" Harold mewled desperately.

The mayor lifted the megaphone. "Let the celebrations begin!"

Harold's shoulders sagged and he was frozen in the middle of the arena. Dragons overhead spurted multicolored fire, and the townsfolk flooded from the stands into the amphitheater. He pinched his ears close to his head as a band struck up a jaunty tune. He normally loved listening to music, but the banjos set his teeth on edge tonight.

Even the smell of food didn't lift his spirits as tables of roast duck, smoked chimera, fruits, and vegetables were unveiled. He particularly liked strawberries but he had no appetite. He couldn't bring himself to join the dragons doing spins and flips. Instead, he tucked his paws over his head and burped butterflies.

Elsa rolled over in her wheelchair and put a hand on his shoulder. "I am so sorry Harold, but this might be a blessing in disguise. You are good at helping others."

A dark feeling brewed in his gut.

He spat at his friend, "This is your fault. If I didn't spend my time hauling you around the runeball field, maybe I would be a fire dragon!"

Elsa gasped and her face wrinkled in shock. He immediately regretted his words.

Tears filled her eyes. "If that's the way you feel, don't bother coming to my next runeball game." Elsa's thin shoulder shook as she spun her wheelchair and disappeared into the dancing crowd.

Harold wanted to go after her but he couldn't bring

himself to chase. Was he worthy of her friendship? No. He gritted his teeth and stalked out of the amphitheater. As he flew back to his cave, he heard laughter, roaring, and music behind him. He flicked his tail and ignored it.

He was the first dragon to return to the row of caves on the hill, but he didn't care. He didn't belong with anyone or anywhere. He got his own "special designation." Only Harold. Alone. An emotional support dragon of all lame things.

This was the most tired he had ever been. He dragged his belly into his tidy cavern and collapsed.

HAROLD'S DREAMS were full of flying through the sky with the fire brigade. So real, he could feel the wind in his ears. The morning sun always brought warmth and hope, and he woke with renewed vigor. He'd never tell a friend they were lame, so why was he talking to himself that way?

Maybe there was more than one way to skin a chimera.

He rolled out of his cave to scheme in the meadow and munch on butterflies. His long tongue nipped out and he swallowed them alive. They were his favorite treat. He rolled onto his back to look up at the clouds. They reminded him of the clouds of smoke from the fire yesterday. Except they were white.

Elsa had another game today. His heart gave a double thump when he thought of his friend's sad eyes. It wasn't fair of him to accuse her of ruining his fire platoon dreams. He wasn't stupid. He knew he was smaller than all the other dragons. But he had twice the heart!

He gritted his teeth. He should return to town and apologize to Elsa. But where had helping others gotten him? Lostmere's first emotional support dragon! A laughingstock. He would prove to Bruno he was a good team member. Unfurling his wings, he ran a few steps for momentum and launched himself into the air.

He flew to the fire hall and saw the dragons relaxing around a big stone slab with an enormous chimera turning on a spit.

Bruno flicked his long scaly tail. "Well, if it isn't our newest emotional support dragon."

The squad roared with laughter. Bertha laughed so hard, she rolled out of the circle.

Harold fluttered his wings and drew himself up to his full height. "I can do this. Give me a chance to prove I can be a fire dragon."

Bruno shushed his squad with a sharp look and flap of his wing.

He sighed, "All right Harold. You didn't come to the final test because you had a runeball game, right? Follow me to our training field."

Stretching his wings as wide as they could go, Harold followed Bruno to an enormous sand pit. The rest of the squad followed, snickering. There was a black line painted on the sand.

"The forest is on the far side and it is engulfed in flame. We have a village on the other side. You need to scorch a burn line right here to save the town." Bruno flew along the line. "Go!" He settled at the side of the field.

"You mean right now?" Harold managed to squeak.

Bruno stomped his thick legs. "Yes, right now. Emergencies don't wait on you."

Harold flew, pumping his little wings hard. He took a deep breath and aimed for the line. He inhaled with all his might, his eyes bugging out. Instead of flames, a puff of smoke and a handful of butterflies came out of his mouth. The butterflies flew in circles, then flitted off.

Bruno's jaw dropped. If the squadron had been snickering before, it was pure hysteria now. The huge dragons rolled with laughter while kicking their talons in the air.

"What are you eating, son?" Bruno asked kindly. "You need substantial protein for flame production. You should be eating sasquatches, chimeras, and buffalo. Big game for big flame."

Harold took a few shuddering gulps of air. "They give me indigestion." He'd given it his all and could hardly breathe.

Bruno lowered his deep voice, "It's okay. The platoon is not for everyone."

Harold's lower lip quivered. This was the blackest, saddest day of his life. He failed. A few final butterflies escaped from his throat when he coughed.

The squad stopped laughing and stared at him uncomfortably. Harold wished the ground would open and swallow him. He squeezed his eyes shut. This was the most humiliated he'd ever been. And that was saying something.

He dug his talons into the dirt and wished he could just vanish. Harold was trying to formulate an exit plan when the ground trembled and he heard a thump.

He opened his eyes and Martha was getting her balance after an awkward landing. She was soaked with sweat and trembling. Her scales were dripping. A froth of white foam stained her leather carrying bag.

She scuttled next to Bruno. "I bring an urgent message from the next town. An enormous forest fire is out of control in Cesterfield, and they can't contain it. They need help!" Her sides heaved.

The squadron sobered up immediately and lined up behind Bruno. Even Bertha. Lunch was forgotten.

"Lostmere Platoon, ready, set, fly!" Bruno commanded.

Harold's ears were blown to the side of his head as the thirteen dragons took flight. The entire sky became a ceiling of muscular bellies, translucent wings, and dust as they launched. The trees rustled from the jet stream.

Martha collapsed in relief beside him. "I've never seen a fire so big. The Cesterfield Platoon can't burn a line fast enough. If they don't find a way to stop the fire, it will destroy their town and then burn up Lostmere. There's only more dry forest between them and us!

Harold sniffed the air and detected the aroma of a bonfire as a thick haze filled the sky. But now wasn't the time to panic. He had to calm Martha down or she would have a heart attack.

He patted her back. "You did a great job, Martha. You've done all you can do for now. You deserve a rest."

She gave him a grateful smile. "You're a true friend."

Harold scuffed his paw on the dirt. Shame flooded him. He wasn't a true friend. The way he'd left Elsa yesterday was worse than unacceptable. It was cruel.

He gritted his teeth and made the hard decision. Some things were more important than his pride.

"I've got someplace to be Martha; I'll see you back in town."

Martha meandered over to the barbequed chimera and picked some meat off the carcass. It was hardly touched. "See you," she said with a full mouth. "I'll meet you at the runeball field"

Harold tried to launch himself straight up, the way the platoon members did, but tripped and tumbled to the dirt. He gave Martha an embarrassed grin and took a running start. This time he successfully flapped up over the treetops.

The runeball game had already begun when he landed beside the sports field. He looked at the bench of spectators but couldn't see Elsa. Had she been so upset she hadn't even bothered to come? His guts churned in self-loathing and he steeled himself to visit her house.

A cheer arose on the field and Harold squinted out on the field. It was Elsa! She'd just scored a goal and was getting high-fives. The referee tossed the stone back onto the field for the next play. Harold's jaw dropped as Elsa tucked her mallet between her knees and spun her wheels in a flurry. She intercepted a pass by bouncing the stone off her forehead.

Harold sat on his bottom and blinked. Elsa had never needed him to haul her around on the field. She was perfectly capable without him. He watched as she used her mallet to pass the ball to a team member and they scored yet another goal.

He gripped his belly, and his lower jaw trembled. He'd ostracized his best friend, didn't make the fire platoon, and wasn't even needed on the runeball field. Where did he belong?

Harold's pity party was interrupted when the crowd gasped. Bruno and his team returned, but something was wrong.

Instead of their usual crisp V formation, they were flying in a confusing clump. Harold could tell they were coming in for a landing on the runeball fields.

"Make way!" Harold called.

The players scattered to the edge of the field and the spectators leaped to their feet.

The thirteen dragons collided, making an uncoordinated landing on the field. They looked disheveled and shell-shocked. Bruno's ear was singed, and Bertha had a torn talon. The rest of the crew had little wounds and were covered in soot. The dragons had no more fight left in them.

Bruno tossed his head. "That fire is out of control. Our burn line slowed it down, but it's raging. I recommend the townsfolk evacuate. I am so sorry."

Smoke and a red glow painted the sky. The smell of bonfire was strong and pungent.

"We can't do it! It's just—" Bruno dropped his head and tucked his tail under his belly.

The crowd in the stands panicked. Some sobbed. Others were rushing home.

Elsa wheeled over to Harold and whispered into his ear. "There's no place for us to go! If the fire reaches our town, we will all die. We don't even have a big lake like Cesterfield. Just a river."

Harold thought furiously. "We have the best fire platoon in the region. If anyone can defeat this monster fire, it's the Lostmere Fire Platoon."

He searched the edge of the bleachers and saw Martha taking a nap under the biggest one.

He had an idea. "Elsa, ask Martha if she can fly back to platoon headquarters and get the chimera off the fire pit. Bring it back here."

ANGELIQUE FAWNS

Elsa nodded. "I'm on it, Harold.

He flapped to Bruno's side and tucked in beside him. "Tell me what's going on, Bruno. What are you afraid of?"

Bruno opened one eye and gave him a baleful glare. "We ran out of energy to make our own fire, and the other platoon was also exhausted."

Harold nodded. "I hear what you are saying and I understand how you're feeling. But the Lostmere Fire Platoon is the best in all the land. Bruno, you are a fearless captain and accomplished firefighter. Your dragons would follow you anywhere. Heck, I'd follow you anywhere."

Bruno raised his head a few inches. "But we are out of ammunition." He roared and a puff of dark smoke rolled right into the spectators on the bleachers. "See? No more flame." The captain let his head hit the dirt again.

Martha, swearing like a banshee, crashed into the grass beside them. Three-quarters of a barbecued chimera was strapped to her back. "That's it! The last thing I deliver today," she huffed.

Harold pulled the rope, and the chimera fell to the turf. "Bruno, you told me yourself, you need a good meal of protein to breathe fire! You responded to the rescue call so quickly, you forgot to finish your meal. Get your platoon to eat."

Bruno gave his massive body a shake. "Harold, you're right. We did engage without eating first. You can't fight fire without fuel."

Harold gave him a hug. "I know you can do this."

Bruno harrumphed, but a grin creased his soot-stained muzzle. "Lostmere fire platoon, dig in! We are

138

heading back to Cesterfield. And this time we are going to create an unstoppable burn line."

The thirteen dragons tore eagerly into the chimera until only a few bones were left. They lined up in a V formation. With a mighty roar, they lifted off and soared toward the inferno. The pink glow was growing and the smoke rose thick and dark over the sun.

"Thank you, Elsa. Thank you, Martha." Harold munched on a knuckle of the chimera and grimaced. It tasted terrible but he choked it down.

He gave himself a running start and launched into the sky. His wings flapped with more power and speed than ever before. Eating meat did make him stronger! But his throat felt like a burning cat was trying to claw out of his belly. Protein heartburn.

His eyes grew huge when he saw the scope of the fire. The forest was a maelstrom of terror. He tried to follow Bruno's squadron, but when the heat curled his whiskers, he settled on a high branch in an oak tree. It was time to think, not be charred.

He watched, heart in his throat, as the Lostmere platoon rejoined the fight and dove and spewed fire with a vengeance. Sparks lit up the sky in a demonic display of destruction. The fire had very nearly reached the town of Cesterfield, and the inhabitants were sitting on boats and rafts in the midtown lake.

Lostmere's dragons worked in perfect synchronicity. They scorched the land at the perimeter of the forest. The local dragons joined in, and a thick black line began forming between the flames and the village. They unleashed the water bags. A viable burn line was created moments before the flames reached the edge of town.

Harold thumped his tail so aggressively, he almost

knocked himself out of the tree. The fire starved, reduced to sparks, and became soot. Warm confidence welled up from his belly. Even without flying in the squad, he had helped save the day.

The smoke cleared as the people on the boats cheered and made their way to shore. Bruno's platoon and the Cesterfield team did a flyover in a double V formation, roaring in triumph. Though most of the dragons were out of flame, their ferocious calls were strong.

Harold reared up to his full height on the tree branch and blew fire with gusto. A thin flame shot into the sky. He grinned. He was getting better. Actual flame instead of undigested insects.

Bruno did a final flyover and then swooped down to Harold and grabbed him with his jaw. With a light flip, he tossed the smaller dragon onto his back. Harold whooped and grabbed onto Bruno's shoulder blades. Harold's ears pinned against his head from the sheer speed of the powerful dragon beneath him. It was like in his dream, but better.

At the front of the V, Harold roared as they circled down to the sports fields. His chest swelled, and he thought he might burst with happiness. The speed was a little scary, but he had a good grip. The crowd clapped gleefully as the team landed.

Harold leaped off Bruno's back, and the scarred platoon leader held up his little wing.

Bruno bellowed, "I designate Harold the official emotional support dragon of the Lostmere Fire Platoon."

Harold grinned and gave Elsa a wink, he couldn't believe he was the star of the final bow! His best friend's smile was like the sun bursting out from clouds. This was the best day of his life. And hopefully, he'd never have to eat chimera again. Butterflies were so much tastier. He'd made the platoon after all.

Even the town's smallest dragon could make a big difference.

A̲ngelique F̲awns has a Bachelor of Journalism from Carleton University in Ottawa and almost thirty years' experience as a commercial producer. She's the author of three guides featuring the speculative fiction market, creates a horror fiction podcast called Read Me A Nightmare, and has sold over eighty short stories. You can find her fiction in Ellery Queen Mystery Magazine, Amazing Stories, DreamForge, *and a variety of anthologies.*

www.fawns.ca
Facebook: https://www.facebook.com/amfawns
https://twitter.com/angeliquefawns
https://substack.com/@angeliquefawns1
https://angeliquefawns.gumroad.com

TO SOAR BETWEEN STARS

CAITLIN BARBERA

No one joined a voidwyrm hunting expedition if their life was going well. Most people tried to steer clear of the hunter ship crews when they came back, a few months older but drinking their pay away in bars twenty years removed from whatever they remembered. They were known to be strange people, and the joke went that, if they weren't lunatics when they signed up, they certainly were when they came back.

Tasha had never imagined ending up on a crew like that. But when she'd made the announcement that she was signing on, no one had tried to stop her. Her parents were gone, her siblings busy with their own families, and what friends she had were limited to occasional drinking buddies. The fact that no one cared if she disappeared for the next two decades was what had made her mind up. If no one would miss her, why not go?

Her mother would have said that she was cutting off her nose to spite her face, but her mother was dead. Tasha's brother and sister hadn't remembered to tell her the location of the funeral until the week before, even though she'd been messaging them almost every day. So she supposed it didn't matter anymore what her mother would have said.

The docks were crowded enough that she couldn't get lost in thought, which was probably for the best. There were people rushing every which way, colliding and shouting and ducking around one another. It was all she could do to keep her heavy canvas duffle bag on her shoulder and her feet carrying her forward toward the berth where she'd find the intimidatingly named *A Heaven of Hell*. When the ship finally came into view, she maneuvered out of the flow of traffic and stood against the wall, watching other crew members go up the gangway.

This was the last chance to change her mind. She could still go back to her old life. She'd quit her job working on the electrical systems for the station's atmosphere scrubbers, but it wasn't as though it had been a particularly good one. She could get something else, stay on the station. She imagined telling everyone she knew that she'd decided to stay after all, and being met with a resounding, "Okay." She just couldn't do it.

She squared her shoulders and stepped out toward the gangway, ignoring the other bodies buffeting her. She stomped up onto the ship with as much determination as she'd ever mustered, and it lasted until she made it into the cargo hold where a glowering, straight-backed man gave her a dismissive look, then turned back to the smaller man he'd been talking to. Tasha couldn't help wilting, slumping against one wall of the cargo hold and waiting to be told where to go.

"Are you Tasha?" someone asked next to her. "Tasha Radek?"

Tasha turned and saw a woman a little older than her, dressed in a boiler suit with "Engineering" on the breast pocket. "Um," Tasha said, glancing back at the two men, who had moved away, talking animatedly as they gestured toward various parts of the hold. "Yes, that's me."

The woman smiled brightly, and Tasha felt her shoulders relax. "Great! I'm Kira Tsai. This'll be my third tour with the *Heaven*. Mister Baines, the XO, asked me to show you around, since you'll be in Engineering too."

"Thank you," Tasha said, rather embarrassingly sincerely.

"We'd better get out of the hold before the captain sees us and gives us something to do," Kira said, lowering her voice and gesturing toward the tall man. "That's him with Mister Baines."

"Oh. I see."

"Don't worry, though. You probably won't have to deal with him much. Follow me!" Kira set off toward the corridor leading out of the cargo hold, deeper into the ship. She launched into an explanation of the time-line of the voyage, the mechanics of cryosleep, and the navigational signals that would be tripped to wake everyone when they'd reached their destination, all at a rapid-fire pace that made Tasha's brain spin trying to keep up. "Then the real work'll start," she finished, a little grimly, as they got to the Engineering Bay. "We're supposed to disrupt the voidwyrm migration routes in the area, drive off any that might be there. You know why, right? Something about the way they move around disturbs the faster-than-light lines, so we need to be sure there are none in the area and that none are going to be coming back in order to lay down a stable line." She turned toward Tasha and frowned slightly. "Sorry for being so serious, but there isn't really any room for error. Disturbed FTL lines... Well, they kill people, so we do have to be on the top of our game. You understand?"

Tasha nodded nervously. "Yeah, uh... That makes sense."

"Courage," Kira said, smiling again and gently punching Tasha's shoulder. "You were brave enough to sign up, you'll be brave enough to pull this off."

Tasha shrugged. "I don't know about that," she said a bit sheepishly. "I've never really been very brave."

"Now's a good time to start!" Kira said cheerfully. "Now, ready to see Engineering?"

Tasha hesitated and, after a nervous moment, cleared her throat and asked, "Will we actually see any voidwyrms?"

She tried not to sound too eager. It was a dream she'd had since childhood, to see one of the great beasts who could live in the vacuum. After her mother's funeral, she'd taken stock and realized that she hadn't achieved any of the dreams she'd gone into adulthood with, and it seemed like the only option was to return to something much older and deeper.

Kira, though, frowned. "Best to hope we don't. Those things can tear through a ship like it isn't even there." She leaned forward, lowering her voice. "That's how the captain lost his last ship, and his last crew. He'd served with them for years. Most people who do this job for any length of time have a list of dead friends. No, it's best if we don't see any in the area. We can disrupt their routes with sound mines and other things that will keep them from coming back."

Tasha felt her heart sink, but she was committed now. She nodded and followed Kira into the Engineering Bay.

TASHA HAD WONDERED if she would dream in cryosleep, but she didn't even realize that it had happened to her. She got in the pod, closed her eyes, then opened them again wondering why it hadn't worked. Except that the lid of the pod was opening, and so were the pods all up and down the row to either side of her. She blinked in confusion, then levered herself up and out.

Kira, stepping out of the pod to the left of her, gave her a slight smile and asked, "Alright?"

"What happened?" Tasha asked. "Did something go wrong with the freeze?"

Kira laughed. "No. Everything went fine. We're here. Come on, let's get to our station."

Tasha pushed herself out of her pod mechanically and followed Kira, waiting for the sensation of a single second passing to resolve itself into an understanding that ten years had passed. It didn't work; the freeze made no sense in her mind.

Her job, as the newest member of the Engineering crew, was as a runner, going wherever there were shorts reported and doing a quick assessment. If it was within her expertise, she could fix it herself; otherwise, she was supposed to call someone more senior. It was just about the smallest amount of responsibility a new crew member could have, but because it was a limited crew where everyone had to do important work, it was still possible for her to really screw up the ship if she did it wrong. She couldn't tell whether she was terrified or proud.

As it happened, the job was tremendously boring, at least at first. There were two more experienced runners, and she was mostly sitting on her hands waiting for something to happen. She was called out to fix a problem with a comms station, and that quick task was about the most interesting thing that happened in the first two hours.

When she was starting to drift off into a daydream, a row of lights along the ceiling of the Engineering Bay flashed red, seeming to bathe the room in blood. Tasha sprang up from her seat, as did her fellow runners. She looked to the senior crew, but they weren't reassuring; they were shouting at one another from their stations. She looked for Kira, but couldn't see her.

Finally, the Engineering Head stepped into the room and raised a hand for silence. She was a big woman with a perpetual scowl, and everyone immediately stopped what they were doing when she walked in. "Everyone to battle stations," she said. "If you do not have a battle station, strap into a crash couch. We are now in a combat situation."

There was a pregnant pause, then everyone sprang into motion, and Tasha found herself buckling herself into one of the crash couches along the side of the room with trembling hands, acting more on instinct than anything else. She closed her eyes and waited for whatever a battle would mean. Maybe there would be explosions? Catastrophic depressurization? Screams, blood, people dying?

There was a long period in which the only sounds were people talking to one another in tense, controlled voices. There were rumbles from elsewhere in the ship that seemed to come from far away. Tasha remembered that the engines were buried deep in the ship, under the strongest shielding and plating, and there was very little chance that any ordnance would get through unless the rest of the ship was basically destroyed. The battle, like the ordinary workday, became just another boring stretch of waiting.

And then it was apparently over. The red lights returned to their regular color, and the senior engineers at their stations slumped in relief. Tasha hesitantly unbuckled herself from the crash couch, hardly daring to believe that she had been in a space battle in her first day on the job, and that it had been *dull*, of all things.

"Is that... it?" she asked confusedly of no one. No one answered her, so she returned to the terminal listing active jobs for runners. There didn't seem to be anything else to do.

It was several minutes later that she stopped to wonder *what* they'd been battling. There couldn't possibly be ships here, they were the vanguard. Had they fought a voidwyrm and lived?

And if so... was there really a chance that she might see one?

When her shift was finally over, she found Kira waiting for her at the doorway to the Engineering Bay. She smiled a little distractedly at Tasha and said, "Come on, I'll show you to the galley."

Tasha didn't think it was even necessary, given the fact that all of the engineering crew getting off their shifts seemed to be going in the same direction, but she was grateful for the company anyway. "Have you ever… been in a battle like that before?"

Kira shook her head shortly, then seemed to return to herself. "No, I haven't… Well, I didn't realize that we could have a battle with a voidwyrm, you know? It's supposed to be over before you realize what's happening, most of the time. I guess we should count ourselves lucky…" She trailed off. They walked in silence for a while, until they reached the door of the galley.

They got their food and settled down with the rest of the engineering crew at a long table. Kira smiled and asked questions about Tasha's first shift, and Tasha answered, but it was clear that they were both thinking about something else.

About halfway through the meal, one of the more senior engineering crew tapped on Kira's shoulder and beckoned her away. They tucked themselves into a corner, talking in a low voice. Tasha watched them for a moment, then realized that they weren't the only ones; there were knots of people sitting or standing together here and there throughout the galley, talking to each other with their heads close together and their hands gesturing expansively. They all seemed to be more senior crew. When Tasha scanned the tables, the people who were sitting, staring at their food or looking nervously around at the conversations taking place, were all junior crew like Tasha. The atmosphere was strange, and she hunched her shoulders and kept her head down.

She was most of the way through her meal, barely tasting it, when the galley went silent. She looked up to see that the XO and several other senior officers, including the Engineering Head, had walked in. They were getting their own food with completely calm faces. Purposely calm faces. They ignored everyone else in the room, but at their arrival, the knots of people having discussions broke up. Kira sat down next to Tasha again and picked at her food.

"Kira," Tasha whispered. "What's going on?"

Kira smiled weakly at her. "Don't worry about it. It'll be fine. We should finish up and head to the bunks to get some sleep."

"Was it a voidwyrm? Was that what we were fighting?"

Kira hesitated, then said, "Yes." Tasha waited, but she didn't say anything else. They finished their food in silence, and Tasha followed the other engineering crew back to the bunks to sleep.

She couldn't sleep, of course. She laid down to stare into the darkness. She tried to close her eyes, but they kept popping back open. There *had* been a voidwyrm, right there by their ship, and Tasha had missed it. It had been right there, soaring through space nearby. Her mind held on to the thought, refusing to let it go.

A voidwyrm. In real life.

She remembered the images she'd seen of void-wyrms as a child, before she'd stopped obsessing over them quite so much. They were massive things, serpentine and crowned with three pairs of enormous, glittering wings growing from their backs. Scientists thought the wings caught and converted solar energy, but there was so much about voidwyrms that no one knew. So much that no one had managed to figure out yet.

She rolled over, shutting her eyes hard. She only had six hours before her next shift. She had to get some sleep.

There was the sound of whispering from somewhere in the bunks and soft footsteps on the floor. Tasha lifted her head slightly, squinting in the direction of the sounds. There was a group of people in the doorway of the bunk talking to one another, tension clear even in the dim illumination from the running lights along the floor. As she watched, the group started filing out of the bunkroom, letting a little more light in. One of them was Kira.

Tasha knew she should just close her eyes and try to sleep. It was the sensible thing to do. The thought of doing something wrong had been tightening her chest all day; she couldn't possibly follow those crew members out into the hall. She was supposed to be sleeping. She was the newest member of the crew. She shouldn't do anything to rock the boat.

But something strange was going on. And there was a voidwyrm just outside, a beautiful creature the likes of which she'd never seen. She didn't think she'd ever wanted anything as much as she wanted to know what was going on.

She rolled off her bunk, took a deep breath, and headed in the direction of the door and the hallway where the others had gone. She opened the door and ducked through it quickly, trying not to let too much light in. She heard raised voices from down the corridor and strode in that direction without giving herself time to think about it.

Kira was standing just around the corner with six other engineering crew members, and when Tasha came into view she was saying, "That message could say anything, we need..." She cut off abruptly, eyes widening, when she saw Tasha. "What are you doing?" she asked.

Tasha couldn't help noticing that none of the other crew members looked particularly happy to see her. She should apologize, go back to the bunkroom. This was a mistake. But instead of doing what she should have done, she swallowed hard against the panicky dryness in her throat and asked, "What's going on?"

"You need to go back to your bunk," one of the other crew members said.

"I just want to know what's happening," Tasha insisted, her heart pounding.

There was a long pause, as they looked at Kira, who apparently communicated something with eyebrow raises and shrugs. Finally, the crew member who had told her to go away sighed and sat back, and Kira turned toward Tasha.

"Caleb heard from some of the bridge crew that it wasn't just a voidwyrm attacking us. There were ships there too. Three of them."

"Sami said the voidwyrm wasn't even attacking us, not at first," Caleb put in. "They sent us a message, and the captain and the XO listened to it without telling the rest of the bridge crew what it said. Then the captain ordered them to shoot at the voidwyrm. It was only then that the other ships started shooting back. The voidwyrm just turned and left."

There was a long silence at that. Tasha imagined the way voidwyrms were said to tear through ships like they weren't even there. The voidwyrm could have killed them. It hadn't.

"How could there have been ships?" Tasha asked, her mind snagging on something else that didn't make sense. "We're supposed to be laying the FTL line. How did they get here without a line?"

Kira shrugged helplessly. "We don't know. It doesn't make any sense."

"We should talk to the Engineering Head," Caleb said, uncertainly. "I think Mister Baines told her what the message said. Maybe she knows how the ships got here."

There was a long silence after that. Tasha waited for someone to agree or argue. It seemed reasonable to her to ask the Engineering Head. After all, their lives were in the balance if the voidwyrm decided to return and attack. Shouldn't they all know what was going on?

But, of course, this was a hunting ship with a clear chain of command. She'd read a bit about that before coming aboard, and officers on ships like the *Heaven* were always on the lookout for potential mutiny. So, there was also a risk, she supposed.

She waited to see what the crew members would decide, but for a long time no one spoke. Tasha couldn't understand it at first; they had to do something, surely. They couldn't just sit there and wait to see whether they were all going to die.

But none of the other crew members answered Caleb. They were all looking at the ground, not meeting each other's eyes. Tasha couldn't even catch Kira's gaze.

Abruptly, she realized that they weren't going to make the decision. They were afraid of being accused of mutiny. They were afraid of what would happen.

But something had to happen. In her mind's eye, Tasha imagined the voidwyrm, beautiful and dangerous, soaring between the stars, perhaps heading their way right at that moment. *Someone* had to be brave enough to make this decision. It couldn't be her; she'd never been brave a day in her life.

But there wasn't anyone else, was there? She shut her eyes for a moment, screwing up what meager courage she had, and said, "Caleb's right. All our lives are at stake, we need to ask the Engineering Head."

Someone snorted. "Oh yeah, newbie? You're going to march in and talk to the Engineering Head?"

"I am," Tasha said, and against all odds her voice didn't waver. "Who's coming with me?"

Silence fell, and she despaired. She'd tried, she'd failed. Just like she'd failed at everything else.

Kira pushed herself to her feet. "Tasha's right. We can't just sit around talking about it. Come on, Head's off shift too. I know where she'll be."

Tasha was relieved she didn't have to lead the group. Once the decision had been made, they moved in a clump down the corridor, and Tasha was able to sink into the background, struggling to catch her breath. She had no idea what had come over her, but she hoped she was done being brave.

THEIR MOMENTUM CARRIED them to the door of the Engineering Head's bunk, and it even gave Caleb the courage to lift his fist and knock on the door. After that, though, Tasha could feel the energy drain out of the people around her as they heard footsteps in the room beyond.

The door opened, and the Engineering Head glared down at them. She was very tall, and Tasha felt everyone around her shrink. "What the hell are you doing here?" the Engineering Head said, making it sound more like a barked order than a question.

No one answered for a long moment. Finally, Kira piped up, "The message, ma'am. We need to hear it."

"You need to hear it, huh? You've just decided that? Get back to your bunkroom. Do it quickly enough and I'll forget this ever happened."

Several of the group took steps back, but Tasha took a step forward. Somehow, having already been brave once made it easier to do it again. "I don't want to die for no reason, ma'am," she said firmly. "I don't think anyone on this ship does either." She held the Engineering Head's stare, and the other woman glowered at her. The longer the standoff went on, the more certain Tasha was that the Engineering Head was about to drag her to the nearest airlock and shove her out into the void. Her stomach roiled and she wondered if she was going to throw up.

But if she was the center of the Engineering Head's attention, the other crew members who had come with her weren't running away.

Finally, to Tasha's incredible shock, the Engineering Head looked away first. "That message doesn't prove anything," she said in a low, angry voice. "Maybe it's just a hoax. Anyway, it's the captain's decision. If he were here, he would order me to put you straight into the brig."

If he were here. But he wasn't. "If the captain is wrong," Tasha said slowly, "we're all going to die." The Engineering Head flinched at that. Tasha didn't.

"Fine," the Engineering Head said, beckoning them through the door. "Come in quickly, before anyone sees you. This is close to mutiny."

They filed into the Engineering Head's quarters. Shipboard accommodations were small, even for such a senior officer. They had to cram together, pressed against the wall, as the Engineering Head crossed to a terminal on the wall facing the door. She looked down at the terminal for a long moment, then sighed and pressed a button.

There was a brief crackle, then a man's voice came over the speaker, slightly warped in the way that audio communications from other ships always were. The man sounded calm, even cheerful, as he spoke.

"Good morning, crew of the *A Heaven of Hell*! My name is Captain Daniel Kalu of the Transport Authority Interception Task Force. We have been deployed to assist with your transition now that you've arrived in the Kepler System. Please be aware that all licenses to hunt or disrupt the movements of voidwyrms have been revoked. I repeat, you are no longer authorized to hunt or disrupt the movements of voidwyrms in this or any system. Please respond to confirm receipt of this message and depower your weapons systems. We are standing by to escort you to the nearest colony."

There was a long moment of silence when the message had finished. They were all looking at one another with wide eyes. Finally, the Engineering Head sighed and said, "The captain did not confirm receipt of the message. Instead, he fired on the voidwyrm."

"Why would he do that?" someone asked behind her, but Tasha already knew why. She remembered Kira telling her that everyone who worked on a hunting ship had lost friends. That the captain had lost his previous ship, and all of his crew. The captain had understood the message, understood that he might be signing their death warrant, but with a voidwyrm in front of him, harming it was more important to him.

"You all know why," Tasha said aloud, and blinked in surprise when everyone turned to look at her. She swallowed hard and kept going, her voice shaking. "If we want to survive, we need to do it ourselves. The captain isn't looking out for our best interests. Not anymore."

There was a sudden explosion of people talking over each other, and Tasha had to step back. Her hands at her sides were shaking and she had to scrub them against her pant legs to wipe the sweat away. She was still in her ship-issued pajamas. They all were. It struck her as absurd, suddenly, that this was happening while they were in their pajamas.

The Engineering Head was looking at her. Tasha lifted her head and looked back, trying to look braver than she felt.

"Everyone, be quiet," the Engineering Head said finally. She didn't say it that loud, but it made the talk fall silent immediately. Everyone turned to look at her. She took a deep breath, then said, "Crewman Radek is correct." Tasha had just enough time to be amazed that the Engineering Head knew her name. "If we want to survive this, we have to take our lives into our own hands."

"Do you… Do you mean…?" Kira started but seemed to be unable to finish the sentence.

"I mean mutiny," the Engineering Head said calmly. "I believe that once we begin the process, the other senior officers will be on our side, but I can't guarantee that. It's possible that we'll fail and be killed. I believe that it's a virtual certainty that we'll die if we don't."

Tasha's heart seemed to be beating out of her chest. She couldn't understand how the Engineering Head wasn't screaming. Tasha had a nearly overwhelming urge to scream herself. She held on by the skin of her teeth.

Forcing the words through what felt like a rapidly closing throat, she said, "I'm with you."

And then Kira said it too. And then Caleb, and then a chorus of voices. And then there wasn't any choice but to keep moving forward.

MUTINY, like battle, was much more boring than she'd expected. They marched back to the engineering bunks and collected more crew members, seeming to convince them by the force of momentum more than anything else, then made their way to the bridge.

Mister Baines saw them first. He and the Engineering Head locked eyes, and there was a tense moment as the captain turned. Tasha froze and wondered whether anything was going to happen now.

Then Mister Baines drew his sidearm and pointed it at the captain's head. The captain gave all of them a poisonous glare.

"What the hell do you think you're doing?" he asked, his voice cold. Tasha was shaking from head to toe by that point.

"I believe you know what we're doing," Mister Baines answered, as eerily calm as the Engineering Head had been.

The captain looked around the bridge from officer to officer, but none of them stood to his defense. He drew himself up, glaring, and nodded sharply. "It's mutiny, then. Perhaps it would be better to kill me, Mister Baines. I don't think I'll make this easy for you, when we return home."

"I think we both know that things will look rather different when we return home," Mister Baines answered. "I'm willing to take my chances."

There was a flurry of activity, taking the captain to the brig, announcing to the crew that Mister Baines was now in command. Tasha found herself pushed to the side of the bridge, seemingly forgotten. She watched it all happen with a feeling as though she was watching a story that was happening to someone else, possibly someone who was very distant from her.

She felt a hand on her arm. She looked up dully and saw Kira standing next to her. "Are you alright?" she asked in a soft voice.

"I… guess so," Tasha answered, trying to wrap her mind around what was happening. "I'm alive."

"That's good," Kira agreed. "We all are, thanks to you."

"Thanks to *me*?" Tasha asked, blinking in surprise.

"Yeah. I think we might all have stood around wondering whether to do something, if you hadn't made us." Kira smiled at her. "You were the brave one."

"I'm not brave," she answered reflexively, and Kira laughed and shook her head. Tasha had never thought of herself as brave before, but maybe…

She leaned back against the wall, her shoulder touching Kira's, and let herself relax for the first time in what felt like hours. For the first time in what *was* hours, she realized.

Mister Baines returned to the captain's station,

159

seemed to steel himself, then pressed a button. "Attention, Captain Kalu of the Transport Authority Intercept Task Force. This is Acting Captain Baines of the *A Heaven of Hell*. We are depowering our weapons and submitting to your escort to... to the nearest colony."

There was a brief silence, then the voice that Tasha had heard in the Engineering Head's bunk filled the bridge. "I am glad to hear that, Acting Captain. I will assume that there has been a change aboard your ship, and that our companion will not be fired upon again?"

Baines hesitated, then answered, "That is correct. By your companion, do you mean the voidwyrm?"

"That's correct," Captain Kalu answered. "Please have your helmsman move your ship into the position I am sending now. Our companion is returning now to help us travel to the settlement."

There was a quiet murmur among the bridge crew, and Baines was struck dumb for a moment before he said, "How? How is that... There isn't an FTL line here."

"We don't use those anymore," Captain Kalu answered, sounding amused. "Don't be alarmed. Rana — the voidwyrm, I mean, has to be pretty close to the ships to bring us along. Keep your weapons depowered, you won't need to do anything else."

"It's the voidwyrms," Tasha whispered to Kira, awe spreading through her chest. "They can pull ships through FTL space. They are *traveling* by *dragon*." She looked at Kira, whose eyes were wide, and they both smiled widely, like children at a festival.

Baines gestured to one of the crewmembers, and a screen showing their position in space relative to the other ships switched to the feed from the exterior ship cameras. They watched as the other ships grew bigger as they approached, maneuvering into the position Captain Kalu had told them to take.

And then Rana came into view. Tasha reached out for Kira's hand, and felt Kira hold on tightly. It was the most beautiful sight Tasha had ever set her eyes on.

Rana was huge, so much bigger than she'd expected, three times bigger at least than *A Heaven of Hell*. Her body looked black, except where the light reflecting off her wings colored her dark green. Her long shape coiled over itself, tail flicking back and forth, enormous head turning to survey the scene. As Tasha watched, the void-wyrm turned to regard the ship, one enormous, luminous, all-white eye coming into view. She had six legs, long and slender, descending from her stomach, but the things that caught Tasha's eyes and held them were her wings, enormous and paper-thin and glowing silver-gold with captured starlight. They spread around her back like light itself was pooling in the blackness, surrounding her. The sight took Tasha's breath away.

"It's magnificent," Kira whispered, and Tasha could only nod and think to herself that she was so, so grateful that she didn't have to kill Rana. She could sail beside her, instead.

Tasha watched as Rana took a position at the head of the formation and tilted her head back, mouth open in some silent exhalation, then those golden wings drifted and flapped, leaving strands of light behind as they released some kind of propulsion. Her body moved sinuously, and then, in the space between one breath and the next, the dragon moved into something *beyond* space, something blindingly white, and pulled all the ships with her as she went.

It was only a moment, a moment that felt as though Tasha was floating outside the bounds of reality, and then she blinked and saw that they were somewhere else, hanging in space above a bustling green planet. There were other voidwyrms, other ships, stations and satellites.

Tasha looked out over the future, filled with magnificent creatures twisting and coiling and swimming their way between stars, and felt tears of joy spill down her cheeks.

CAITLIN BARBERA IS a lifelong lover of reading and writing science fiction and fantasy. Her first story was about a girl velociraptor going on an adventure and fighting androids. She is currently a student in the Genre Fiction concentration of the Graduate Program in Creative Writing at Western Colorado University. A native of Colorado, she currently lives in the Denver metro area with her spouse, child, and dog, and spends much of her time coming up with more story ideas than she could possibly write in a lifetime. She can be found at caitlinbarberawrites.wordpress.com.

JEYHONE

LORNA JANE HANSMANN

J oseph sighed as he filled in the next test bubble. The room was quiet as all the students' heads were bent working on their tests. Joseph would finish first, as usual. He was attempting to go slower when the sensation of lightning shot through his spine. He arched his back and clamped his mouth shut as he dropped his pencil; it rolled toward several desks in front of him. Sweat beaded on his forehead as he swallowed a large lump and let out a long breath as the pain dissipated.

Damn! Not now. Not after all this time. He stood from his desk and grabbed his backpack. Trying to appear ill, which wasn't difficult given the aftershocks of electricity now running from his spine to his sides, he stumbled to the teacher's desk.

"Mr. Anderson, I'm not feeling well. Can I go to the nurse's office?"

His teacher's brow furrowed with concern. "Yeah, you don't look too great. Go ahead. Do you want someone to walk you there?"

"No, it's okay. I can make it."

"Alright. Get better."

Once out the door, Joseph jogged down the hall despite his suffering. By the time he reached the office his face was covered in sweat, his breath was shallow, and his hands shook.

He didn't talk to the secretaries or go see the nurse. Instead, he went straight to the phone that was set up for students. He dialed his mother's number. "Hey Mom, I'm not feeling good. I feel like I've been hit by a truck."

The last line told her everything she needed to know. "We'll be there in five."

He sat on the bench, elbows on his knees, head in his hands. The shocks kept coming and his breathing was still hollow.

True to her words, Mom showed up in five minutes and checked him out with the office ladies. The moment they were outside, they ran to their van. Their doors slammed shut, and Dad took off toward the freeway. His twin sisters were in the back, behind them in the trunk were their emergency bags.

Joseph lay down across the middle seat.

"Did the warning pain happen again?" Dad asked.

"Yeah," Joseph choked out as another spike shot down his spine. Through gritted teeth he added, "You are gonna want to go faster. They're close."

Mom turned around in her seat, she rubbed his shoulder and held out a water bottle. "Drink a little, it will help."

Taking the water, he awkwardly drank while half lying down and half sitting up. When he finished, he gave the bottle back to Mom before plopping his upper body back on the seat. He groaned again.

"Mom?" Nora said from the back.

"Yes, dear."

With a quivering voice she asked, "Will Maxine and I have this happen to us too, when we get older?"

The last time Joseph had an "episode" they had been two years old. They didn't remember what it was like, and it was obvious that seeing their older brother as he was now scared them.

"Sweethearts, I –" Mom turned toward Dad, their faces grim. She took a deep breath. "We don't know. It might be Joseph's special gift, or it might be a new generation's way of trying to survive. We just don't know."

"I hope we don't have it," Nora whimpered. Maxine held her hand and whispered in Nora's ear. A smile spread on Nora's face and soon the girls were playing make believe in the back without having the world's burdens on their backs.

Twenty minutes later, the last aftershock began and faded before reaching Joseph's sides, and he knew it was done. He took a deep breath and let it out slowly before pulling himself back to a sitting position.

Joseph pulled off the thick glasses he didn't really need and unbuttoned the top of his too tight plaid shirt, both a part of his stereotypical nerd disguise, before leaning in between the front seats. "What's the plan?"

Dad answered. "We are going to head north. Once we know we've lost them we'll go east."

"Did you already decide on what city we'll be in?"

"Yes," Mom said while finishing putting her blonde hair into a ponytail. "We decided after we'd settled in last time. It's a smaller town called Weeping Storm."

"Smaller town? It'll be harder to stay under the radar that way."

"We know," Dad said. "We are hoping the DEF won't expect us to settle there." Joseph didn't remember a time when the Dragon Elimination Force wasn't chasing them.

Joseph hesitated. "Can I choose my persona this time?" Three years they'd been able to stay in the same place. It was the longest they'd stayed anywhere. Joseph knew it was because his parents had created his persona, making him shy and nerdy, an outcast. But he wasn't shy or nerdy, though he was certainly intelligent.

"You'll have to run it by us." Joseph felt his chest tighten with disappointment at his father's words. He understood why. They 'd been discovered every year, sometimes twice, until they stepped in. It took time to understand how the DEF's machines worked. But they knew now. The more they interacted with others, the more their dragon essence permeated an area, which is exactly what their tools searched for. An outgoing young dragon who made friends easily created a disaster when trying to stay hidden.

"How about my name?"

Mom smiled, despite the worried lines on her face, and touched Dad's arm. "You can definitely choose your name."

"Okay, thanks."

Joseph leaned back into his seat. He closed his eyes so he wouldn't be disturbed but he didn't sleep. His body felt tight. He needed to stretch it out. Push out the tension using his real form. What he wouldn't give to fly freely.

THE MOTEL STANK and the beds were uncomfortable, but no one complained. Dad went out to meet his contact to get the family's new identification papers. True to their word, Joseph got to pick his new name. He chose the name Johnny. He hadn't had that human name since he was in kindergarten. He liked it the best since it used almost every letter of his real name, Jeyhone.

Johnny could hear his sisters playing with their dolls on one of the queen beds. Mom was on a secured phone talking to their soon to be landlords. He closed the bathroom door and shook out his hair. It had grown out a bit. He'd deliberately put off getting a haircut. He preferred it longer. When they stopped for supplies, they'd told him to pick out a new hair color. He chose black, much to his parents' chagrin. What they didn't know was that he'd also pocketed a dark blue. He got to work, hogging the small bathroom, as he bleached his hair, put the black color in and added the dark blue to a thick strip in the front.

As he was finishing up, a knock came at the door. "Hey," Dad called. "I brought pizza. Come get some before your sisters eat it all."

His sisters, whose new names were Nikki and Molly, were in the middle of a growth spurt. They were constantly hungry and could eat a whole sheep, let alone an entire pizza.

Johnny used the cheap blow dryer that was connected to the wall so he could really see his new look. He nodded, firm in his decision, and braced himself before stepping out of the bathroom.

His family encircled the tiny table that only could fit the two pizza boxes stacked on top of one another.

Mom had a chair, and the second chair the sisters shared. Dad stood with a paper plate in his hands. Johnny pulled out a slice and his mother gasped. Everyone halted their movements as they stared at him.

Dad's jaw twitched as he clamped his teeth together. The anger in his eyes as he inspected Johnny could have put fear into anyone. Johnny's hands began to sweat.

"Explain. Now." The calm manner in which the words flowed only made Johnny more nervous. It didn't matter if he had known this would happen, it didn't prepare him for his father's intensity.

He rubbed his palms down his pants. "I have been far from who I actually am for the last three years. It's been torturous. I needed something to remind me that I'm still me."

"With a punk look?" Dad asked incredulously. "That's how you are going to begin in our new home? With this new community?"

"I'm sure I won't be the only one with this kind of look."

"That just shows your ignorance. Weeping Storm is a small community built on tradition. They are small-time farmers who work hard, and you are going in there like that? I already gave in to your mother to allow the black hair. This is too much. You will change it."

"Dad, please understand I need it."

"No, *you* need to understand. I am trying to keep my family safe from those who would experiment on you. Cut you up and see how you work."

Nikki whimpered. Molly put her arm around her. Nikki had always been more sensitive.

"Dear," Mom said as she knelt before the girls. "Let's not go into details."

"Take the pizza and go eat at the playground across the street. I need to finish this chat with our son."

"It's not a chat, it's a lecture," Johnny said, shaking his head in disbelief.

The girls followed Mom out. Dad waited a few more seconds before continuing his reprimand.

"You can't possibly understand the pressure of keeping us all safe. Everyone needs to do their part and that includes blending in. We will get more black dye and fix this. I will not risk your mom or your sisters because of your selfishness."

"It's not selfishness. It is a need. I am losing myself here."

"Don't be dramatic."

"I'm not. You don't get it. I have spent more time as a human than I have as a dragon. I know this face better than I do my real one. It has me all twisted inside. I need this, Dad. I need the blue. I need it as a reminder of my scales, of who I really am."

His father rubbed a hand down his face. "Listen, I'm sorry this is our life. It's not like your mother and I wanted it to be this way. I hate how the Dragon King trusted that peace was possible between us and the humans. He should have been more cautious. If he had, each hidden land of ours would still be intact and you could live how we were meant to. But wishing that doesn't make the reality less true. I don't want you standing out."

"We can tell them we're from the city and I'm the rebellious teenager that you are trying to give perspective to. Hence our move to a smaller community. Can't we do that?"

"It's too much of a risk. We don't know how many people they pay to notice anything odd."

"I know that. But hell, if I'm the one who has the agony every time they are close, shouldn't I have some say."

The crease in his father's brow deepened. They stood silently for a long moment before Dad let out a breath and his tense frame relaxed. He put a hand on Johnny's shoulder. "You have a point. Ever since your ability has manifested, we've had more time to flee. How about a compromise? I'll let you keep the blue, but if people in the community bring it up to your mother or I, then you change it."

The heaviness in Johnny's chest eased. A compromise, it was something.

"Deal. Thanks, Dad."

"I know it's tough," his dad sighed. "Come on, let's go get the girls. Hopefully there's still some food left."

NOT ONLY WAS Johnny used to being the new kid, but he was also used to coming in midyear. The stares. The whispers. Always the same.

He walked into his first period class a few minutes late. He wore black jeans with a black dress shirt tucked in and sleeves rolled up. A loose tie hung around his neck, one that matched the dark blue in his hair. Each of his hands had several silver rings. This was his style, one that his dad may have been nervous about drawing too much attention, but now knew Johnny needed.

He handed a slip to his English teacher, Mr. Gordon. "Welcome. Go ahead and take an empty seat."

All the seats in the back two rows were taken, so he slipped into a spot in the second row next to the windows.

Mr. Gordon began his lecture. They were starting a new unit on famous speeches and the students would be required to write their own in the upcoming weeks.

As he spoke, Johnny gazed out of the window. The sky was clear, a bright blue. How he longed to sprout his wings; to see how fast, how high he could go! To dance on air. To feel the cooler temperature on his scales. The longing always sat in his belly.

A flash of orange ran past the window. He turned his head quickly to see the back of a girl with reddish orange hair and an orange dress that looked like it came out of a sixties movie. She turned the corner and was gone.

Johnny turned his attention back to the teacher. Mr. Gordon was pulling up one of Winston Churchill's speeches when the orange-haired girl ran in.

"Sorry Mr. Gordon, I overslept," she said breathily.

"That's alright, Sasha. Start with putting the grades in for last week's tests."

"Yes, sir."

Sasha went to Mr. Gordon's desk and sat down. She opened a large green gridded notebook and picked up the first paper in the stack that sat next to it. Her finger ran down the page and then across before she marked the book. Then she picked up the next paper in the stack. Johnny guessed this little town didn't have the computer system the big cities did for school.

There was something about her orange hair that completely captivated him. Or maybe it was the freckles he discovered she had. He didn't generally find humans attractive, so he pushed that thought aside, but he was feeling some sort of pull that made him curious about the girl.

He didn't realize how intently he was staring until her eyes flashed to his. He probably should have dropped his gaze; he knew most humans would have. But her irises were such a beautiful deep blue that he couldn't help but stare at the depths of them. Sasha didn't look away either.

An urge hit him so suddenly, Johnny gripped his desk to anchor himself. The desire to turn into his true form and surround this girl with his fire grew the longer he stared into her eyes. Eyes that seemed to widen with their own surprise, but that must have been because some creep was staring at her!

Johnny wasn't sure how long he could keep himself in check. He'd never experienced anything like this. He'd never felt the need to lose control and to let his dragon fully take over before today. His heart pounded and he could admit to himself that he was indeed truly scared, knowing the danger of such an outcome.

The breaking point was coming, Johnny could feel it. But by some sweet miracle, Mr. Gordon walked between them, blocking the view and severing the connection. The relief that spread through his body was acute.

Mr. Gordon tapped his desk. "Do I have your attention now, Johnny?"

"Yes."

"Good, because I asked you to come up and take a turn reading Mr. Churchill's speech. The last two paragraphs. Let's see if you can put in a bit more passion than the others. It is the climax after all."

Johnny went to the podium on shaky legs, deliberately avoiding eye contact with Sasha. His deep voice rumbled as he spoke the words, "…Turning once again, and this time more generally, to the question of invasion…"

When he finished, he quickly sat, keeping his head down, afraid to risk a glance at the girl. The rest of class was uneventful, despite the pull he still felt tingling along his skin.

The bell rang and Johnny quickly gathered his bag and headed toward the door.

"Johnny, could you wait a second?" Mr. Gordon asked.

Halting, Johnny slowly turned around as the rest of class exited, except for Sasha. He kept his focus on Mr. Gordon.

"Yes, sir?"

"This is my TA, Sasha. I looked at your transcripts and it looks like you are missing grades from only one unit. I'd hate to have you go to summer school for such a small thing. I want you to work with Sasha. There were only a few turn-in assignments. We mostly read lots of poetry in class. Sasha will explain the assignments and I'll retroactively put them into the grade book."

Johnny cleared his throat, still avoiding Sasha's eyes despite feeling her gaze burn into him. "That is thoughtful of you, but I don't want to give anyone extra work to do. I don't mind just going to summer school." The very idea of having to interact with this girl who affected him in such a way terrified him. He was dragon enough to admit that freely.

"It isn't a bother to help you." Sasha's lilt sent a pulse through Johnny's chest. "Half the time Mr.

Gordon doesn't have much for me to do and I end up just reading."

"That's true," Mr. Gordon said. "And I often give time in class to work on things, so you can discuss the requirements then."

Johnny nodded, now keeping his gaze to the ground. He'd have to get out of this later. More students were filing in for second period, and he still needed to get to his own class. Though, more importantly, he just needed to get away from Sasha.

"Okay, thanks."

With that he hurried out of the room. In the hall he took a deep breath and let it out slowly. What was happening? Even now, the desire to turn around and embrace this human girl pulled at him. Not embrace, that was a human idea. No, it was a desire to dance in the sky with fire all around them creating the song of their movements.

He made it to second period on time. As he sat, Sasha walked into the room. *Bloody hell*, they shared this class too. He kept his head down, until through his peripheral he noticed she'd sat down in the front row. The back of her hair reminded him of a sunset, orange and red and even a few natural highlights of blonde. Johnny was grateful she was in the front row. He was in the back. He doubted he could have made it through all of class without touching her hair if she'd sat any closer.

The rest of the day, each class resulted in the same. He'd get there first and sit in the back. She'd come a moment later and sit in the front. Every. Single. Class. What were the odds? It wasn't until period six that he realized most of the kids in his classes were the same, not just Sasha. Small school meant fewer students, and this was the smallest school he'd ever attended.

By the last class, having spent all day with the back of Sasha's head in front of him, he felt like his body was going to combust. The pull to her never ceased. It was bizarre and sometimes painful, sometimes eager. It was the most intense physical reaction he'd ever had, and certainly the most mental. He wished to run from her, not because this was all new, but because his desire had increased. If he lost control, he would surely frighten her.

When the bell rang, he darted out of the school. His parents had gotten him a cheap, used and beat-up motorbike to make the twenty-mile trek to and from school. He hopped on, fired it up, and accelerated with as much force as the bike could handle.

As the wind whipped around him, his knuckles white from gripping tightly, an ache in his chest burned. The further he distanced himself from her, the more it deepened.

The drive home should have taken about twenty minutes but instead he booked it in ten. Hopping off the bike, he ran into the little house.

"Mom!" She was sitting on the floor with the girls as they finished up a worksheet.

"What is it?"

His face must have been considerably fierce, because she immediately told the girls to go to their room and went to him. She grabbed his shoulders. "What is it? What's happened?"

He explained what had occurred with Sasha, pacing back and forth as he did. Her brows furrowed, and her lips pressed into a tight line as she slid to the couch.

"Well, what do you think?" he asked.

"You couldn't possibly be …I mean, it's unheard of with a human . . ."

"What is?"

A knock at the door made them both jump.

Mom stood. "I'll get it."

Johnny followed her. When she opened the door, to his shock, Sasha stood there.

Mom spoke first. "You must be Sasha."

Her face lit up. "You've already heard of me. That's unexpected, but nice." Sasha's focus flicked to his face and immediately he was once again zeroed in on her with an intensity that made his yearning increase. "Hello, Johnny."

He swallowed hard. "Hi," he let out with a hoarse breath.

"May I come in?" she asked, keeping her attention on him. He couldn't seem to say anything at that moment. He didn't want her here, but he definitely didn't want her to leave either.

"What can we help you with?" Mom asked stepping in front of Johnny. Her tone was pleasant, but her stance protective.

Sasha's voice was light. "It's the other way around. I'm here to help you. Please, may I come in and explain?"

Mom didn't move. Johnny figured she must be going through her options. Then Sasha spoke again.

"Please" she pleaded softly. "I've had to stay away from him all day. It's been difficult, knowing he was sitting behind me. Feeling his eyes on me but knowing he'd not look at me if I turned around, which is completely understandable, but here, he can. Here, we can . . ."

Johnny moved to see her face. "Can what?"

Mom pulled her inside and closed the door. "Go on."

Sasha let out a relieved breath. Those blue eyes of hers snatched Johnny's before he could stop them. Once again, the vision of him as a dragon and her, with his fire all around them, burned in his brain.

He choked on the intensity of it and felt his mother's hand on his back in comfort. Then he felt Sasha's hand on his cheek.

"It's alright, Johnny. I see it too, and I feel it."

"You really are his mate," his mother's voice said in awe.

"Yes," she said as her cheeks flushed.

Mate? But she's human!

"I'm from the family of Eli."

"What?!" His mother practically shouted, yet Johnny still didn't say anything, still didn't move, holding himself back from the desire to transform. But he'd been taught the way of the dragons, he too was in awe of this revelation. His mother's wonder matched his. She continued. "We thought you were all slaughtered like the rest of the dragons!"

"I'll explain, but first . . ." her words drifted away and suddenly her mouth was on Johnny's. Not just a mere human kiss, no, she breathed into his mouth, but what came was not just air, but a cleansing of his loneliness. That ache had burrowed inside him for so long and now in this moment it had been flooded with her warmth. Her light filled it completely. It was the most glorious feeling he'd ever felt. On instinct, he let some of his fire spark and travel into her mouth. She breathed it in without fear. Back and forth the cleansing and the fire danced along their tongues; each time bringing them greater understanding of who the other was. An exchange that deepened their connection.

When she pulled away, the vision he couldn't shake while looking into her eyes disappeared. Her countenance shined delightfully as she kept trying to tamp down the huge grin on her face. An image of her embracing a ball of his fire passed through his mind, a representation of her acceptance of all of him.

"I'm yours," he said in a daze.

"Yes, Jeyhone."

To hear his true name on her lips was overwhelming and confirmed that the kiss had sealed them together. Johnny took her hand and kissed it gently before placing it on his heart. Traditionally, dragons mated much older; to have found a mate at all was a miracle.

Mom shook her head in disbelief. "Mates as dragon and human. It's never been. And, from the family of Eli. Are your parents alive?"

"They are."

Mom turned her attention to Johnny. "Alright, I'm calling your father and we are all going to Sasha's home." Mom turned toward the hall. "Nikki! Molly!"

The girls ran out of their room. "Yes," they said in unison.

"Get your shoes on, we are going out."

As they grabbed their sneakers Molly whispered to Nikki. "Why is Johnny holding that girl's hand?"

Nikki shrugged. Then turned to her brother. "Did you get a girlfriend on the first day of school?"

Johnny chuckled and Sasha smiled wide. "Something like that," he said.

"Weird."

Mom had stepped to the side to call their father. "What's your address, Sasha?"

"I'm going to take you someplace better than my house. Tell him to go to the outskirts of town, to the abandoned mine. My parents will be there."

As Mom finished her conversation, and the girls finished lacing their shoes, Johnny stepped closer to Sasha. He reached up and touched her hair, the silky feel flaming his desire for her, before leaning to whisper in her ear. "I've never found a human enchanting before, but you are so very beautiful to me. It is surprising."

When he pulled back, Sasha's cheeks were a lovely shade of pink. "I find you attractive in your human form as well, but I am most eager to see your vibrant blue scales with my own eyes." She tugged at his dark blue tie, not breaking her gaze.

"Alright," Mom said, unaware of her interruption. "Let's go." She ushered them all out the door and into the car. Once on the road, Mom started with the questions.

"Do you possess the magic of Eli?"

"Yes."

"What about government sensors?" Mom asked. "They've developed some fancy stuff to find us."

Sasha sat up straighter. "The more they create such things, the more our power grows."

"What power?" Molly's voice was so soft. It was rare for her to talk, so it surprised them all.

Sasha twisted in her seat so she could see Molly and

179

Nikki. "I come from the bloodline of Eli. He was a great mage whose sole job was to make sure the dragons were safe from humans. His family was given that responsibility and we hold it still."

"Then why do we have to run?" Nikki asked.

"Well, the humans were sneaky. They convinced the Dragon King that they could be trusted, so my family had orders to stand down. But my grandfather had his misgivings, so he sent my parents away in case they were needed. Having not heard the order by their king, they didn't have to obey it. The only problem is any dragons who escaped were scattered. But don't worry. In this little town, there are eight dragon families. My oldest brother has left again to search for more."

"Eight!" Mom exclaimed, a hand clutching her heart while the one on the steering wheel swerved slightly on the road. "We thought we were the last. We didn't think anyone else got out."

"The fact that you're here is quite amazing. All eight families have moved here because we found them. You are the first dragons to show up on your own. It is quite exciting. Everyone will be thrilled."

They reached the abandoned mine. An old sign with red letters hung at the entrance with the words DANGEROUS KEEP OUT. The beams at the entrance were rotten and unstable. Dad was already there and climbed out of his car as they did the same.

Having to be discreet on the phone, Mom took Dad aside and explained all that had happened.

Nikki grabbed Johnny's arm and started tugging. "Can you stop staring at Sasha and give me a piggyback ride?"

Johnny laughed. "I don't know, sis. She pretty much has all my attention."

"Ugh."

He let go of Sasha's hand and picked Nikki up, swinging her over onto his back. She laughed happily. "Come on, Molly, you know what to do," Johnny said.

Molly giggled and jumped into his open arms. She wrapped her legs around him and over Nikki's legs. One of Johnny's shoulders had Molly's chin resting on it and the other had Nikki's. "Hold on tight ,you two, I'm doing this with one hand." Nikki's grip was solid, so he shuffled to make sure he had hold of Molly before taking Sasha's hand again.

"This is good practice," Sasha said.

"Oh? For what?"

"Our own."

Johnny's eyes widened and it was his turn to blush. There was no time to respond as his parents stepped closer.

"Hello Sasha, it is an honor to meet you," Dad said, still reeling from the turn of events. "We will properly welcome you to the family later, right now, let's meet your parents."

Sasha's face lit up with excitement. "I'm happy to meet you, too. This way."

Nikki and Molly stayed clinging to Johnny as they followed her into the mine. It was dark for about twenty feet. Then the "mine" disappeared and before them was a great meadow with a lake in the distance.

"Whoa," Nikki said, sliding off Johnny's back. Molly turned and followed suit as everyone's steps slowed.

Johnny dropped to his knees. Before them were dozens of dragons. Some laid out on the grass, others were in the sky. He was just a hatchling when his parents fled with him from the DEF. He had no recollection of other dragons. Rarely had he seen his parents in their true form and only a handful of times had he made the change.

Nikki and Molly began jumping up and down, jostling Johnny from his shock at the sight.

"There are so many colors!" Nikki said.

Molly pointed to one area of the open sky where several dragons raced. "And they're so fast."

Dad was holding Mom in an embrace as tears of joy streaked down her face.

"What do you think?" Sasha asked Johnny.

"How?" He felt too taken aback for words.

"The power of Eli," she said. She began to wave, and Johnny noted that there were two humans by the lake. A man and a woman climbed on the back of a yellow dragon and flew to them.

The dragon landed in front of the newcomers. A particularly large dragon. Most, as far as Johnny's parents explained, were the size of a horse or a little larger, but this dragon was at least two horses tall. It was magnificent.

Sasha gestured toward the humans as they dismounted, using the dragon's scales as holds to climb down. "These are my parents, Gig and Catherine."

"Welcome," Catherine said with a smile. "It's so wonderful that you've found us."

Johnny's parents shook both their hands while Johnny gathered his faculties enough to rise from the ground.

"We are a bit overwhelmed," Dad said. "This feels impossible."

Gig nodded. "Most usually are. Sasha phoned to tell us we'd be having visitors here and we were quite surprised."

Johnny's thoughts swirled this way and that. He landed on one and bluntly asked, "Aren't you worried a human will enter the mine?"

Sasha squeezed his hand, a motion that caught her parents' notice. Catherine raised her gaze. "No, we aren't worried. If anyone but us or a dragon enters, they will find what they expect, an abandoned mine. We have this whole area concealed."

"Even the town is protected, so no DEF can detect dragons here," Gig added.

Johnny gasped. *No more running. No more being a loner at school. No more being trapped in only this form!*

Catherine's attention went again to the entwined hands of Sasha and Johnny. "I think you may have left something out in your call, sweetheart."

Sasha's face flushed bright red, almost matching the reddish part of her orange hair. "I didn't know how to share discreetly over the phone. We've —" she swallowed and leaned into Johnny. "We've mated."

Not being able to help himself, even while both their parents were standing right there, he leaned over and kissed the top of her head tenderly.

The yellow dragon roared. Johnny, Nikki, and Molly all jumped at once. His parents didn't, even after all these years. And the family of Eli were certainly accustomed to those sounds.

The dragon's shoulders moved up and down and Johnny realized the creature was laughing. "Sorry," he said in a deep growly voice. "I have a habit of letting my enthusiasm get away from me. I am Thersh, the elected dragon leader. It is always a happy occasion when a dragon finds their mate, but this is unique, and I am pleased to witness it."

"Thersh," Gig began, "Would you like to gather everyone and introduce them?"

"Of course, but perhaps, our dear new friends would like to be themselves when I do."

Johnny's heart pounded. How many years had it been since he transformed? At least five. Going into dragon form left more of their essence for the DEF to find. It was rarely risked.

His parents spoke quietly to his sisters but soon they changed, becoming two different shades of purple. Dad's maroon shimmered in the light moments later and Mom's teal soon followed.

Sasha wrapped her arms around Johnny's neck. He hugged her back. "Let me see the real you," she whispered in his ear before giving a quick kiss on his neck. She stepped away, excitement buzzing all around her.

How fast joy could be felt. How fast years of anguish could be extinguished. A meadow full of dragons and a beautiful young woman who helped protect them. A woman that was his.

He closed his eyes and felt his lungs enlarge, filling them with fresh air that aided his transformation.

His skin pulled apart swiftly, painlessly, making way for the dark blue scales to take their place.

His limbs changed shape, his hands and feet now claws.

His face elongated, his snout now its proper form and his teeth now sharp.

Lastly, his wings, those blessed wings shot from his back, the elation of it being almost unbearable.

Sasha ran the few steps to him, kissing his dragon face. Using his scales as steps, she climbed on his back.

"My darling, Jeyhone," she said laying forward to wrap her arms around him. "Fly. Fly!"

The dragons were gathering to welcome them, but Johnny paid no mind. His mate's request mirrored his own desire. He blasted himself into the sky with Sasha hanging on tightly, his wings slicing through the air; his claws tucked in close to his belly. Her joyful laughter rang out over the meadow.

LORNA JANE HANSMANN was named after the novel Lornadoone. So, perhaps, it is no wonder that her mind and heart turned to stories. Lorna believes in the power of storytelling in all its forms. Whether through dance, acting or writing she loves to do them all. Stories change lives and enhance our ability to be better humans. She has been writing stories for over ten years. She's written six novels and dozens of short stories, as well as flash fiction. Her number one fan considers her to be "Better than Brandon Sanderson." That is saying a lot, even if it comes from her youngest son. You can visit her website at lornajanewrites.com or follow her on instagram @lornajanewrites.

STRENGTH OF SPIRIT

NICHOLAS SAMUEL STEMBER

The four members of the adventuring party took a moment as they looked over the carnage of their recent battle. They all had minor cuts and scrapes, but none had been hurt too severely in their battle with the six grax that had attacked them.

"They weren't so tough," the dwarven warrior said as he flicked a piece of skull out of his long blond beard and rested his axe on the dead creature below. It looked all gnarled and darkened with almost simian features and dull yellow eyes that caught the moonlight, even though the creature was dead.

"Easy for you to say, Torsten," the vale elven archer grumbled as she brushed her sky-blue hair out of her eyes and tried to decide the best way to remove the arrow that was lodged in her thigh. "A little help, Clove?"

The forest elven mystic was pulling her long cloak out from under another grax body that had pinned it down as she looked over at the vale elf and nodded. "Give me a moment, Cass."

Cassava played with the arrow shaft a bit, tentatively testing how bad it hurt when it moved.

"Keep playing with that and you'll go blind," chimed in their human rogue with a smile.

"Yes, Cass, stop playing with that," Clove said, scolding the archer. As she pushed the rogue aside, she said, "And Fox, you be quiet."

The mystic tied her long mint-green hair into a ponytail and then came over to her companion and looked at the arrow. She concentrated for a moment and her hazel eyes began to glow blue, as did her hand. "May the power of the water phantasm heal you."

The blue glow moved from her hand to the wounded leg as the magic caused the arrow to pop out and then quickly heal the elf's damaged skin. The mystic's eyes returned to their normal shade as she glanced around at her other companions. "Anyone else?"

The human rogue playfully stroked his thin copper colored goatee and looked as if he was going to say something, but when he saw the glare from Clove, he kept it to himself.

"The phantasms are still with us," Torsten said in his deep dwarven voice. "We'll need the power of the gods to see us through this." He accented the statement by patting the ground with his free hand. "May the earth phantasm keep our feet sure."

Cassava slung her longbow back over her shoulder and recovered what arrows she could. She glanced at the large cave mouth that was situated in the dense forest they had been traveling through for days. "We came here to find the dragon, and this is its cave."

"Well, we don't have to find the dragon, just its

hoard," Fox said with a smile as he cleaned off his longsword and put it back into his sheath. "The duke is paying us to retrieve his emerald scepter. I might be able to sneak in, grab it, and get out and then we're rich… and alive."

The dwarf let out a grunt. "The duke also said this dragon had been terrorizing his town for a long time, maybe we should stop that."

"For a terrorized town, they didn't look all that scared," Clove commented as she picked up her long birch staff from where she had set it down. "In fact, they looked healthy and well fed."

"We go in prepared for anything," Cassava said, taking the lead as she usually did. "And we do it smartly. We sneak in, see if the dragon is even in there, and then try to spot the scepter."

The other three nodded, gathered up the last of their belongings, and entered the cave. The slick rocks that made up the floor were quite wet, and the sound of dripping water grew louder as they moved deeper into the cave. Many of the stalactites and stalagmites had been broken, evidence of something big moving through the cave.

Soon, what little light coming in from the moon was gone. This wasn't as much of a problem for the elves and the dwarf, but their human rogue was grumbling.

"I'm going to have to light a lantern if I don't get some help."

"Of course," Clove said with a smile. Her eyes lit up once more and she touched his longsword as he drew it out, transferring the pale blue light to the blade, which gave them all some light to see by.

The light began to spread and as their eyes adjusted,

they realized there were some gold and silver coins scattered along the rocky floor. As they moved deeper into the cave, the scattered coins grew in number and started to build into a slope.

Fox motioned for them all to stop, as he held out his sword and let the light play on the dragon's hoard that sprawled before them. He looked up, but there was no sign of the dragon. "The phantasms are with us tonight for sure," he said. "Let's find that scepter."

Torsten, Fox and Clove began to climb the small mountain of treasure as Cassava circled around the other side of the mound, trying to make sure they really were alone in here.

"It must be out hunting," Torsten said in his gruff dwarven tone. "We may have gotten very lucky."

Just as Cassava started to circle to the back, her sharp elven ears heard a sound above them. It was high up…it was…sobbing?

"Do you hear that?" she asked, noting the sound was coming from a high ledge behind the treasure hoard.

The rest of them stopped — Well, three of them stopped but Fox was putting coins and gems in his backpack.

"Who is that?" Clove called out.

For a moment the crying ceased, then a large scaly head peered out from the ledge and the four of them froze.

The dragon was bigger than they expected it to be, for as it pushed out from the ledge and towered over them it seemed as if it was at least twenty feet from nose to tail, all covered in shimmering purple scales with black highlights and big eyes that shone like amethysts. It unfurled huge wings as it brought its two front claws to the edge of the ledge and looked down at them. Both large eyes were glistening with tears that rolled down the creature's large face.

The four of them looked at each other, stunned. Cassava began to climb to the top of the hoard, and she looked up at the dragon. "This is not exactly what we expected," she finally said. "Um, are you alright?"

For a moment, the big purple dragon looked down at the four invaders as if trying to judge them, then shook its head. "No," the deep voice said, and they instantly realized it was female. "I'm not alright."

"You're a dragon from the spirit phantasm," Clove spoke up. "I'm a mystic of the water phantasm."

"Earth, water, fire, air or spirit, does it matter what kind of dragon she is?" Fox asked. "She's still huge and we have a job to do."

"Dragons born from the magic of the different phantasms have different temperaments," Clove reminded him. "Spirit dragons are unpredictable."

"Stop being such a jerk, she's obviously hurting." Cassava said to the human. "My guess is it's a guy, right?"

The dragon's mouth opened a bit, then closed. "How did you know?"

The vale elf gave a shrug and smiled. "I've cried once or twice for that reason too. I guess maybe we're not all that different deep down."

"We don't eat people," Torsten grumbled.

"I don't either," the dragon said, her voice a bit hurt. "I'm certain that you don't taste good."

Fox was about to reply with a clever retort, but Clove glared at him, and he kept it to himself.

"I'm Astra," the spirit dragon said. "I've been

courted by a young male that is roaming the country-side, but he seems to have lost interest."

"Maybe we can help?" the vale elf said from the top of the hoard.

"Help?"

"Sure. I mean, we've all had problems like that before. Maybe you just need to say the right things to him."

The dragon cocked her head to the side and lowered her huge face to the blue-haired elf, then her voice became very quiet. "That's just it. I don't say anything to him. I don't even know *what* to say to him."

"Found it," Fox said as he reached into the huge pile and pulled out the emerald scepter.

The dragon's face turned to the human rogue and her eyes narrowed a bit. "Ahem. That's mine." Wisps of smoke came out of her nostrils as she brought her head down to face him.

Cassava quickly moved across the hoard and put herself between Fox and Astra, "Maybe we can help you, and then…maybe you can help us?"

"How?" the dragon asked, her voice a mixture of suspicion and curiosity.

"Men are easy to handle," the vale elf said with a big smile. "You just need to start talking to this dragon. We'll help you do that, and you give us this scepter, and then you and your handsome dragon guy live happily ever after."

"Hmmm," Astra said as she seemed to mull it over. "It is a very pretty scepter, and I hate to relinquish any part of my hoard. It was a gift from the duke to leave his city alone. But if you really think you can help."

They all blinked a few times. "Gift?" Cassava asked.

Astra shrugged. "I had no plans to bother his city anyway, but I like gifts."

"Oookay," Cassava said as they all looked at each other. "So, I guess the duke just wants his scepter back."

"So, you can help?" the dragon asked hopefully.

"We can," Cassava assured the dragon, then looked at her companions. "Right?"

The response was less than enthusiastic as Torsten and Fox just shrugged and Clove tried to smile and then finally nodded.

"Okay, let's go over it," the vale elf said as she sat down on top of the hoard and the others gathered around. The dragon slid off the shelf and draped herself around the mountain of treasure, her head resting next to the adventurers.

For an hour they talked about this male spirit dragon that had come and gone, occasionally stopping at her cave for a few moments, waiting for her to say something, but each time she said she was at a loss for words.

"Nothing?" Clove asked.

"I can't get out a word," Astra admitted. "He quickly loses interest and leaves again."

Cassava seemed to think about it for a moment and then smiled. "He's not losing interest.... He doesn't think *you* have any interest."

"Me?" the dragon said in obvious shock. "But I keep summoning him!"

"And then say nothing," the vale elf said with a smile.

"Yeah, that would annoy me to too," Fox said with a laugh as he rolled his eyes.

"Well, this time will be different," Cassava said with

a sense of self-assuredness as she flashed Fox a glare. "Here's what you're going to say to him…"

The two elves — though mostly Cassava— went over possible conversations for the next two hours, while Fox and Torsten sat at the base of the hoard playing with various pieces of treasure.

Finally, as they went over it the last time, Cassava stood up and placed her hand on Astra's snout. "Do you think you have it?"

For a moment the dragon looked at the elves, then nodded. "Yes, I think I do."

"Alright," Cassava said, "You said you can summon him?"

"Sort of," she said. "I put out a scent and he knows that I want to mate. He'll pick it up from leagues away."

"What if it attracts the wrong kind of dragon?" Torsten asked.

"Dragons don't mix," Clove assured him. "I doubt there is more than one other spirit dragon anywhere near here. If he's still around, that means he wants to be near Astra."

"Let's do it then," Cassava said.

"Let me put the four of you up on my ledge so he doesn't see you," said the large dragon.

From her front claw up to her body, she created a ramp for the four of them to climb up onto the ledge above. Once up there, they saw she had even more treasure that she had formed into a bed of sorts.

It was then that the scent hit them. It wasn't unpleasant at all, like being in a field of lavender that was in full bloom. It wasn't long before they heard the loud flapping of wings from outside the cave. They kept low but Cassava found she couldn't resist peering over the edge of the ledge as the other spirit dragon came into the cave. He was slightly smaller than Astra, but still quite large.

"I'm here…again," his deep voice stated almost tentatively. "Hopefully you'll want to talk."

She stared at him, her face not far from his, her mouth opened…and nothing came out.

He looked at her for a moment as her mouth opened and closed a few times. "Nothing?" he asked, his voice laced with regret. "Again, nothing?"

Cassava could see the panic in Astra's face, even from her vantage point above. Suddenly an urge hit her, and she picked up a gold coin and tossed it over both dragons' heads to clink against the rocks back near the cave entrance.

His huge head snapped around to the sound of the noise, and in that instant Cassava slipped off the shelf and landed on Astra. She slid down behind her large left ear flap, picking an angle where the male dragon wouldn't see her when he turned back around.

"You can do this," she whispered into Astra's ear.

Astra shook her head frantically and Cassava almost lost her footing, grabbing onto the flap to steady herself.

"So, still nothing?" the male dragon asked as he looked back. "Perhaps I'll come back again in a few weeks," he said with a disappointed tone, then turned to leave the cave."

"Stop," Cassava whispered, "I don't want you to go."

"Stop," Astra suddenly said, finding her voice, "I don't want you to go."

The male dragon turned back around and raised up his head. "You *do* speak."

"Of course I do," Cassava whispered. "It's just you make me nervous…I'm shy."

"What?" asked Astra.

"What?" asked the male dragon.

Cassava poked the back of Astra's ear hard.

"Ow…I meant, of course I speak," Astra said louder. "It's just you make me nervous…I'm shy."

The male dragon's amethyst eyes smiled, and he came closer to her. "I make you nervous? I never meant to do that."

Cassava slunk lower as she tried to slide off Astra to slip around to the other side of the hoard.

"Did you know you're crawling with elves?" the male asked with a lighthearted laugh.

"Oh," Astra said, then looked down at Cassava and then up to where Clove had raised her head. "Yes, well…they're friends."

"Good friends, it seems," he said. "Come, let's fly together."

"Together?" she asked, a smile growing along her long lips.

"Yes, we have dragons to make." He leaned forward and rubbed his snout along hers, nuzzling them together.

"Yes," she agreed, the joy evident in her tone.

He started to lead her out of the cave, and she quickly scrambled off her hoard to follow him.

"Um," Cassava called to her as she was almost out of the cave.

"Oh, yes," Astra said as she glanced back at the four adventurers. "Take the scepter. Heck, take whatever you can carry, we'll have a new hoard to build together."

And with that, the two dragons flew off into the

night sky, leaving the elves, the dwarf, and the man sitting there with huge smiles and whoops of joy.

Born in New York City, Nicholas Samuel Stember spent most of his life growing up in the suburbs of Princeton, NJ. His father, Charles H. Stember, was a published professor of sociology at Rutgers University, and his mother, Sue, was a professional singer and later a portrait photographer. With two creative influences, and a profound love and appreciation of the genres of fantasy, science fiction and horror, the directions his writing took were firmly set. His short stories have appeared in various online magazines and anthologies over the years including three upcoming anthologies. He also joined the Horror Writers Association in 2024. His love of those genres also found him a wife from across the Pond, and he ended up marrying her and moving to the Faroe Islands, where he resides today. For more information check out his website at https://nsstember.com or https://www.facebook.com/ nicholassamuelstember

STONE MOTHERS

CHIP HOUSER

Temenlith flew along the stone peaks of Ruln, the tails of the four cows she carried in her taloned feet flicking in the unsettled air. She had bartered with man, trading labor for cattle by pulling trees, digging out their roots, and clawing long furrows for a new field. Three full days of work. Longer than she expected, much longer than she wanted to be gone from her egg, which would hatch soon. But her daughter's first meal would be red meat, just as hers had been.

Temenlith glided along a rain-varnished granite face. Ahead, something long and thin hung from the mouth of her nesting cave, writhing in the wind, slapping against the stone. It looked like a tail, but it smelled of sun-parched grass and—

She gave a single piercing cry and flung the cattle into the cave.

Her egg was gone.

She crawled into the cave, running her snout along the cool stone, pushing aside grass and cow. The scent was faded, days old, but unmistakable: *man*.

Why would they steal her egg? She had hunted only in the mountains, she had bartered with them, just as her mother taught her, rather than simply taking their meat! She was no thief, despite the lack of prey near Ruln, despite her growing hunger, despite the nearness of her egg's hatching. She had done nothing to man, taken nothing from him, yet he had still stolen her egg.

Thieves!

For this, man would suffer. She swung her tail, scales scraping rock, sweeping nest and cattle out into open sky. She leaped from the mouth of the cave and dropped along the granite face, wings tucked, scales nearly touching her shadow, following the scent of her egg toward the ground far below. Her egg's rich musk lingered on the scuffed stone.

She spread her wings, catching the air with a sharp snap, pulling her up and back. She landed on her hind legs in the wide grassy sward that ran between Ruln and the vast forest to the east. She smelled her egg, its life, the heat of its growth: it had somehow reached the ground unbroken. She also smelled the thieves, six of them, each a blend of iron and salted hide, wood and soft man-flesh, sweat and sand – and something she didn't recognize, something sharp and bitter. She cried out again, scorching the rock with the unintended flame of anger.

She should not have been gone so long – she thought her egg was safe.

Temenlith shrank down, pushing her chest toward her tail. She tensed her hind legs, pressing them tight against her sides, and sprang into the air, up and out over the forest. She skimmed the treetops, heading east, following her egg's scent.

THE THIEVES HAD TAKEN her egg into the forest without an ox or cart. She would catch them easily. They had made no effort to conceal themselves as they traveled the path, which looped frequently to avoid scores of circular, boulder-studded clearings. In the brief time Temenlith had known her mother, she had spoken of these clearings. She had called them resting places, but they were not resting places. Ruln would never rise from her slumber, nor would her mother. Man had seen to that. The clearings were graveyards. Temenlith would tell her daughter the truth.

In her first hours, Temenlith had flown with her mother, learning how to take off, how to glide to save energy, how to land without injury, how to find the nest by sight and scent. Her mother said she would teach her how to hunt the forest, the mountains, and the sea, so that she could avoid man. "They are small and weak, my daughter, but they are powerful. We are few, man is many. Never steal from him, never threaten or harm him, or he will send you to your clearing."

Temenlith had been eager to hunt with her mother. "Tomorrow, little one. Today you must stay here, hidden, and rest while I hunt."

Her mother flew away, crimson scales glowing in the sun as she glided over the trees. Temenlith never learned what to hunt in the forest because she never saw her mother again. Though she searched for many years, she never found her mother's clearing.

Once she had her egg back, Temenlith would not leave her daughter alone until she had raised her to be strong and smart, to understand the world and the dangers of man.

THE PATH RAN alongside the river, which flowed slower and broader here than where it spilled from Ruln. A group of men hauled long nets glittering with red-silver fish from the river. They yelled with each pull. Together, their weak cries sounded almost fearsome. Other men hung the fish from long lines of sticks driven into the ground a short way up the bank. The smell of fish was strong, but not strong enough to hide the scent of her egg. The fish-men did not have it.

When her shadow crossed the river and the men looked up, they dropped their nets and ran into the woods. Dozens of fish flopped on the muddy bank, in and out of the tiny footprints. She wanted to land, to ask them questions about the thieves. But man did not treat with dragons for free, and she did not have the time to do whatever they might ask.

She flew on, following the path past many small villages hunkered among the trees. She circled each, but the thieves had not stopped in any of them.

MANY MILES FURTHER EAST, the scent left the path and lingered in a large, grassy clearing in the forest. Hulking in its center was a massive chain of granite hummocks. Time and weather had broken apart the enormous stone dragon, split the vast chest from the flanks, worn away the tail to a series of rounded mounds studding the field, sanded the head and horns smooth. Temenlith wondered which of her ancestors rested here. She would have been ten times Temenlith's size, surely a mother of many. Temenlith landed near the foremost stone. She bowed her head, pressing her forehead against the weather-smoothed slope of the ancient brow.

"Stone mother," she whispered, breathing in the scent that still clung to the crumbling granite. The smell reminded Temenlith of her own mother, though this dragon was far larger.

The thieves would have been tiny against the great bulk of stone. Their fire, weak and dirty, had slicked her ancestor's neck. The char highlighted a triangular indentation there, in the shadow of her great jaw. A missing scale. Temenlith's mother had been missing a breast scale, she had forgotten. It was freshly lost, still crusted with blood.

It was no coincidence that these thieves built their fire against the mother. They knew she would follow; they were taunting her.

Temenlith washed the stone with flame, burning away charcoal and droppings, cleansing all evidence of man so the stone mother might rest again in peace. She rose into the sky and followed her egg's scent across the forest.

As THE SUN dropped toward the trees far to the west, the path reached the edge of the forest, where a cliff dropped sharply into the Dry Waste, a landscape of hardpan swells and valleys dotted with thousands of stone spires. Temenlith had never flown this far east; there was nothing here to hunt.

The spires below were of some softer stone, not the granite of dragons. The spires looked like ranks of enormously tall men wearing broad caps, their bodies thinned by time and weather. Had men once been nearly the size of dragons?

She swept down into the valley, passing low over the flat stone caps of the spires, breathing the many scents. Strongest of all was her egg, but there were many others to sort: loam on the cool air from the forest; clean, hot sand from the Dry Waste; the moist reek of man-sweat; the cold stink of iron; long-dead wood fires; the musty reek of leather tents; the nauseating smell of man-foods, of baked wheat and rotting plants; and that mysterious bitter smell. She also smelled something unexpected: other dragons. Not the burgeoning life of her egg; this smell was weaker somehow, faded. Not unlike the muted scent of stone mothers. Perhaps a battle was fought here long ago, and the blood lingered in the dust. Yet, despite the ranks of spire giants, she smelled only the blood of dragons.

A sudden rush of fear drove her higher into the sky. Something wasn't right about that dragon smell. It seemed an odd choice to stop here: she had thought the thieves were fleeing to the Dry Waste to rejoin their people, to hide her egg among the mud and offal of their tiny nests, or perhaps to challenge her fury with an army of their kind. But she smelled only the six here. Perhaps they chose this place because the spires would protect them and keep her from her egg. Perhaps it was a trap; men were small and weak and wingless, but they were cunning. But she was a dragon, and they had her egg.

Temenlith circled back over the spires. All but their weathered caps lay deep in shadow. She cupped her wings, swung her legs forward, and hovered a moment, motionless, each hind leg above a spire, before landing softly. The spires groaned and popped beneath her weight, like winter ice on a high tarn.

She dropped her head and hissed, smoke seeping from her jaws. She didn't see her egg, but it was close, somewhere in this confusion of spires and shadows. She did see the thieves down there between the spires. Five of them looked up at her, raised arms holding iron spears, the sixth knelt behind them.

Did they think to threaten her with their tiny barbs?

She said, "Where is my egg?"

The thieves tensed but said nothing. Each wore a brightly colored chest plate: cobalt, vermilion, silver, jade, and ocher. A shimmering blue light now rose from the hands of the kneeling thief, showing his hair to be gray, not black like the others. The gray-haired thief's blue light was the source of the bitter smell. His chest plate was larger than the others, a warm auburn the color of sunset beyond the mountains.

She inhaled deeply. Yes, her egg was close. Very close. But where, and why couldn't she see it? "Where is my egg?"

The thieves drew their spears back. As their armor creaked and shifted, Temenlith realized their chest plates were dragon scales. The smell was revolting: complex and sad, a jumbled mockery of her lineage. The scales were ancient, their scent tainted by generations of Man. The gray-haired thief's scale smelled familiar – it belonged, Temenlith thought, to the mother of many mothers. Temenlith remembered the missing scale on her neck, the stone coal-charred by these thieves' weak fire.

Temenlith roared, "How do you have dragon scales?"

The thieves shrank back, all except Grayhair. The blue light around his arms pulsed to his laughter. The sound was surprisingly deep for something so small. "Surely your mother explained."

"Explained what?"

"The scale gambit."

Temenlith waited. Whatever a gambit was, it didn't sound good.

"My twice-great-grandfather ransomed you for your mother's scales. Like her mother, and her mother's mother, she gave us what we asked."

Was their plan then to enrage her, to goad her into attacking and tangling herself in the spires? Surely they wouldn't bother throwing those tiny metal barbs. They had traveled too far, planned their theft too carefully, for such nonsense. Temenlith roared, fire washing the stone caps. "Where is my egg?"

The thieves glanced back at Grayhair, who moved his hands through the air, muttering words. Bluish-white light flickered in his palms. The bitter smell suddenly fouled the air, sharp and heavy. Unknown magic was rarely good magic.

Too late, Temenlith opened her jaws.

Greyhair pushed his palms forward. The air rippled and folded toward her as the thieves threw their spears. With the folding wind came a suffocating bitterness – and the spears. They leaped from the thieves' hands, impossibly fast and true, pushed by the magic.

Temenlith tensed and drew her body in, but she couldn't avoid all the spears. She hadn't thought she would need to, they were so small – but moving this fast even tiny sticks were dangerous. One flew wide, one glanced off her neck, another off her haunch. One tore through the membrane of her wing. One struck her chest with a loud crack, knocking her back. She roared, flexing her wings for balance.

One of the spires she stood on gave way. Temenlith lifted into the air as it crumbled in a chaos of stone and dust. Two of the thieves, the wearers of the silver and jade scales, were too slow, their screams muffled and brief. Grayhair disappeared behind rippling blue waves into the dust. The other thieves scattered. She caught two in her flame, enveloping them so long that what little was left of them – larger bones and their stolen scales, ocher and cobalt – skipped across the hardpan.

Through the charred flesh, all she smelled was her egg. She landed, scrabbling between spires. The spires were too closely spaced for her to move easily. She pushed one to the side to clear her way. Too late, she realized her mistake, roaring as she tried to stop the spire's fall. It fell into another spire, and that into others, and others, a toppling wave of crashing, booming stone widening as it spread outward. She breathed deeply over and over again, until she was certain her egg hadn't been damaged.

Suddenly her left hind leg exploded in pain. One of the thieves had darted from behind a spire and rammed his spear up between her scales. He was too fast, the spires too close together, for her to catch him in her jaws. She curled her head around, sweeping flame, but he was gone.

Her leg pulsed from the cold iron. She buckled and lost her balance, arching her back so she fell backward. The air filled with the sharp cracking of spires, then with thick dust. She tried to rise but her injured leg wouldn't bear her weight. She bit down on the shaft protruding from between the scales, hoping to pull it out, but it was buried deep, the shaft too small. She bathed it in fire until the iron ran glowing red onto the hardpan.

Temenlith hopped as best she could with one leg, fanning her wings for balance. The dust coiled away between the spires. She smelled the thief close behind her, her egg and Grayhair, or at least his noxious magic, somewhere just ahead.

She turned and roared, hoping to keep the vermilion thief at bay. She pulled down only enough spires to allow her passage, careful they each fell backward. Ahead, between two spires, Grayhair floated in the center of a broad, circular clearing. He was fifty feet above a forest of spears jutting up from the ground, arms stretched out, writhing spheres of blue light in each hand. The bitter reek lay heavy about him. No, he was not floating – he was standing on something. Her egg, she realized, able to make out faintly its outline hovering above the spears.

As if her seeing it spoiled the magic, her egg slowly reappeared. It was whole, undamaged. Temenlith didn't realize she was cooing softly until Grayhair chuckled.

The thieves had suspended her egg between the spires of the clearing, in a thin harness of grass-tails high above a forest of spears jutting up from the ground.

The grass-tails creaked, straining against the downward push of his magic. If she breathed fire on him, the grass-tails would burn, and Grayhair would live just long enough for his magic to skewer her egg on the spears below.

Stretching up on her good hind leg, Temenlith spread her wings and hissed at the thief. His eyes flicked down, not at her injured leg, but behind her. She lashed her tail and struck something soft, mannish. It made a small noise as it hit a spire, another as it slapped the hardpan.

Grayhair called out, "Barter with me, beast!"

Temenlith said. "It is too late to barter, sand-man."

"I will destroy your egg." He peeled his lips back and showed his teeth.

"You cannot destroy my egg so easily."

"My magic is strong enough to split your scales," the thief said, his eyes falling to her breast briefly. "I would think eggshell far softer."

Though her lungs boiled with flame, though she yearned to roast this weak creature, Temenlith forced down her molten breath. "What is it you want?"

"Scales," he said.

"Scales. Like my mother's?" With time, she could solve this thief's gambit. She must keep him talking. "How many?"

"One for each of my men you have killed."

"One, two, three—" Temenlith slowly slid her tail backward, feeling the ground "—four, five?"

"Is that sarcasm, dragon?"

"I do not know that word. Does it mean five of something?" Her tail found the base of a spire.

Greyhair laughed, but he was watching her closely.

She hoped he couldn't see through her as she pressed her tail against the base of the spire.

"I want my egg." She looped her tail slowly back and forth, back and forth, keeping pressure on the stone. "I have many scales."

"Very wise," he said. The magic flickered in his palms. His eyes slid from hers down her neck, to her chest, down her shoulder. She flexed it; he looked back up at her. "First, a matching pair, one from each shoulder, by the wings."

Curving her neck out, she lowered her head to her shoulder, keeping one eye on the thief. She kept her tail tensed. She slipped a tooth under a scale, bit down, and pulled. It didn't come free. She pulled harder, feeling skin and muscle stretch. The scale tore free; nausea lanced through her. She dropped the scale on the ground in front of her.

"The same from the other side."

She ran her snout along the other shoulder, down to the elbow and back up. "What will keep me from killing you once I have my egg?"

"Scales first."

Temenlith turned her head away, letting her hip on that side slide back, settling most of her weight on her unwounded leg. Grayhair's eyes remained on hers. She pulled the scale, pulled against the searing in her flesh, and dropped it next to the first.

She waited, watching, as he surveyed her. Wet joy was building in his tiny eyes. "Now, one from each foreleg."

As she lowered her head, she drew in a deep breath and turned back to Grayhair. Her entire body tensed. "That will be delicate work."

"And painful." His eyes dropped to her chest. "A shame about your breast plate, it would have made a fine shield for one of my lesser warriors."

Temenlith leapt forward, pushing off with her coiled tail and her good hind leg, clawing forward with her front legs, shattering the spires before her, breathing fire. Blue light erupted from the thief's palms. Her dragon-fire washed the field of spears as the thief's magic drove him and the egg down. The grass-tails snapped. Egg and man plunged toward the spears, into the flames, well ahead of the surging Temenlith.

The thief laughed as the egg slammed into the spears. But Temenlith's fire had softened the iron and, instead of piercing the egg, the spears sagged and slumped, cradling the egg in glowing red arcs of iron.

Temenlith stepped forward, looming over the thief. "Your plan has failed!"

"Has it?" He raised his hands and the blue flame rose and rippled toward Temenlith. Temenlith exhaled a long gout of fire that consumed him. When she stopped, the crackling flames sounded like his laughter.

Temenlith's triumphant peal echoed through the dust-shrouded spires. She dipped her head and nuzzled her egg. She lifted it with her forelegs, held its soft curve tight to her shattered breast.

As the flames died, Temenlith realized she still heard laughter. She scanned the enclosure. Grayhair, his naked, pale flesh traced with glowing blue lines, stood just inside the far spires. He held one of her scales, her blood angling across its curve. She leaped forward, washing the man with flame. He should have been cindered, but instead he kept laughing as he shot above the spires. His magic carried him east, blue rings dissipating into evil stench. Temenlith did not follow. Her egg was safe, but night was coming, and her nest was many hours away. Even if she flew fast and straight, she wouldn't make it back to her nest before the thief stonebound her.

She clawed through rubble, searching out the mothers' five scales. She brushed off the bits of charred leather and metal and stacked them atop her egg. Their curvatures were similar. She gathered them in her front legs and lifted off the ground.

In the warm light of dusk, Temenlith rose slowly into the sky and flew west, chased by her shadow.

TEMENLITH FLEW until the sun disappeared behind the spiny humps of Ruln and the treetops below were only vague shadows. With sundown, the air grew cool, and her body began to stiffen. Not just her wounded leg now, her whole body. A sensation she had never felt before, a creeping numbness, crawled slowly up her limbs toward her shoulders. Thinking she must be cold, she gave herself a fire-bath. She flew on, but the heat didn't loosen her muscles.

Flying was becoming difficult; she couldn't feel her tail. She locked her numb forelegs around her egg and the scales and flew as best she could. She was still hours from her nest when she accepted that she wouldn't make it back. She pushed on, determined at least to reach the mother of many's clearing.

As she soared above the forest, Temenlith's wings grew heavier and heavier; soon it took all her strength to raise and lower them. How long could she hold her egg?

She knew what would happen to her egg if she dropped it, but what would happen to it if she died before her daughter hatched? She could not die, she had too much to teach her egg – about dragonkind, about flying and hunting, about the treachery of man. She would reach the stone mother and rest.

When she could no longer move her wings, Temenlith forced them straight out and glided. She was high above the forest and could see the clearing ahead. But she was losing height. She dropped lower and lower, closer to the forest canopy, as she neared the clearing. Her hind legs dragged through the treetops. Branches, then limbs, then trunks, snapped and split.

Then she was past the trees and in the clearing. She struck the ground, cradling the egg as she rolled awkwardly over the grass. Temenlith's breathing was labored, her chest constricted. She could no longer smell her egg or the mother and was so stiff she could barely stand.

Temenlith pressed the mother's missing scale into its place on her neck, just above the stone ridge of her shoulder. She leaned her brow against the mother's great sloping forehead. "Be whole again, Mother of Many."

Temenlith curled around her egg, breathed in its scent, the scintillating warmth of growing life, and fell into an exhausted sleep.

TEMENLITH WOKE STRUGGLING TO BREATHE. She was still curled up, but the warm cocoon of her egg no longer pressed against her. She stood – or tried to, but nothing happened. Her whole body was heavy and cold. She tried to lift her head, to at least look for her egg. Temenlith could only raise her eyelids enough to see a narrow slit of the grassy field. She tried to call out but made only a weak mewling.

She drew air in slowly, hoping for her daughter's scent. She smelled something, the warm spice of dragon, but it wasn't her daughter.

"You are strong," a deep voice said, its power resonating through Temenlith's stiff body, an echo of the warmth she had lost overnight. "I did not expect you to wake."

"My daughter—" Temenlith rasped.

The mother lowered a great auburn-scaled foot, the egg cradled safely within its talons. Temenlith drew in the vibrant warmth of her egg. She pushed out a single word: "Safe."

"She is," the mother said. "I will tell her of you and bring her often to visit."

The mother of many lowered her head to the dew-covered grass so Temenlith could see a vast yellow eye. "Man may have bound you with your scale, but their gambit has failed this time." The mother's hot breath was soothing. "Rest now. I will find the others you have saved, and we will wake you after we have repaid the treacheries of man."

The mother kept speaking, but a rushing numbness tugged at Temenlith, pulling her somewhere quiet and peaceful. She fell into stone-sleep watching the grass glow in the mother's shining yellow eye, feeling the deep thrum of her voice, and smelling the hope of her egg.

· · ·

CHIP HOUSER currently lives in northern Colorado by way of Missouri, Kansas, Italy, and Germany. He attended the Odyssey Writing Workshop, has an MFA in Creative Writing from UMSL, and was Associate Editor for the literary journal, Natural Bridge. *He's read slush for* Amazing Stories *and coedited, alongside Carina Bissett and editor Julie C. Day the anthology "Weird Dream Society."*

His stories have appeared in Bourbon Penn, PodCastle, Molotov Cocktail, The Drabblecast, Pulp Literature, *and many other markets. His flash collection "Dark Morsels" was published by Red Bird Chapbooks in 2023.*

When not day jobbing as an architect, writing, domesticating, or forming new, mostly unpronounceable words, Chip enjoys hiking in Colorado's front range with his wife. Find him on the socials as chazzlepants *or at* chiphouser.com.

CREPERUM

VONNIE WINSLOW CRIST

H alla removed a candle stub from the stone alcove behind the altar and dropped it into her bucket. She replaced it with a fresh candle, then glanced at the dragon.

"Last one, Tarald," she said.

The dragon nodded, became airborne with a few wing flutters, and hovered in front of the nook. After he had gulped a mouthful of air, Halla spotted the slight swelling in Tarald's throat. With precision learned from years of performing the task, the dragon exhaled just enough fire to light the candle. Carefully, so as not to extinguish the flame, he flapped his sapphire wings and descended to the church's floor.

"Let us hope we will hold back the Darkness once more." Halla adjusted the strap of her pouch of new candles. She picked up the stub bucket and her lantern. With nearly silent footfalls, she walked from the apse through the sanctuary, chancel, and crossing. In contrast, the slap of Tarald's feet and clicks from his claws echoed throughout St. Betina of the Waves. They had just entered the nave and begun walking down the center aisle when squeaks from the north transept caught Tarald's attention.

I will be back in a few minutes, thought the dragon as he took to the air.

Halla kept walking. Seconds later, she heard squeals and saw two flashes of light.

By the time she'd reached the narthex, Tarald strolled beside her once more. She raised her lantern. The dragon's tongue flicked around his lips. She noted all evidence of splattered blood and torn flesh had been licked away.

Rats. Tarald picked a morsel from between his teeth with a claw, then popped it into his mouth. *Two fat ones,* he added.

"I don't need the details," responded Halla.

The mind-speak between them was so natural, she didn't need to talk out loud. But they garnered enough glances and whispers from the sisters, novices, clergy, and monks that Halla didn't want to draw additional attention to exactly how she knew what the dragon was saying.

In front of others, Tarald obliged her request for squeaks, growls, and rumbles. Halla would tilt her head and appear to understand. Then, she'd "translate" for whichever member of the religious community stood nearby. It was a waste of time, but appeased the suspicious residents of St. Betina.

As they pushed through the front doors, Tarald reminded Halla, *There is one more fire to light.*

She sighed. Setting ablaze the heap of wood at the top of the north tower filled her with dread. Not only were the walkway and steps always slippery from sea mist, but the shadows there seemed ready to rise up, take form, and drag her to their dark world.

I am with you, the dragon reminded her. *I will always keep you safe.*

"I know, it's just..."

Before she could finish, Sister Margete appeared in the hall. Per usual, the nun strode with a deliberateness that caused Halla's heart to race. And the nun's face, as always, wore a scowl.

Sister Margete had been one of the two nuns who'd found Halla more than ten years earlier.

Halla had been delivered to St. Betina of the Waves by a stranger. He'd thumped on the metal-studded doors of the abbey with the handle of his sword, then looked at her from behind a helmet visor.

"The sisters will take care of you," he had assured her. Without further comment, he'd walked to the gate. Just before exiting the courtyard, the stranger had glanced back and called in a gruff voice, "I *am* sorry about your mother."

At the mention of Mater, Halla had felt tears leaking from her eyes. Using her blouse's sleeve, she'd wiped away their dampness.

"We must be strong, Tarald," she'd told the creature in her apron pocket.

In answer, the bright blue dragonet had popped his head out. He'd started to crawl from her pocket.

Not yet, she'd warned using mind-speak.

Halla had communicated with Tarald via her thoughts since before she could talk. The day before she was born, a dragon egg had appeared in her cradle. It had hatched at the moment of Halla's birth. Viewing the dragon business as a blessing from a magical entity, her parents had done nothing to deter the friendship. Thus, since their first breaths, Halla and Tarald had been inseparable.

Soon? Tarald had asked from his hiding place.

Halla had thought, *Yes*. Then, she'd stepped back as the huge doors swung open.

Two women dressed in dark robes had stood before her. The tallest had asked, "Who are you?"

"Halla," she'd responded.

"Where are your parents?" the shorter woman had inquired.

"Dead," Halla had answered. "One of the soldiers who killed Mater left me here."

"Oh, dear." The shorter woman had reached for her. Before she could step away, Halla had been wrapped in the woman's arms and pulled into the abbey.

The other woman had shaken her head and warned, "Sister Birgit, Abbess Mary Verita might not be so welcoming."

Luckily, Sister Margete had been wrong.

"GOOD EVE, SISTER MARGETE." As a sign of respect, Halla lowered her head briefly.

Not only did Tarald lower his head, but he folded his wings as the nun approached.

As she passed, Sister Margete said, "It is late. By now, I expect all candles and fires are lit. Foundlings must earn their keep or be cast out."

Halla chose not to answer and mentally warned the dragon against any response. As the abbess aged, it had become clear Sister Margete was first in line to replace Abbess Mary Verita. Halla suspected her time at St. Betina of the Waves was coming to an end. What the future held for Tarald and her was as predictable as a toss of the bones or a tarot card reading.

As they continued down the hall toward the entrance to the tower passage, they went by the cells of the nuns. Each cell was the same, except for the one belonging to the abbess: a bed, chair, side table, chest, shelf, hooks for hanging clothing, and a candle. Each door had a small, shuttered window at chin height which could be opened to allow in more light. Though the nuns' cells were furnished with a mattress, blankets, and pillow, they were far from comfortable. Halla knew, because she and Tarald shared the cell nearest to the kitchen.

Although most of the nuns were in their cells by this hour and they surely heard the dragon's claws clacking on the polished stone floor, no one spoke to Halla. Even Sister Birgit was reluctant to call attention to herself as night swallowed the abbey.

We must hurry to the tower, urged the dragon.

"Give me a minute," she said. Careful not to dump out any of their contents, Halla placed the candle bucket and sack in front of their cell.

Tarald trotted ahead of Halla and exhaled a stream of fire. *Something is different,* he thought.

"Different?" she shook her head. "Every night has been the same for years. Every day for that matter."

Halla couldn't imagine what Tarald meant by *different*. For more than a decade she'd risen early, eaten breakfast with the sisters, and helped clear the dishes. Then, she'd gathered her first sack of candles, picked up the stub bucket, and with the dragon at her side, began the daily task of replacing all the candles in the abbey which had melted into flat slabs of wax. While they were in the various rooms and halls, Tarald was also responsible for flying up to the rafters and incinerating webs, spiders, and bats. Though some of the fatter, juicier bats were roasted and eaten by the dragon rather than incinerated.

Different, Tarald repeated as he once more broke into a trot.

Luckily, Halla only carried a lantern. The extra weight of the bucket and sack would have prevented her from keeping up with Tarald. Even now, it was challenging to match the dragon's pace.

Hurry, he whispered in her mind.

"I am hurrying," she replied.

At last, Halla reached the foot of the stairs which circled up the inside of the north tower. Tarald waited for her on the twentieth step. Moving the lantern to her left hand, she grabbed the iron railing bolted to the tower wall and began the climb. The dragon moved up the stairs ahead of her, regularly exhaling flames to help light Halla's way. Leg muscles burning from the rapid climb, Halla finally stepped into the north tower. Tarald waited for her.

It is the Darkness. The dragon's eyes surveyed the west horizon where it met the vast waters of Ever Sea. Then, he lowered his gaze to study the boiling surface.

Halla gasped. *We must hold back the Darkness at all costs* was the first and most important rule of St. Betina of the Waves. Every abbess, nun, novice, and servant knew this. Every priest who stepped inside the stone and timber buildings of St. Betina's embraced the abbey's role. Which was why when Halla and Tarald had been abandoned outside its ten-foot-thick walls, they'd been allowed to stay.

Abbess Mary Verita had taken the arrival of a red-haired child and her fire-breathing dragon as a sign St. Betina of the Waves would prevail against Creperum. Creperum, who was darkness manifested, had destroyed hundreds of towns a thousand years before. Creperum, who was repelled by St. Betina herself, was expected to return. Halla feared tonight was the night Darkness returned.

Following the direction of Tarald's gaze, Halla looked for the shadow creature who longed to destroy the coastal cities and villages. She spotted something black and monstrous swimming toward the abbey.

"Shouldn't we light the fire?" she asked in a quavering voice.

It will not be enough. The dragon looked at her with his eyes glowing. *We must call for help.*

"Yes! We must wake the abbess. She will know what to do."

No. Tarald coughed a shower of flames onto the tower's neatly stacked logs. The bonfire sprang to life. *We must call St. Betina's dragon.*

"What are you talking about?" she asked as Tarald disappeared down the stairwell. Upon receiving no response, Halla ran down the steps after him. Panting by the time she reached the foot of the stairs, she managed to gasp, "*Did* St. Betina have a dragon?"

Of course. How else could she have held back the Crepera? The dragon studied her face.

"Crepera? Don't you mean Creperum?" she asked as she felt her pulse slow to near normal.

No, replied Tarald. *There are hundreds of Crepera. St. Betina and her dragon only repelled one beast. Tonight, I spotted at least four of the foul creatures swimming toward the abbey.*

"What do they want?"

To feed, answered the dragon. He paused long enough for his words to sink in. Then, he thought, *Now, to visit St. Betina's relics.*

Before Halla could protest the idea of disturbing the saint's remains, Tarald dashed down the hallway.

Lantern swinging, Halla followed the dragon. She made no attempt to quiet her footfalls. The nuns and abbess would have to be awoken if the abbey was to defend itself from the Darkness. And apparently, it wasn't Creperum who they would face, but a foursome of demons from the depths of the sea.

By the time Halla reached the narthex of the church, Tarald had made his way to the corner pillar where the south transept met the chancel.

Your slowness endangers us all, the dragon scolded.

Halla gathered her strength and dashed down the aisle. Wheezing slightly, she reached Tarald. Without hands, the dragon couldn't open the false panel and access the spiral staircase to the tunnel which led to the crypt hidden below the crossing. But Halla could.

On several occasions, she'd witnessed Abbess Mary Verita guide an important visitor to the crypt. Once, she'd followed them as they traversed the tunnel and entered the dark burial chamber. There, kings and queens, noblemen and noblewomen, as well as a few bishops were entombed in large stone coffins. On top of the coffins, a likeness of the dead had been carved in marble. As the abbess walked, she had lit torches secured on the walls at regular intervals. But there was no need for light at the tomb of St. Betina.

Dressed in a white veil, bandeau, coif, guimpe, and pleated habit, the saint was displayed in a glass coffin. She appeared to have not aged though she'd been dead for a thousand years. And most astonishingly, St. Betina glowed as if she were lit from the inside by fireflies.

The memory of the saint clear as the water in the sacred spring in the abbey's prayer grotto, Halla manipulated the carvings in one of the columns, slid back several locking mechanisms, and opened the false panel.

The dragon pushed past her and darted down the stairs.

"Light all the torches," she called to Tarald as she set her lantern on the floor of the south transept. It would be easier for her to descend the narrow spiral of steps with both hands free, but she still needed to see.

Halla slipped inside the wall. As asked, the dragon had lit the torches. The stairs and tunnel were brightly illumined. Moving as quickly as tired legs would allow, Halla hastened to the crypt and stepped inside.

It was as she remembered. Whether queen, bishop, or duke, blazing torches highlighted the features of dead royalty captured in stone and set eerie shadows dancing. And there, on her elevated platform in a glass box, glowed St. Betina.

Tarald had placed his front paw on the top of the saint's coffin. With one sharp claw, he was meticulously scraping a circle in the glass above St. Betina's chest.

"What are you doing?" Though Halla wasn't a novice or nun, she still held sacred the relics of a saint. To disturb a saint's body seemed a sacrilege.

Getting you what you will need to call forth Betina's dragon, thought Tarald as he completed the circle. The dragon licked the bottom of his foot, placed it in the circle, pushed gently, then pulled up. Miraculously, the glass adhered to his foot. As soon as the circle was above the rest of the coffin top, the dragon slid it to the side and released it.

Now, comes your part. He pointed at the third finger on the saint's right hand. *We need the ring.*

Feeling queasy, Halla stepped to St. Betina's coffin. The thousand-year-old nun appeared to be sleeping. There was no smell of death. There was no drying of skin.

"How is this possible?" she said.

The corners of Tarald's mouth curled up. *She was dragon-bonded. Even now, should she choose, her dragon could return and awaken her.*

"Awaken her!" Before she could step back, Tarald used his front foot to push her closer.

The ring, he mind-spoke, *take her dragon ring.*

With trembling hands, Halla reached inside St. Betina's coffin and picked up her right hand. It felt cool, but alive. Pressing her lips together to keep from crying out, she tried to slide the small, silver ring from the saint's finger. It wouldn't budge.

It is as I feared. The dragon sighed. *Only Betina can remove the ring.* He tapped the glass with a claw. *We must cut off her hand and take it, bearing the ring, to the courtyard.*

"Cut off her hand!"

It is the only way.

"I will *not* do it," stated Halla.

Then, you loose Darkness upon the world, condemning St. Betina by the Waves and thousands of men, women, and children to a cruel death.

"Can't you do it?" If Tarald removed the saint's hand, it would still be awful, but at least Halla wouldn't be actively involved.

No, responded the dragon. *It must be a clean cut made with a silver blade like the one you carry in your boot for trimming wicks.* Observing her hesitancy, the dragon added, *time is short. You must decide if you want to save the world or let it fall into the grips of Darkness.*

It was then, Halla heard the words not of the dragon, but of the nuns, the priests, and most loudly, Abbess Mary Verita echoing in her head: *We must hold back the Darkness at all costs.* She reached inside her boot and grasped the dagger. This was the moment for which she and Tarald had been born. Blade held firmly, she leaned over St. Betina. This was the moment Abbess Mary Verita had foreseen—the reason she'd allowed Halla and her dragon to stay at the abbey. She took the cool, pale hand of the saint, whispered, "Forgive me," then sliced through the flesh.

Expecting to strike bone, Halla was surprised when St. Betina's hand, ring and all, parted from the saint like a plucked bloom parts from the plant. There was no blood. In fact, where she'd cut the saint's wrist, the limb was sealed and still glowing.

To the courtyard, the dragon yelled in her mind.

More rapid than wind, Tarald and she sped from the chamber. They didn't slow until they'd reached the courtyard.

Place Betina's hand on the ground, said the dragon.

Halla obeyed. As she did so, she noticed all the nuns and novices were standing in front of the abbey's front doors holding candles. Abbess Mary Verita stood in the center with a fierce expression on her face. She was flanked by Sister Margete and Sister Birgit.

Tarald locked eyes with Halla, inhaled deeply, then exhaled a ball of fire. Though encircled by flames, St. Betina's hand did not burn. Instead, it glowed brighter.

Suddenly, the sky opened. An enormous dragon with feathers as white as the clouds flew from the portal and landed beside the fire.

"Betina," called the white dragon in a voice like a building storm, "awaken. The Darkness has returned."

The nuns of St. Betina by the Waves parted as the glowing saint, who'd slept for a thousand years in their abbey, stepped from their midst. She walked to her severed hand, knelt, took the ring from its third finger, then slipped the dragon-shaped ring onto a finger on her left hand. Next, still holding the hand, St. Betina stood, smiled at Halla, Tarald, and the white dragon. Then, she returned to the nuns. Appearing to barely touch the steps with her pale feet, the saint went to Sister Mary Verita and gave the abbess her severed hand.

"The abbey will still have a relic," said the saint. Then, almost as an afterthought added, "I trust you will keep my hand safe until I return."

"It is our honor," replied Mary Verita.

Halla, whispered Tarald. *It is time for you to decide whether you want to be dragon-bonded with me and fight Darkness, no matter its form, until we perish.* He pulled a ring shaped like a dragon from between two sapphirine scales.

She surveyed the nuns standing like a row of soldiers holding their small lights up against the coming Darkness. They were brave, strong women who had sheltered her.

But Halla was not one of them. She stared into the eyes of the abbess who had known from the first that Halla and her dragon were special. Allowing her gaze to drift to Sister Margete, she knew the abbess-to-be would mold a miraculously religious tale to explain whatever happened this night. For despite her sour manner, Margete was perhaps the most sensible and strongest of them all.

Looking at Tarald once more, Halla said, "Yes, I will bond with you." She took the ring, slid it onto her finger, and felt it tighten.

St. Betina scrambled onto her white dragon, whom Halla now realized was a wyvern. "Step back," she told Halla. "It is time Tarald assumes his rightful place beside his kin."

As soon as Halla obeyed the saint, a wave of azure flame poured from the wyvern's mouth and washed over Tarald. Sparkling like sea-shimmer, Tarald grew to nearly the size of the white dragon.

Climb aboard, he said to Halla. *We go to fight the Crepera.*

Halla did as he asked. Once on top of her dragon, she tightened her legs and gripped several small spikes that had sprouted from Tarald's neck. In the blink of an eye, the sky once more ruptured. Two more dragons appeared: a scarlet, wormlike dragon and an emerald, bat-winged drake. Both carried riders.

Without another word from reptiles, saints, or humans, the four battle-ready dragons swooped over the abbey's walls and sailed to where the Ever Sea met the sand.

Halla swallowed a scream. Crawling from the surf was a horror of unimaginable size. If such a thing were possible, the Creperum was a hundred shades of dark-ness. Its flailing tentacles ringed by stinging nettles shone like the eyes of dead fish. Its corpse-black beak snapped with such power, she had no doubt it could crush stone and shatter bone. But unlike the beaks of birds, the Creperum's beak was filled with rows of jagged obsidian teeth. Adding to the terribleness, the Creperum had a multitude of oral arms sweeping everything in its path into its beak.

Hold tight and pray, Tarald shouted as he and the other dragons dropped to the Creperum.

Repeating every prayer she could remember, Halla clung to her dragon and beheld Darkness. As the dragons spewed fire at the ebon monstrosity, she saw the beast had hundreds of pulsating, pitch-black eyes and a plethora of stringy, tentacle-like appendages which flailed and writhed.

Halla had expected Darkness to have some human-ness to it. The demons in the frescoes painted in plaster adorning the abbey's walls had horns, fangs, and pointed ears. Even so, there was a humanness to them. There wasn't a scintilla of humanity about the bellowing Creperum. Its grim presence sent waves of evil in all directions. Halla was certain it had no compassion, no empathy, no pity, and no intention of allowing anything to survive when it crept and slithered onto the land.

Use your weapon, said Tarald.

"Weapon?"

Your silver dagger, thought her dragon.

Looking at the other riders, she observed each was wielding a silver blade. Whether axe, sword, or spear, the other dragon riders were slicing and stabbing any part of the Creperum which came close. Doubting she could do much damage with her knife, nonetheless she drew it from her boot.

Still breathing fire, Tarald dove near the back of the Creperum's bulbous head. When one bulging eye was within her reach, Halla leaned to the side and dragged her dagger's tip across the pupil. She felt a painful tingle creep up her arm, but kept the knife against the creature's eye as long as possible.

Time seemed to move slowly. Halla's ears rang from the thunderous roars of the Creperum, her nose and mouth were filled with the smoke from dragon fire, and her eyes hurt from trying to follow the movements of dragons and tentacles. Minutes later, or perhaps it was hours later, the wounded Creperum backed from the shore to the shallows, and then, to the deeper waters.

Before the dragons and their riders could celebrate, a second Creperum rose from the depths. It lashed out at the green drake with a darker-than-death tentacle. The tentacle found its mark and badly wounded the drake and rider. The chorus of screams from the other three dragons shattered the night. So poignant was their cry that Halla felt the ache in her bones.

And that was when the sky opened.

Like in a wonder tale repeated by generation after generation of storytellers, the heavens filled with light. Then, a multitude of dragons burst forth. Some collected the green drake and rider and lifted them into the blinding brightness. Others attacked the Crepera with claw and fire.

It was over in a few dozen beats of Tarald's wings.

Singing a victory hymn, the heavenly dragons vanished into the light leaving nothing in the night sky but the waxing gibbous moon, the stars, three dragons, and their riders.

Tarald, the white wyvern, and the scarlet worm landed on the beach.

St. Betina, astride the wyvern, turned to Halla and asked, "Will you and your dragon be joining us?"

"I'm not sure." Halla was at a loss. She wondered, *What am I joining? Where will it take me?*

I will honor your choice, promised Tarald.

"We must hold back the Darkness at all costs," said the one-handed saint. "Though we have pushed back the Crepera from this shore, there are other shores, forests, deserts, and mountains where far more loathsome creatures of Darkness plot to decimate our world."

Halla recalled the nuns, some elderly and frail, holding their candles on the steps of St. Betina of the Waves determined to defend goodness, light, and the life of common folk from beings of the dark. Could she do any less?

Voice barely above a whisper, she replied, "Tarald and I will go with you."

St. Betina smiled, then turned to speak with the rider of the ruby-red worm.

Do not be afraid. I am with you, Tarald reminded her. *I will always keep you safe.*

"We will see," Halla answered as the trio of dragons sprang from the sand, faced north, and sailed toward the unknown.

VONNIE WINSLOW CRIST, SFWA, HWA, is author of Dragon Rain, The Enchanted Dagger, Beneath Raven's Wing, Owl Light, The Greener Forest, Murder on Marawa Prime, the Shivers, *Scares series, and other award-winning books. Her speculative writing appears in hundreds of publications including* Asimov's Magazine, Amazing Stories, Cast of Wonders, Chilling Ghost Short Stories, Weird-book, Twilight Tales, *and* Cirsova. *Believing the world is still filled with mystery, miracles, and magic, she strives to celebrate the power of myth in her writing. For more information about Vonnie and her books: https://www.vonniewinslowcrist.com https://www.facebook.com/WriterVonnieWinslowCrist*

REACTOR

L.N. HUNTER

B enson Strickland was staring at an animated dragon's head on his computer screen.

Three days ago, the world's first commercial fusion reactor had been switched on, producing enough power to run an entire city. Benson, along with the rest of P-Gen Reactors' staff, had partied long into the night, celebrating their success.

Now, there was a dragon on his computer.

"Hoy, alien lifeform. Can you be hear we?" it asked.

At least, Benson thought that's what it said, over the hissing and crackling on his headphones, as if the creature were standing in a furnace—not the Rachmaninoff he'd been listening to right before the dragon took over his computer. He waggled his mouse and clicked the button a few times, then tapped the 'escape' key. Nothing changed. After hitting 'escape' twice more, and 'enter' and 'space,' he pulled his headphones off and whipped around in his chair. "Come on, Geoff, stop mucking about!"

Geoff, at his desk on the other side of their shared office, turned to face him. "You what?"

"Give me my screen back."

"What're you talking about?"

Benson pointed at his screen. "This."

Geoff squinted at the dragon. "That's not me, mate." He wheeled his chair across to peer at the screen. "How'd that happen? What did you do?"

"I didn't do anything—it just appeared. I was working on the survey spreadsheet when the screen went blank and this appeared. I can't do anything to make it go away." Benson put his headphones to his ear then unplugged them so that the sound would be routed to his desktop speakers. "Look, it's speaking too."

"—ello. Can you be hear we?"

Geoff's eyes widened. He called, "Hello back at you. Who are you?"

"We are be"—sequence of clicks and pops—"and wish to be know what name you are be."

"Who is this really? Simon? Beth?"

The dragon's brow furrowed. "What be simonbeff? We are not be simonbeff. We are be"—clicks and pops.

Benson put a hand over the microphone and whispered to Geoff. "Stop, don't say anything else. We've been hacked. We need to shut this down." He removed his hand and leaned close to the screen. "Look, I don't know who you are or what you want. I'm calling my manager." He turned to Geoff. "Go get Penny?"

As Geoff left, "What be 'manager?'" came through the speaker. Then the dragon blinked. "Not matter. We are find you three planet rotates past, when you make life reaction. Same as in life home. We are excite to find lifeform."

Life reaction? Benson frowned. "Reaction, like fusion reactor?"

The dragon looked puzzled. "What be 'fusion?'" Its eyes widened. "Yes, yes. Like fusion deep in life home. You are call 'sun'—we are live in you sun."

Benson snapped, "Stop messing about. Who are you and what do you want?"

"We are lifeform. We are not know other lifeform until you are make fusion. We are want know you."

Could this be real? "The sun? Come on, nothing can exist there, not even atoms. The temperature and the pressure…"

"You word for life reaction be 'plasma.' We are of plasma, and we are speak you in lower dimensions. You are exist in four of dimensions, and we are of ten. You are not hear we until we talk in lower number."

Like in Flatland, Benson thought, before saying, "I don't believe you. This is a trick. What do you really want?"

The dragon tilted its head left and right, as if having a conversation with someone else, fading into a mess of flickering reddish-yellow pixels before reappearing. "We are want meet, no trick. Look. Watch pattern. We count you base ten."

The screen pulsed off for a second, then back on for two before going blank again. The cycle repeated with periods of three, four, and five seconds, all the way up to ten.

The dragon head reappeared. "Light is take short time from we to you. You be watch sun. We leave now and come back in light time."

Benson's computer screen blanked, then returned to

normal. Classical music resumed through the speakers. He turned the volume down.

He squinted at the spreadsheet on the display, closed the application and reopened it. Everything looked perfectly OK. He was still hunting for anything unusual when Geoff returned with Penny.

"What's up?" she asked. "Geoff said something about a dragon taking over your computer."

Benson shrugged. "It's gone now. My screen… my computer…" He scratched his head. "Look, I don't know what happened."

Penny sighed heavily. "You've been working hard. Maybe you need—"

"Geoff saw it too," Benson said.

Geoff nodded.

Penny pursed her lips. "But everything's normal now, right?"

"Seems to be."

"Tell the IT guys. Get them to check your machine over. You haven't opened any emails with weird attachments?"

Benson shook his head.

"Dragons," Penny muttered as she left the office. "Idiots."

Geoff sat back at his desk.

Blowing out his cheeks, Benson reached for his phone, but what would he tell the IT guys? A dragon—it sounded stupid. He let his gaze roam across the office as thoughts rattled around his head. After typing a detailed email to IT Support, explaining the strange conversation, he deleted it—they'd send the men in white coats round after they read it.

As he began a more coherent email, realization hit

him that sunlight takes just over eight minutes to reach Earth. He checked the clock in the corner of the screen. Seven minutes since that weird counting message. He picked up his mobile phone and opened the office window. If something was going to happen to the sun, not that he actually expected anything, he was going to record it.

Geoff looked across and asked, "What're you doing now?"

"Probably nothing," Benson muttered, looking out at the clear sky. "Just something the dragon said."

Geoff joined him at the window. "Come off it, there's nothing there."

Benson held his phone up to capture a video of the sky. Minutes passed as he squinted and blinked in the direction of the sun. Everything looked as it should: totally normal.

Geoff said, "See, nothing."

Sighing, Benson slumped into his chair and played the video back. A minute in, the light from the sun pulsed—not a complete on-off, but a small dimming then brightening. The hairs on Benson's forearms rose. The timing matched the pulsing that had occurred on his screen. Could the camera have picked up something his brain filtered out from his vision? *People don't normally notice clouds drifting across the sun, do they? I guess this could have happened.*

"Geoff, Geoff, c'mere." He held out his phone. "Look at this."

They were watching the video for the fourth time when the dragon reappeared on the computer monitor. It somehow looked smug and was saying something.

Benson turned the speaker volume up.

"—believe we?" the voice said.

"Are you really real?" Benson asked. "Are we talking with someone in the sun?"

The dragon nodded.

"Nothing can go faster than the speed of light. How can you talk to me when radiation takes eight minutes to reach here?"

"In you dimensions, yes, but we are in more dimensions. We are can be in all places with life reaction at simultaneousity. We are travel by quantum tunnel to all places you are say fusion."

They have instantaneous travel? Between fusion sources? Can they travel between stars? "Wait, you're in our reactor right now? No way!"

"Not be there yet. We are communicate first. We are want see what are you before we come, and we look at you planet radiation—that be how we are learn you language. We are want see if you like we. We are want meet alien lifeform. You be first lifeform we find that are not we."

"Oh wow. This is incredible," Geoff said. "First contact! And it's us." He turned to Benson. "You, I mean. I need to capture this." He pulled out his mobile phone, pointing it at Benson and his computer screen. At the same time, he fumbled with the desk phone. "I'm getting Penny, too," he said as he dialed. "Go on, talk to it."

"Why me?" Benson said to the dragon.

It shrugged. "We talk many, you first answer. No other be answer. This exciting for"—the clicking noises from before were repeated—"and we not think life exist in place—not right word, in matter, no, in *density* so close to vacuum. You be like nothing we are ever find before.

We are interest to see what you be." The dragon smiled, showing long, glowing teeth. "You are look strange to us, but must be effect of low density."

Geoff laughed. "You look damned strange to us, too. Dragons—what you look like—are creatures of myth here." He tapped his chin. "Do you live solely in the sun, or have you ever flown past our planet? I wonder if our ancestors saw you and that's what created the stories."

"Yes, yes." The dragon seemed to be bouncing excitedly. "We are explore planets many time ago with remote bodies—remote bodies are... drones you are say. Like we, but not need life reaction. We are seek high mass elements since not in home-sun. We are use what you are call asteroid belt for element now, not planet. Easier. But we never think there be life on planets. Not enough dense."

Just then, Penny stepped into the office.

"What the blazes is that?"

Benson said, "Blazes is right. It's the dragon I told you about. It lives in the sun."

"Oh, come off it. Someone's pulling your leg."

Benson turned to the screen. "Can you do the sun flashing thing again?"

The dragon nodded. Benson said to Penny, "In eight minutes, point your phone out the window and video the sky. In the meantime, our friend here will repeat what he, er, she—it said to us. Are you an 'it?'"

Penny asked a question Benson hadn't thought of: "How many of you are there?"

The dragon pursed its lips. "One who is many. Thirteen billion bodies, and one mind."

Benson blinked. "You mean like a hive mind?"

The dragon looked blank for a moment, then nodded. "Please, it be time—light reaching you now."

Benson jumped up. "Come on, everyone, get your phone cameras out."

In silence, they videoed the sky for a couple of minutes.

When Benson directed Penny to look at the recorded video, she said, "You know this is stupid, right? Nothing lives in the sun." Then she gasped as the sun seemed to dim and brighten again. "No, this can't be real. Someone's controlling our phones."

Benson grimaced. "There must be some way to verify it."

Geoff blurted, "Astronomers! Someone must be looking at the sun—we can ask them."

Penny said dryly, "Do you have any astronomers' phone numbers to hand?"

Geoff shook his head.

"Proof is we!" the dragon exclaimed. "We are come now. Reactor be small—much smaller than sun space. Smaller than we. Difficult fit, but we are go where life reaction be."

"Wait!" Benson called. "What do you mean 'difficult fit?'"

The dragon blinked.

"Hold on, you're going to transport yourself *into* our reactor?" Benson asked.

A confused expression crossed the dragon's face. "Where else be we go? We are exist only in life reaction. We come, you are see we! We are see you!"

As Benson's screen returned to normal, Geoff leaned back in his chair. "Wow, a real dragon. In our reactor."

Penny waved her hands dismissively. "Pfft. Dragon, schmagon. Nothing's going to turn up in the reactor. It's just the IT guys, they're winding you up." She headed toward the office door. "I'm going to have a word with them."

A thought started to tentatively wend its way through Benson's mind about what might happen if a foreign body suddenly appeared within the reactor. He glanced down, as if he could see through the five floors between the office and the core.

Especially a large *foreign body.*

"Wait," he shouted at the screen, leaping to his feet. "Is that safe? Send drones instead."

Penny and Geoff stared at him. Geoff looked confused, and Penny appeared to be about to say something.

"Stop!" Benson yelled, hoping the dragon would hear him, "How big are y—?"

Alarms blared throughout the building.

Way too big, Benson thought, as the floor launched him and the others into the air to thud against the ceiling. As he fell, he saw an outline appear on the floor, first black as it charred, then burning white hot. An outline of a smiling dragon's face. As his senses went into slow motion, he saw the face expand and grow, tightening and distorting as if it was squeezing into a space it could never fit.

Oh, sh—

An expression of surprise on a city-sized dragon burned into his retinas, and then his whole world exploded.

. . .

L.N. Hunter's dragons first appeared in his comic fantasy novel, *The Feather and the Lamp*, which sits alongside works in anthologies such as *Best of British Science Fiction 2022* and *Detectives, Sleuths, and Nosy Neighbors*, as well as several issues of Short Édition's *Short Circuit* and the *Horrifying Tales of Wonder* podcast. There have also been papers in the IEEE *Transactions on Neural Networks*, which are probably somewhat less relevant and definitely totally devoid of dragons. When not writing, L.N. occasionally masquerades as a software developer or can be found unwinding in a disorganized home in Carlisle, UK, along with two cats and a soulmate.

https://linktr.ee/l.n.hunter

https://www.facebook.com/L.N.Hunter.writer

PADRE JORGE AND THE DRAGON

JAMES RYAN

P adre Jorge nearly split his head open as he grabbed hold to keep tumbling off the quarterdeck.

"I thought you said this would be smoother than the Atlantic," he said to the captain of the vessel.

"Si, she is, Padre Jorge," the captain replied. "Can you not tell the difference?"

Padre Jorge had to gulp down the contents of his stomach once more, as the carrack continued to list from starboard to port and back. He knew he'd scrubbed it well, but every time he looked at the left sleeve of his brown robe, he could still see the splotch where he had vomited on it.

"You see," the captain continued, "in these waters, we don't go back and forth the way we did before. That was much worse than this was. Notice also, much lighter clouds. Notice how they are not dark as night, like it is in the Atlantic."

Padre Jorge started to glower at the seaman, maybe half his age or at least fifteen years younger than him, wondering what he had done that God would put him on this journey west as well. He didn't care for the captain and had started to loathe him, despite Saint Francis's teachings by the time they got to Sevilla la Nueva.

"And if you think this is the work of the dragon, no, it's not," the captain offered.

"How do you know this isn't the Tenocha asking us to stay away?"

"We'd be in Heaven by now if it were. But I thought they knew you were coming; didn't His Holiness send them a letter asking to meet?"

"For our sakes, I hope they read the Pope's letter, and that this is only the 'calm seas' you claim they are."

Padre Jorge pulled the rosary from his robe and muttered repeatedly as he held the crucifix, "Oh Lord, make me an instrument of Your peace." In the past, doing this a few times allowed him to refocus and calm himself.

It was only after the twenty-eighth invocation that he started to feel more charitable toward the captain.

THE FIRST TIME Padre Jorge saw the Tenocha god was on the road to Cempoalati.

He had read about the deity, of course; the descriptions of the survivors of Cortez's expedition that were wiped out at Cempoalati twelve years earlier were clear and precise. To a man, they described it as a few hundred feet in length, a large snake with scales each the size of a shield, a green shade like jade. Each wing that spouted from either side of its body was nearly as long as the god was from snout to tail. The head was described as frightening, like a lion's more than a snake's.

But seeing it fly overhead was entirely different. The color green he witnessed was more vibrant than any mineral from the earth; it seemed closer to the foliage that lined the road inland, but almost emitted its own light, not merely reflecting the sun. The descriptions never noted the sound the god made as it flapped to stay aloft, like sails being battered by a hard wind. Perhaps the row of feathers running down the spinelike ridges weren't noted by others, as those witnesses may have survived by not studying the deity too long. And while the head of the god was fearsome, as Padre Jorge and his party were there not as conquerors but emissaries, its countenance projected more nobility than menace.

The woman leading the landing party turned her head to avoid looking at the god. She wore a blouse with wide sleeves that could have been wings themselves had she held out her arms and let the wind carry her, her headband adorning her dark hair with green feathers.

As the god left, Padre Brown tried to ask, "Um, if I may, Zo... Zo..."

"It is Xiloxochitl," she replied.

"Thank you, yes. If I may, I notice you turned your face from your god as he flew overhead."

"It is a sign of respect that all priests practice."

Padre Jorge tried not to let the idea of women being priests be a distraction to him, and asked, "And the rest of the people also turn their heads as well? Is it a requirement?"

"We encourage it ourselves. Quetzacoatl has not told us what he prefers, but better to be on terms with him with a granted permission than with a request for better behavior."

"I see." Padre Brown added, "Your Spanish is very good."

"Gracias," Xiloxochitl replied with a hint of annoyance in her voice.

"I mean, I didn't expect a member of the order to be able to, um…"

She sighed. "I would assume that in Espania, that I would be greeted by someone who studied Nahuatal to be with me when I visited."

"Yes. Well, yes," he ultimately offered.

"I was asked to study Spanish when we sent our reply to your letter from His Holiness, Clement, in anticipation of the arrival of his delegate."

"That must have been a lot to ask, to take up such studies."

"I was asked as I showed great talent in studying both Maya and Quechua. The fact that Quechua uses a writing system similar to your own made studying the languages faster than it would have been had you used the glyphs we do."

"Languages?"

"The other one that was in the letter. Et lingua Ecclesiae."

Padre Jorge nearly lost a step in response to her perfectly pronounced Latin.

"I presume that were we to say we were coming, we would receive as warm a response as we have shown so far."

"Ah. Well, we don't have many speakers of Nahuat with us."

"Nahuatal," she corrected.

"Yes, yes, you see our problem. We might find it hard to reciprocate, as we have not had as much contact with you as you've had with us."

"I suppose the fact that we have contacts with islands taken off our coasts as colonies gives us some advantage."

"Well, I do see——"

"So, would we have to do the same then? Would we need to claim your neighbors' lands as ours for you to learn our tongues?"

Padre Jorge said nothing, and by the time the sting in the air had faded they were in sight of Cempoalati.

The city seemed older than Toledo, dominated by step pyramids that rose higher than the guard towers along Toledo's walls, and seemed to hold nearly as many people. Looking closer, he made out the tops of a set of pillars grouped in a circle, close together without a roof atop them.

As they got even closer though, Padre Jorge started to see buildings that looked abandoned in between the lush fields of produce and the city center. Many of these were just four walls of baked mud with roofs missing, at best the remains of wood that held pieces of thatch here and there.

"If I may ask, Zo-zi——" Padre Jorge took a breath to catch himself and continued, "Xiloxochitl, I notice the columns that do not seem to have a roof on them. Is there a reason for that?"

She took her own exasperated breath before she replied, "There is no roof for these. They are markers we use to note the stars, to let us know when the moon will appear, and how full she will be."

"Ah, ingenious." He considered how exasperated she

was with his question, and decided not to ask about the abandoned buildings yet.

In front of the largest step pyramid, Xiloxochitl introduced Padre Jorge to an elder gentleman wearing a cape that was tied to his shoulder. The pattern of the garment, green diamonds stacked atop each other, was eye-catching, and the way he wore it reminded Padre Jorge of a Roman senator's tunic.

She spoke to the gentleman in her tongue, but he did catch her mentioning his name, "Padre Jorge de la Madrodjos, Ordo Fratrum Minorum, Apolistic delegate in the name of His Holiness, Clement the Seventh, Romanus Pontifex."

She then said, "Padre Jorge, may I present the Tlamacazqui Cuitlauac, representative of the Tlatoani of Tenochtitlan," at which he bowed to Padre Jorge.

"It is an honor to meet you," Padre Jorge said to him.

The Tlamacazqui spoke to Xiloxochitl, who translated, "He hopes your trip was comfortable, and asks you about it."

Padre Jorge took a moment to realize just what Xiloxochitl's role was going to be, then told her, "You may let him know— Do I need to specify whether I'm talking to you or him every time I open my mouth?"

"Oh no, I should be able to tell if you look at the Tlamacazqui as you speak if it's for him or me."

"Very well," he said as he looked at his host, trying not to feel self-conscious in what he was doing. To help him concentrate on the arrangement, he closed his hand around the rosary as he answered. "It was a long journey, about nine weeks from Spain to these shores. It was very rough most of the way, and more than once I thought we were going to be taken by our Lord."

Tlamacazqui Cuitlauac asked Xiloxochitl a question, looking Padre Jorge in the eyes as he did so, which she relayed, "I do not understand what a 'week' is."

"Ah. A week is seven days, the time between days of rest. So nine weeks becomes — give me a minute — 63 days."

Tlamacazqui Cuitlauac nodded, and replied, "You have come a long way to talk to us. Did you by any chance make a stop at the lands Quetzacoatl had rested in before coming to us?"

He turned to her and asked, "The lands Quetzacoatl had rested in, did he say?"

"Our beliefs hold that he is of the eastern sky, where the sun rises, and that he had been the morning star before he came here."

Padre Jorge said to him through the translator, "We did not pass by the lands of Quetzacoatl. Between Spain and here, there was only the Atlantic Ocean."

"So perhaps the lands he rested in are further to the east than you are, then?"

"You could come to that conclusion, I suppose."

"Your Romanus, he mentioned wanting to open a spiritual dialog with us. I am glad we are starting off almost immediately."

"My Romanu — Oh, we refer to him less formally, as the 'Pontiff' or 'Pope' when we refer to the head of the church."

"So he is not as formal on titles, I take it?"

"Excuse me? I don't understand the question?"

"I ask, as I sometimes find titles to show your position get in the way of discussing it. If you would like, please call me 'Cuitlauac' as we need not remind ourselves who we are with every breath."

"Thank you. As for me, simple 'Jorge' is more than enough."

Jorge noticed Cuitlauac's smile as he threw away his title as well. As they smiled, the nine weeks at sea felt as though they were not in vain.

THAT NIGHT, Jorge retired to quarters provided close to the main pyramid. He noticed that this was at the edge of the abandoned buildings he saw on his way into town.

Unlike the others he saw, this single structure had a thatched roof, looking new compared to the walls. There was another house with a new roof nearby; in between the two was a brick oven in the shape of a dome that had an encampment set up around it by the bearers who had accompanied him since he came ashore.

"I will be in the house across the way," Xiloxochitl stated. "I've instructed attendants in a few basic Spanish words; if you point to something and say what you need, they will do their best to help you with your request. If not, I am available to translate."

Jorge looked around and asked, "I did notice something I didn't say earlier. It looks like the buildings here were abandoned; this wasn't from the battle, was it?"

"It was tied to Quetzacoatl's return, yes."

"I knew that some of the residents were sympathetic

to Cortez, but I can't imagine many of them dying in the conflict."

"Some were directly involved in the battle, yes. All of those who took up arms and were in the fight died alongside the Spaniards who did not flee as the day went against them."

"I am surprised."

"How so?"

"Your god is so big, I'm surprised that he didn't do more damage to the houses. Many of them just look to have been abandoned."

"They were. Those who sided with the Spanish afterward were captives and were brought to Tenochtitlan."

"All of them? At once?"

"Yes. It took many days for so many people to be brought up the steps of the Hueyi Teocalli. It was said the blood in the streets below would come up to the height of everyone's ankles during the busiest time of the offerings."

Jorge wasn't prepared for that answer. He knew of their practices in war, how captives would be sacrificed to their god; he was told this by the Cardinal's prelates many times as he prepared to go west.

It was the casual manner in which Xiloxochitl described the event, though, with only a mere shrug, that made him retire early for the night, ill at ease.

Jorge wasn't expecting the third day of talks to be as great a breakthrough as it turned out to be.

The previous two days felt superficial, mostly an

exchange of basic background information regarding each other's practices. The hardest part was when it came to describing Toledo Cathedral to Cuitlauac; that took most of the second afternoon and was hampered by Xiloxochitl not having the vocabulary to describe stained glass and vaults, as well as Jorge's having to give details about something he took for granted his entire life.

When the third day of talks started, they made the climb with two attendants holding shades made of palm leaves over them, and accompanied by Jorge's wheezing; try as he might, it was difficult to talk while he addressed the steps, and the whole effort was for naught.

When they reached the high point, Cuitlauac gave Jorge a chance to catch his breath before he asked through Xiloxochitl, "How do you petition your god?"

The surprise question made Jorge take a moment to answer. "Prayer. We ask God for his intercession through prayer."

"And you use rituals for this, I gather, to let him know you have a request."

"Oh, well, there are rituals, such as the Mass, but we can also speak to God through prayer."

"Ah. Small incantations, I guess? Maybe a totem?"

"We believe God is everywhere, so we don't put God into an object."

"And yet you have a representation that you hold with you a…" As Cuitlauac pointed, Xiloxochitl seemed to be struggling for a word.

Jorge realized he had noticed the clutched rosary in his hands. "This is a 'rosary,' a set of beads we use to count out how many prayers we've made, if we need to do a whole series of —"

Jorge noticed that Cuitlauac was still pointing at his hand, his finger being more specific.

"Oh, this part of the rosary," Jorge replied as he held it up. "This is the 'crucifix,' and yes, it does have a representation of Our Lord. It shows the moment when He gave up His life for us to free us from sin."

"And does he answer?" Cuitlauac surprised him.

"That's… Well, there is the idea we hold, that God can sometimes move in ways we cannot see. There are psalms where we ask God to explain what He is doing, and sometimes we do not realize what He's done for us until long after we've asked."

"So, your god walked among you then?"

"This was many years ago, yes. About 1500 years, in fact."

Cuitlauac nodded. "And do you know if he's coming back?"

"Ah; well, it's an article of faith that when the last moments come, that He will be with us as the world ends and bring us to paradise."

Cuitlauac nodded again, then asked, "So you do not know what would make him come back, then? Not what you would need exactly to do so?"

"This… is an odd line of questioning."

"And you have never met your god here, in person."

"Well, as I said, God is all around us."

"But you have never touched your god, nor your god you, physically."

Jorge was trying to come up with a proper response. He tried to remind himself that these were people who may have only heard some of His word and would have questions the innocent would ask. The fact that Cuitlauac was likely only a few years older than he was shouldn't upset him. He'd seen young ladies almost as old as his translator still having problems with the idea of an omnipresent God, and a few some years older than that not quite getting the idea of the trinity —

Suddenly, everyone around Jorge bowed their heads. They stopped looking at him, casting their gaze to their feet.

He had a brief clue as to what was happening as he quickly turned to look skyward.

The first time Jorge beheld Quetzacoatl on his way to Cempoalati, he had a moment of dread as he flew above him so far in the sky. Watching as the winged serpent came closer, blotting out the sun with his extended wings, he nearly evacuated his bowels in the face of sheer terror.

The hour of his death upon him, Jorge suddenly felt a surreal calm. Every account of the martyrs who were about to die for the glory of God, their calm in their last minutes, he suddenly, truly understood, like nothing he'd ever understood before.

He abandoned his first choice of action, to cower and scream, and instead stood to look their god in the eye.

For so big a creature, the winged serpent landed softly on the opposite corner of the roof, coiling up his body while extending his wings. Up close, Jorge could see his features better. The scales covering his body were hard feathers, still as steel plates, but clearly plumage. Seen this closely, the face of their god had features other than those of a snake and lion; a mouth shaped like a beak but covered in hard scales, sharp teeth visible if it moved its lips.

The eyes, however: This great god had eyes with

irises like a man's, with bands that were spinning bolts of lightning, circling in his eyes like wheels with sparks that crossed his pupils.

Jorge raised his hand with his rosary still clutched and held it out in front of him. If this was the hour of his death, he decided, it would not do to show any fear.

For comfort in his last moments, he recited Saint Francis's *Laudes Creaturarum* to die by. He was nervous as he started, not getting his voice up until a few lines into the song:

Be praised, my Lord, through all your creatures,
especially through my lord Brother Sun,
who brings the day; and you give light through him.
And he is beautiful and radiant in all his splendor!
Of you, Most High, he bears the likeness.

PRAISED BE YOU, my Lord, through Sister Moon and the stars,
in Heaven you formed them clear and precious and beautiful.

PRAISED BE YOU, my Lord, through Brother Wind,
and through the air, cloudy and serene,
and every kind of weather through which
You give sustenance to Your creatures.

PRAISED BE YOU, my Lord, through Sister Water,
which is very useful and humble and precious and chaste.

PRAISED BE YOU, my Lord, through Brother Fire,
through whom you light the night and he is beautiful

and playful and robust and strong.

PRAISED BE YOU, my Lord, through Sister Mother Earth,
    who sustains us and governs us and who produces
    varied fruits with colored flowers and herbs.

PRAISED BE YOU, my Lord,
    through those who give pardon for Your love,
    and bear infirmity and tribulation.

THE LACK OF EXTREME PAIN, the absence of the sensation of blood running through open wounds where limbs had been, the failure to feel bits of him being ground into meal; when Jorge realized something was missing, he forgot to say aloud the next few words. He tried to make up for it with more:

Praised be You, my Lord
through our Sister Bodily Death,
from whom no living man can escape.

BUT THERE WAS NO PAIN, no sensation, not even the threat of any, that made him stop and open his eyes.

The Tenocha god was staring at him. The look on his face was not very *And-now-I-have-you-for-lunch*; it seemed more contemplative, more interested in listening to what he had to say than how he tasted.

Jorge noticed the head move closer and again readied himself to be another martyr celebrated for the faith…

254

But Quetzacoatl kept his mouth closed. He brushed Jorge's outstretched hand, the rim of his nostrils stoking him the way a human might pet a dog, and then stared into Jorge's eyes.

The gaze of the god filled Jorge with sensations and thoughts that he could not name, feelings he could not express; he felt as though he lived a few years over the course of a second, trying to catch up with himself.

And before he could grasp it all, there was a sudden downward pressure upon him. He closed his eyes briefly in reaction but forced them open to see the feathered serpent going skyward, his wings and body leaving Jorge's sight as he flew toward the sun.

Jorge saw that his hosts were no longer looking down at their feet but at him. He refused to return their glance as he bounced more than ran down the steps of the pyramid.

———

"I understand you must feel upset."

Jorge heard Xiloxochitl on the other side of the blanket that served as his door of the reclaimed house. It was the first he heard from her since his audience with the dragon that morning.

Prayer and contemplation from that moment until long after the sun had gone down were not helping him come to terms with what he went through. He lost count of how many times he chanted, "Oh Lord, make me an instrument of Your peace," and only sometime around reaching the tens of thousands did he control his inner reflexes to either attack or run away. It was about at that moment he realized that, because he was so far away from everything, at least weeks to sail to Sevilla la Nueva if he could get aboard a ship right there, that neither course would serve him well.

He gave a few more chants, though, just to make sure that he could speak to her without some latent resentment complicating things.

"Are you all right, Jorge?" she asked, just as he emerged.

"May I ask a question?" he finally said to her. "What made him think that that was a good idea?"

"I'm sorry?"

"I have… no animosity toward Cuitlauac. I can forgive what happened; if the Sainted Francis were atop the pyramid instead of I, he probably would have forgiven him faster than I could, so who am I who follows him to do less?"

"But… but he thought you wanted to meet him."

"Pray tell, *please*, what I could have said to Cuitlauac to make me want to have that encounter? Why did he think I wanted to do that?"

Xiloxochitl looked confused before she replied, "But Cuitlauac didn't suggest that that take place."

"Who then? Was it you, dare I ask?"

"No, of course not!"

"If not you or him, then who?"

"Quetzacoatl; he thought you wanted a direct audience."

Jorge did his best not to let the sudden apoplexy nearly fell him. "He suggested it, you say."

"Yes, he did."

"And when did he tell you this?"

"I was only told this morning that he wanted to meet."

"So he said something to you just before he landed."

"He didn't talk to me directly, no."

"And who did your god speak to then?"

"The Tlatoani of Tenochtitlan; the two spoke late yesterday, and runners came this morning from the capitol with word."

Jorge took a breath and asked, "So, if your god… spoke to you, what does his voice sound like? Because I don't recall hearing him up there. I felt him, yes, but I didn't hear him."

"He has… other ways of speaking. It's not how we do it."

"How does he do it, pray tell?"

"You… you <u>feel</u> it. If you look him in the eyes, he… I don't have the words, not in Spanish, Latin, Nahuatal; there is no way to describe it in words."

Jorge looked closely at her and asked, "You've spoken to him, then?"

"Yes. It was a few years ago, shortly before the letter from your Pope arrived. I was scared when he asked to meet me atop the Hueyi Teocalli, and I thought I was going to be a sacrifice to appease him for something I could not imagine. Instead, he landed there, looked me in the eyes and I…"

"Go on," Jorge finally prodded before the silence was too much.

"Time did not exist as I had feelings fill me up when he looked into my eyes. I didn't understand it all then, but when the letter arrived, and the materials left behind by Cortez's men that we had, it made translating your languages much easier. I don't know if I could be holding this conversation with you now had he not 'spoken' to me."

There was another silence, during which they both started flowing toward the fire in front of the oven in the courtyard; both sources of heat kept the creeping chill of the night at bay when they started to talk again.

As he looked into the fire, Jorge finally said, "So it's not words, it's… the gift of tongues, I imagine?"

"The gift of tongues?"

"When Our Lord went back to Heaven, and his apostles were gathered, there was a wind that blew onto them, tongues of flames lighting each one. And they went out form there, able to proclaim His message in all the languages of the world."

"I see."

"Somehow, I imagined a fire breathing dragon would be something else entirely."

Xiloxochitl started to ask, but stopped herself with a shake of her head. Instead, she stated, "I was wondering why I was being asked to go to the temple, even though I hadn't asked to be sacrificed."

"No one asks to be sacrificed. Do they?"

"There was the Tetlauhtilli."

"Which was what?"

"Just as the Spanish came, our king, Moctezuma, had a vision that the world was coming to an end, and assumed that we would be swept away. But in a moment of bravery and compassion, he volunteered himself to be sacrificed to the gods."

"Oh…"

"Yes, he felt that only with so big a gift to the gods as a king willingly giving up his life on the altar that he could somehow save us all."

"And how soon after that did Quetzacoatl show up?"

"Three days later, at sunrise. We assumed that he'd

come because at dawn the next day, Huei Citlalin was not rising before the sun.

"Huei Citlalin?"

"Yes, the morning star, which was Quetzacoatl's place in the sky."

"You mean, a really bright, almost like the moon in intensity, that morning star?"

"Why do you ask?"

"Because we call it Venus, and that hasn't appeared in the sky for twelve years. Which means…"

The two of them sat in silence.

"There's something I don't understand," Xiloxochitl finally spoke up. "The letter from your Clement."

"The Pontiff's letter, you mean?"

"Yes. He made reference to something that didn't make sense. He talked about 'understanding the means to make the divine corporeal,' which he asked if we could share with his representative, promising... You look pale, Jorge."

"Corporeal…"

"Is there some enemy facing you as were against us, that threatens to invade you too?"

Jorge suddenly shuddered physically with spasms. Xiloxochitl called to the camp for help, but as they reached her, he was able to speak.

"God forgive us all," Jorge finally said. "I never would have…"

"What? What's the matter?"

"The enemies. It's not from without. The Germans who follow the heretic Luther. The Germans who sacked Rome, who turned their back on the Pope. There was even talk of Henry of England being tempted into dissent before I left. It all makes sense now, a horrible, horrible sense."

"We called our god to come to us," Xiloxochitl said as she understood, "and he wants to be able to call his to him…"

———

JORGE DID NOT SLEEP that last night.

He prayed, hard, deep. He took no rest until the first purples of sunrise started to streak the sky.

He rose from his room and headed for the main pyramid.

Every step on the way up, he would stop and repeat the same admonition the Sainted Francis made in his letters:

And you should desire that things be this way and not otherwise. And let this be an expression of true obedience to the Lord God and to me, for I know full well that this is true obedience. And love those who do these things to you. And do not expect anything different from them, unless it is something which the Lord shall have given to you. And love them in this and do not wish that they be better Christians.

And he continued up the steps, proclaiming this on each one, as he went up.

He was preparing himself for his next conversation with god on earth…

JAMES RYAN (HE/HIM) has published the novels Raging Gail *and* Red Jenny and the Pirates Of Buffalo, *a collection of stories from Rooftop Sessions entitled* Alt Together Now, *and the monograph* The Pirates of New York. *His forthcoming novel* Statues to Silence *will be published soon by Golden Story-line Press. His work has also appeared in the anthologies* Gabba Gabba Hey!, Trees, The Fans are Buried Tales, Conspiracies and Cryptids Volume I, *and* Ruth and Ann's Guide To Time Travel Volume I , *and the publications* Rebeat, Pyramid Online, Dragon, The Urbanite, Dream Zone, *and* Rational Magic. *His column "Fantasia Obscura" about obscure older sci-fi, fantasy, and horror films runs at* Forces of Geek. *His website is https://raginggail.wordpress.com/, and his Linktree is https://linktr.ee/jdanryan.*

CELESTIAL CRACK

RODNEY HATFIELD JR.

T he entire world was tilting their heads upward, staring at the sky. No one could quite wrap their head around what was happening, but the same question echoed in everyone's mind.

"WHAT IS THAT?"

As I lounged in the backyard with my wife and kids, our eyes were fixed on the moon. A prominent dark scar marred its surface. I craned my neck to the sky, feeling a mix of wonder and unease tightening my chest. The unknown loomed above us. My thoughts raced, grappling with the sheer magnitude of what lay before our eyes.

"What do you think it is, Dad?" my son asked, eyes wide with curiosity.

"I don't know," I replied, my voice tinged with the same uncertainty I felt. "But it's something big."

My wife shifted uneasily beside me. "Do you think it's dangerous?" she asked, her voice barely above a whisper.

"I hope not," I said, trying to sound reassuring. "But until we know more, it's hard to say."

Our daughter, always the inquisitive one, chimed in. "Maybe it's aliens! What if they're coming to visit us?"

I chuckled softly. "Well, if it is aliens, I hope they're friendly."

We sat in silence for a few moments, each of us lost in thought. The news and, of course, the internet were abuzz with various theories. Some folks speculated about a shift in the moon's plates caused by a moonquake, while others floated the idea of a secret Nazi moon base. Then there were those who entertained the notion of peculiar space debris.

"Can you believe people actually think it's a Nazi moon base?" my wife chuckled, trying to lighten the mood.

"I know, right?" I said. "People come up with the wildest theories."

"I heard someone on TV say it might be a giant alien ship," my son added.

My daughter giggled. "Or a moon monster!"

I smiled. "The giant turd theory is still my favorite."

"The giant turd theory?" my daughter giggled. "Really?"

"Yes, really," I said with a laugh. "People have some wild imaginations."

The whole situation had us all on the edge of our seats, eagerly awaiting more information. We sat together, our eyes still fixed on the moon, wondering what answers the next day would bring.

"Do you think the scientists will figure it out soon?" my son asked.

"I hope so," I replied. "They'll probably be working around the clock to get some answers."

My children are constantly bombarding me with questions, their wide eyes pleading for answers. "Daddy, is it dangerous? What is it?" they inquire anxiously.

I find myself repeatedly reassuring them, "It's just a moon worm, kiddos! It's harmless, merely lounging on the surface, scavenging for some space food."

I do my best to paint a whimsical picture for them, hoping to dispel any fears and replace them with a sense of wonder. The notion of a moon worm on a cosmic quest for sustenance seems to captivate their imaginations, and I'm relieved to see their anxious expressions transform into curiosity and amazement. Their laughter rings out, echoing in the night as we go through the routine once again. Each time, I would come up with the weirdest explanations.

"You know, I've been thinking. Maybe it's a moon bug with big old wings, with fuzzy antennae dangling about. It eats moonbeams and meteors."

I also suggest it's a moon canyon, moon pond, or meteor impact. At one point, I even declared it to be a fallen moon tree. It is a silly game, a parental practice to keep their worries at bay. We gather around the flickering flames of the fire pit in our backyard, a cozy haven beneath the vast night sky. As a family, we embark on the simple pleasures – roasting hotdogs over the open fire, crafting gooey s'mores, and simply soaking in the cool night air before the inevitable bedtime calls. These moments filled with laughter, warmth, and a touch of whimsy become cherished memories in the tapestry of our family life.

As the night wore on, we continued to watch the moon, its dark scar standing out starkly against the familiar surface. The more we looked, the more questions seemed to arise.

"Maybe it's just a shadow," my wife suggested, though she didn't sound convinced.

"Could be," I agreed, though I knew it was unlikely. "But it's a pretty strange shadow if it is."

Our daughter yawned and snuggled closer to her mother. "Whatever it is, I hope they tell us soon. It's kind of scary not knowing."

I nodded, wrapping an arm around her. "We'll find out soon enough. In the meantime, let's just keep hoping for the best."

"Do you think they'll tell us on the news tomorrow?" my son asked, his voice tinged with hope.

"Probably," I said. "They'll be working hard to get answers. Scientists, astronomers, everyone will be looking into it."

"What if it's something bad?" my daughter asked, her voice small.

"We'll handle it," I said firmly. "No matter what it is, we'll face it together."

We stayed outside a while longer, until the chill of the night air drove us indoors. But even then, the image of the scarred moon lingered in our minds, a mystery waiting to be solved.

THE NEXT MORNING, the first thing we did was turn on the news. Reporters were still speculating, experts were being interviewed, and everyone was eager for answers. My kids sat glued to the screen, their breakfast forgotten.

"Do you think they'll figure it out today, Dad?" my son asked, his eyes never leaving the TV.

"I hope so," I replied. "But these things take time. It might be a while before we know for sure."

My wife nodded. "In the meantime, we just have to be patient."

"Do you think it's aliens?" my daughter asked, her voice filled with wonder.

"Who knows?" I said with a smile. "But if it is, I'm sure we'll find out soon enough."

As the day went on, we continued to follow the news, eagerly waiting for any new information. The scar on the moon remained a topic of endless speculation and conversation, not just in our household, but all around the world.

In the evening, as we sat down for dinner, the topic came up again.

"Did you hear what the latest theory is?" my wife asked. "Some scientists think it might be a giant asteroid that hit the moon."

"Wow, really?" my son said, his eyes wide. "That would be so cool!"

"Or maybe it's a giant alien base," my daughter suggested, giggling.

I chuckled. "Well, whatever it is, we'll find out eventually."

After dinner, we went back outside to look at the moon again. The dark scar was still there, a mysterious mark on an otherwise familiar surface.

"It's still there," my son said, his voice filled with awe.

"Yeah," I said. "But remember, whatever it is, we'll face it together."

As the night went on, we continued to watch the moon, our imaginations running wild with possibilities. The scar on the moon had brought us closer together, giving us something to wonder about and discuss as a family.

"Do you think they'll have answers by tomorrow?" my daughter asked as we got ready for bed.

"Maybe," I said. "But even if they don't, we'll keep hoping for the best."

We turned off the lights and lay in the darkness, the image of the scarred moon still fresh in our minds. It was a mystery waiting to be solved, and we were all eager to see what the next day would bring.

ROUGHLY TWO DAYS had gone by since the perplexing celestial incident, playfully labeled "moon-poo" by humanity. Leave it to us humans to take a momentous occurrence and infuse it with a touch of humor, even if it's in the form of a poo joke. In the face of the inexplicable, sometimes humor becomes our way of grappling with the unknown, offering a lighthearted perspective on what might otherwise be a perplexing situation. Curiously, there had been a conspicuous lack of official information from our government or NASA about the nature of this lunar phenomenon. Fortunately, one need not be a NASA insider to snag a decent snapshot of the moon.

The days following the celestial spectacle unfolded like a cosmic puzzle, each passing moment offering new enigmas and revelations. People from all walks of life gathered in impromptu moon-gazing parties, telescopes and cameras in hand, capturing every conceivable angle of the moon's peculiar blemish. Social media overflowed with an eclectic mix of lunar observations, ranging from awe-inspired poetry to comical memes featuring moon worms clad in space helmets. As the moon continued to hold its enigmatic secret close, a wave of lunar-themed merchandise flooded the market. Moon worm plush toys, lunar-themed board games, and even "moon-poo" merchandise adorned the shelves of stores, turning the mysterious event into a pop culture phenomenon. It was as if the entire world had embraced the absurdity of the situation, finding solace in humor amid the uncertainty.

In the midst of this lunar fervor, my family and I found ourselves attending a local moon festival. The community-organized event featured moon-themed decorations, games, and even a contest for the most creative moon-inspired costume. My children, wide-eyed and filled with infectious enthusiasm, insisted on dressing up as space explorers, armed with makeshift telescopes fashioned from cardboard tubes.

"Look, Dad! I'm an astronaut!" my son exclaimed, holding his cardboard telescope up to his eye.

"You sure are, buddy," I replied, smiling at his excitement.

As we navigated through the festival grounds, we encountered fellow moon enthusiasts sharing their own whimsical theories about the lunar anomaly. From the imaginative tales of a moon wizard casting spells to the playful notion of an intergalactic game of celestial tic-tac-toe, the creativity of human minds seemed boundless.

"I heard it's a moon wizard," a man dressed as an alien said to his friend.

"A moon wizard?" his friend laughed. "That's a good one. I was thinking it's an intergalactic tic-tac-toe game."

Laughter echoed through the air as families, friends, and strangers alike reveled in the shared experience of embracing the unknown with a spirit of lighthearted curiosity.

"My kids think it's a moon bug," I said, joining the conversation.

"That's a great one," the alien man said, chuckling. "I think my favorite theory so far is the moon worm."

"Yeah, that one is pretty popular," I agreed.

Amid the festivities and merriment, a subtle under-current of anticipation lingered. The absence of official information fueled a collective yearning for clarity. It seemed as if the entire world held its breath as it waited for the experts to unravel the mystery that hung in the night sky. It cast a surreal glow over our lives.

"Do you think they'll tell us what it is soon?" my daughter asked, her eyes wide with curiosity.

"I hope so," I said, kneeling down to her level. "But sometimes these things take time. Scientists need to make sure they have all the facts before they can tell us anything."

She nodded, her face serious. "I just want to know what it is."

"We all do," I said, giving her a reassuring hug. "But in the meantime, we can enjoy the fun of guessing."

And so, we continued to gaze at the moon, our ques-tions lingering like echoes in the cosmic expanse, as we navigated the uncharted territory of this extraordinary lunar phenomenon. The festival continued around us, a celebration of human curiosity and the enduring mystery of the universe.

As night fell, we gathered with other families around a large bonfire, the flickering flames casting a warm glow on our faces. Stories were shared, songs were sung, and the sense of community was palpable.

"Remember when people thought the moon was made of cheese?" someone joked, eliciting a round of laughter.

"Yeah, and now we have moon-poo," another person quipped.

Despite the humor, there was a shared sense of wonder and anticipation. What could the scar on the moon mean? What secrets did it hold? The lack of answers only fueled our imaginations further.

"I bet it's a sign," an elderly woman said, her voice carrying a hint of wisdom. "Something big is coming."

"What kind of sign?" a young boy asked, his eyes wide with fascination.

"Who knows?" she replied, smiling mysteriously. "But whatever it is, we'll face it together."

As the festival wound down and we made our way home, I couldn't help but feel a sense of unity. Despite the uncertainty, we were all in this together, sharing our hopes, fears, and dreams under the same enigmatic moon.

Back home, I tucked my children in and went to bed. As I lay in bed staring out the window at the moon, I felt a deep sense of connection. The moon, with its mysterious scar, had brought us all together, reminding us of the vastness of the universe and the boundless potential of human curiosity. We didn't have all the answers yet, but we had each other, and there was a kind of magic in that.

Finally, NASA came forward, it turns out that the moon-poo-worm is, in fact, a significant crack etched into the lunar surface. This canyon, stretching across the moon's expanse, is colossal. With some basic measurements, it becomes apparent that not only is the surface disrupted, but the distinctive shape and circumference of the moon has become disstorted. Many speculated that it might be the result of a meteor impact, given the visible damage. However, this hypothesis was swiftly dismissed as there was no evidence of space debris, and NASA reported no detection of any meteors capable of causing such extensive lunar harm. The mystery deepens as the moon reveals a side that defies conventional explanations.

Days passed, and the enigmatic crack on the moon grew larger and larger. While the naked eye struggled to detect the change, a telescope revealed the gradual expansion. Many of us remained blissfully unaware of any issue, and I'm uncertain if NASA was aware of the unfolding anomaly. That is until the moon experienced a cataclysmic break up in real time. It took one observant person to bring attention to the sky, and suddenly everyone was gazing upward, witnessing the horrifying spectacle. As I stood outside, the TV inside relayed the unfolding events, describing what NASA had uncovered. The air was thick with tension as the moon, a constant and comforting presence in our night sky, underwent a transformation that none of us could have anticipated. The description of the discovery traveled through the air, blending with the surreal visual of the celestial breakup, leaving us all in a state of shock and awe.

The passing days seemed to stretch into an eternity as the lunar drama unfolded. The crack, initially a subtle aberration, now dominated the night sky, casting an eerie glow that replaced the once-familiar face of the moon. Telescopes were trained on the celestial event, capturing the intricacies of the moon's disintegration in agonizing detail. Conversations buzzed with speculation, fear, and a sense of the unknown. What was once a distant, serene orb in the sky had become a cosmic canvas, depicting the fragility of celestial bodies. As the news spread, the world collectively held its breath. NASA, thrust into the spotlight, scrambled to provide explanations for this unprecedented lunar catastrophe. The airwaves crackled with updates, scientific analyses, and somber reflections on the significance of the event. The moon, a symbol of constancy and beauty, was now a fractured relic, a haunting reminder of the unpredictable nature of the cosmos.

The emotional weight of the situation hung heavy in the air, a palpable mix of sorrow and disbelief. Families gathered, eyes glued to screens, as the moon underwent a metamorphosis that transcended the boundaries of our understanding. Children asked questions that had no easy answers, and adults grappled with the profound implications of a shattered moon. The once-unassuming crack had become a chasm, a cosmic wound that exposed the vulnerability of the celestial bodies we had long taken for granted. The world watched as the moon, in its broken state, became a symbol of the impermanence woven into the fabric of the universe. The description of the discovery traveled through the air, blending with the surreal visual of the celestial breakup, leaving us all in a state of shock and awe.

A shared revelation reverberated worldwide, dismantling our prior comprehension. "We were wrong; it wasn't a moon. IT WAS AN EGG."

The global realization marked a turning point, challenging our assumptions about the celestial bodies that have adorned our night sky for eons. The world held its breath as an unprecedented spectacle unfolded before our eyes. From the remnants of the shattered moon-egg emerged a creature of mythical proportions — a dragon, majestic and awe-inspiring. The skies themselves seemed to resonate with astonishment as humanity grappled with the staggering reality of legendary beings manifesting in our midst. Each majestic beat of the dragon's wings left a trail of wonder and disbelief, as if the very fabric of reality was woven with threads of fantasy. Scientists found themselves in a frenzied pursuit of comprehending the profound implications of this extraordinary event, while the global community stood united in collective amazement.

As the dragon soared through the heavens, its presence became a living testament to the convergence of myth and reality. Its eyes, pools of ancient wisdom, gazed down upon the earth with a mix of curiosity and regality. The once-stable order of the cosmos had been irreversibly disrupted, heralding the advent of a new era — one where the boundaries between the extraordinary and the mundane became beautifully entwined in the tapestry of our everyday existence. Pandemonium seized the earth, an abyss of chaos unfurling in the wake of the moon's rupture, triggering a cascade of catastrophic events. An electromagnetic pulse (EMP) wave surged relentlessly across the globe, mercilessly wreaking havoc on our technological infrastructure. Cities plunged into darkness as power grids crumbled under the relentless assault.

Deprived of the moon's stabilizing force, tides rose with unchecked ferocity, inundating coastal areas and reshaping landscapes in a watery dance of destruction. Earthquakes echoed through the continents, their magnitude heightened by the upheaval in gravitational forces. The once-predictable cadence of nature now spiraled into a disorienting abyss of unpredictability, as the familiar patterns were replaced by disconcerting chaos. In the aftermath of this celestial disruption, humanity found itself thrust into a harsh reality, grappling with the profound repercussions of a world plunged into turmoil. The reliable comforts of modern life crumbled, and the very foundations of our existence trembled under the weight of cosmic upheaval. The absence of the moon, once a serene and unwavering presence, had birthed a maelstrom challenging the resilience of both nature and civilization.

Amid the turmoil, people confronted the harsh reality that the celestial order they had long taken for granted now lay shattered. Above them, the dragon born from the fractured moon-egg soared majestically, yet ominously, through the turbulent skies, a silent witness to the chaos it had unleashed. As humanity grappled with the repercussions of this cosmic upheaval, the world teetered on the precipice of a new and uncertain era. The familiar rhythms of existence shattered, replaced by an uncharted realm where the resilience of both nature and humanity would be tested in the crucible of celestial disorder.

Amid the bedlam, the dragon finally departed, leaving behind a once-dominant civilization to face a world plunged into chaos and uncertainty. The absence of the moon had unleashed havoc on Earth's delicate balance, causing once-stable foundations to crumble like ancient ruins weathered by time. Scattered remnants of humanity now struggled to survive in a landscape reshaped by the celestial crack, grappling with the profound changes that had befallen their once-familiar world. The dragon's majestic departure lingered in the collective consciousness, becoming a symbol of both awe and foreboding. As the remnants of civilization sought to navigate the uncharted territory of a trans-formed Earth, the memory of the dragon's presence cast a shadow over their endeavors.

The skies, once a canvas for the moon's gentle glow, now held echoes of the mythical being's flight, a silent witness to the upheaval it had witnessed. In the after-math of the dragon's departure, the remnants of humanity faced the daunting task of rebuilding amid the ruins of their past. The celestial crack, now a permanent scar on the earth's surface, served as a constant reminder of the cosmic forces that had reshaped their existence. The struggle for survival unfolded against a backdrop of uncertainty, as those who remained sought to adapt to the harsh realities of a world forever altered by the absence of the moon and the enigmatic presence of the dragon.

In the absence of the dragon, survivors found them-selves thrust into a harsh reality reminiscent of ancient times. The loss of advanced technology, courtesy of the EMP wave, compelled people to adapt to a simpler, more primitive way of life. Once-thriving cities now lay dormant, overgrown by nature as humanity returned to the fundamental principles of survival. Small groups emerged, each forging their own path in this altered world. Some embraced nomadic lifestyles, traversing the transformed landscapes, while others sought refuge in pockets of safety, forming tight-knit communities. The knowledge that had once been meticulously stored in digital archives and advanced libraries was now passed down through oral traditions and rudimentary written records.

The survivors faced the daunting challenge of rebuilding not only their physical surroundings, but also the intricate web of human civilization. In the quietude of abandoned cities, whispers of a bygone era lingered, carried by the wind through crumbling buildings and overgrown streets. Nature, once held at bay by concrete and steel, asserted its dominance over the remnants of human ingenuity. Amid this primal landscape, a tapestry of new stories began to unfold. Nomadic groups, once strangers to the land, became adept at reading the signs of the altered terrain, honing survival skills that transcended the conveniences of the past. Tight-knit communities, fortified by necessity, worked together to cultivate the land, rediscovering the ancient art of agriculture.

As the survivors adapted to this simpler way of life, a profound transformation occurred within the collective consciousness. The ephemeral glow of screens was replaced by the warm light of communal fires. Oral storytellers became the custodians of knowledge, weaving tales of the world that was, passing down wisdom from one generation to the next. In the absence of the dragon, the survivors embarked on a journey of rediscovery, uncovering the resilience ingrained in the human spirit. The remnants of advanced technology became artifacts of a distant past, and the survivors learned to thrive in harmony with the reshaped Earth. As they ventured into the unknown, a new narrative unfolded — one where the strength of community, the wisdom of tradition, and the simplicity of survival formed the backbone of a world reborn from the ashes of a once-dominant civilization.

Above, the shattered remnants of the moon drifted aimlessly in space, a poignant reminder of the cataclysmic event that had reshaped their world. The cosmic debris served as silent witnesses to the upheaval that had altered the very fabric of their existence. As the remnants of the celestial body floated in the void, they cast an ethereal glow against the backdrop of the cosmos, a haunting testament to the fragility of celestial bodies. The tides, no longer governed by the moon's gravitational pull, surged unpredictably, reshaping coastlines, and presenting the survivors with the constant challenge of adapting to ever-changing environments. Coastal settlements, once firmly established, found themselves on the frontline of this tidal dance, grappling with the ebb and flow of the now unpredictable seas. The survivors, attuned to the rhythm of the reshaped Earth, became adept at reading the signs of the ever-shifting tides, their lives intricately woven into the tapestry of the transformed landscapes.

As the remnants of humanity navigated this new, primal existence, they carried with them the memories of a bygone era, determined to carve out a future in the wake of celestial upheaval. The oral traditions and rudimentary records passed down through generations became the compass guiding them through the uncharted territory. The tales of the moon and the dragon, once mythical, now served as anchors in a world adrift. In the quiet moments beneath the unfamiliar constellations, survivors would gather around communal fires and share stories of the world that once was. The shattered moon above, a cosmic relic, became a symbol not only of loss but also of resilience. It stood as a constant reminder that from chaos, a new narrative could emerge—a narrative where humanity, stripped of the comforts of the past, forged a path forward with an indomitable spirit. And so, amid the cosmic echoes and the ever-changing tides, the survivors embraced their primal existence, recognizing that in the remnants of the shattered moon, there lay the potential for a future shaped by the collective resilience of those who dared to navigate the uncharted cosmos.

As the survivors ventured forward in this trans-formed world, they not only faced the challenges of nature, but also encountered the emergence of mythical creatures that had once existed only in the realms of folklore and myth. Strange and wondrous beasts now began appearing across the lands, a living testament to the shattered boundaries between reality and myth. Creatures of majestic proportions roamed the reshaped landscapes, their presence captivating and bewildering the survivors who had once believed them to be nothing more than the stuff of legends.

In this rediscovery of the Iron Age, humanity adapted to harness the resources of the altered Earth. The survivors honed their skills in crafting antique tools and weapons, embracing the craftsmanship of eras long past. They cultivated the land for sustenance, turning

the once-wild terrains into thriving pockets of agriculture. As the survivors delved into the arcane knowledge
passed down through generations, they learned to
coexist with the newfound mythical inhabitants and
navigated the intricate dance between survival and
harmony with these otherworldly beings. Forming
alliances became a crucial aspect of the survivors'
newfound existence. As communities adapted to the
presence of mythical creatures, they realized the importance of unity against both the unpredictable forces of
nature and the fantastical inhabitants that now shared
their world. Bonds forged in the crucible of adversity
became the bedrock of protection, as humanity stood
resilient in the face of challenges that transcended the
mundane and ventured into the extraordinary.

Though the dragon had departed, its ethereal presence lingered, woven into the fabric of the survivors'
stories and beliefs. The dragon became a symbol not
only of the cosmic upheaval that had birthed this new
and fantastical chapter in human history but also a
reminder of the potential for coexistence between the
mundane and the mythical. As the survivors navigated
the uncharted territories, the legacy of the dragon
became a guiding force, a testament to the indomitable
spirit that could arise from the remnants of a shattered
world.

*RODNEY HATFIELD JR. is a freelance writer from West Virginia,
known for his vivid storytelling and unique narrative voice. A
natural-born creator, Rodney began crafting stories even before he
learned how to read. This early start fueled a lifelong passion for
writing that has since blossomed into a diverse body of work.*

Rodney's background in freelance writing spans a range of genres, blending elements of suspense, mystery, and emotional depth. His stories often reflect the rawness and complexity of human nature, with a flair for the unexpected. Whether penning short stories, long-form fiction, or other creative pieces, his work consistently captivates audiences with its authenticity and intrigue.

THE COLLECTOR

KEITH J. HOSKINS

I *smell lunch.*

Phlogiston stirred from his age-old slumber, lifting his head with a deliberate grace. His cavernous nostrils widened, catching the alluring scent that permeated the air, rousing him from the depths of his winter repose within the heart of his mountain abode.

"Yes," murmured the ancient wyrm to himself, his voice a rumble like distant thunder. "The northern passage harbors an unexpected guest, drawing nearer with each passing moment. Oh, I do love it when food delivers itself."

In his youth, Phlogiston would have reveled in the chase, finding delight in the pursuit and the final, decisive strike. The thrill of the hunt, the scent of fear that preceded the kill—these were once his sustenance. But now, in the twilight of his days, he found solace in the simplicity of easy prey and the tranquility of slumber.

Phlogiston sniffed the air. "Closer it draws yet lacking in fear. Perhaps unaware that the mightiest of all dragons claims this mountain as his realm." He sniffed once again. "But there is something else… something familiar…"

The flickering light of a torch entered the cavern held aloft by a figure dressed in vibrant clothing. The visitor bore no armor, nor a weapon of any sort, only the torch that illuminated his path and a leather satchel that hung from his shoulder. Then again, Phlogiston's eyesight wasn't as keen as it once had been. He relied more on his nose than his eyes these days. The aroma from the visitor carried with it many scents, but not that of iron or steel from a weapon. "A fool or a wizard, perchance?"

"I am neither," the visitor retorted, catching the dragon off guard with his response. "Although the former is debatable."

Phlogiston's lips curled into a wry smile, a glimmer of amusement dancing in his age-old eyes. "It matters little, for your fate shall mirror that of the last interloper who dared to trespass upon my domain."

With a sinuous motion, the ancient dragon coiled his neck, preparing to unleash the fiery wrath that lay dormant within him. The glow of embers flickered to life along his scales as he readied himself to engulf the audacious intruder in a torrent of flame.

"Nor am I a thief," the man declared, holding up his hands in a desperate plea. "I come on behalf of King Oladel, bearing tidings of kingdom business."

Phlogiston paused, intrigued by the mention of the human king. "Kingdom business?"

"Yes, oh mighty one." The small human swallowed, his voice trembling. "My name is Jervis, a humble servant of the king."

Phlogiston emitted a disdainful snort. "Oladel, you

claim? What does the pitiful human king seek from me this time? A host of foes to be vanquished, mayhap?"

"No. Nothing so dire." Jervis stepped deeper into the cavern, his eyes taking in the enormity of the dragon's home, the hoard of treasures encompassing the dragon, and of course Phlogiston himself. "Actually, my visit is more of a bureaucratic nature."

"Explain yourself—and speak plainly; my patience wanes in these twilight years." Phlogiston's draconic visage drew nearer to the diminutive figure before him. His sinuous neck arched like a serpent, encircling the frail mortal.

"Very well." Jervis cleared his throat, his gaze tracing the serpentine movement of Phlogiston's head, wary of making any sudden movements. "The kingdom's coffers languish in the depths of poverty. It is the king's decree that every subject within his realm must offer a yearly tithe, proportional to the scale of their abode and the riches it harbors."

"Ha!" scoffed Phlogiston, his maw agape in incredulity. "You're a tax collector. A fool, indeed. Consuming you will now be twice as fulfilling."

"Before you do anything in haste," Jervis interjected, hands raised again, "you should be warned that my death will only anger the king."

"And why, pray tell, should his wrath concern me?" Phlogiston countered.

"Should I fail to return, another shall take my place, bearing the same decree. And if he, too, should vanish, the king shall unleash his legions."

"Legions?" Phlogiston pondered, a glint of amusement twinkling in his eyes. "I have quelled many such hosts, feeble men upon their steeds. Their flesh kindled by my breath, their ashes my repast. Your king invites them to my banquet."

"Yet the king's new army bears an uncommon potency, unknown to most," Jervis cautioned, edging further into the dragon's lair.

"And how so?" Phlogiston inquired.

"King Oladel charged his sorcerers with crafting a spell of dreadful might, devised to sunder even the mightiest of dragons. All have failed, save one. A spell long forgotten, ensconced within a tome of ancient sorcery believed lost in the annals of time. Its name: Dragon's Bane."

Phlogiston peered intently at the tax collector. "The book and spell are a myth, whispers of legend told in tall tales about the spell that imbues weapons with the power and might to inflict unnatural damage unto dragons."

"Alas," countered the tax collector, his tone solemn, "the truth is far more grim. The king's high wizard now possesses this book and has practiced the spell. Be it arrow, blade, or spear, each strike fueled by this enchantment assures certain doom for any dragon."

"So, you come to me with threats, tax collector?" Phlogiston brought himself up to his full height and peered down at the diminutive human. The orange glow increased beneath his scales.

Jervis retreated a few paces. "Not at all, oh mighty one. A simple warning is all. None within the realm seek conflict with you. There's been enough death and destruction these past decades, we don't need any more. We have brokered peace with our neighboring kingdoms, and I'm certain that all wish to remain amicable with you."

Phlogiston lowered his head to within a few feet of Jervis's. The dragon inhaled deeply, taking in the myriad of scents lifted from the human.

There was now fear—not too much, but it was unmistakably there. The scent of honeysuckle, possibly from a female companion. The smell of various fruits and meats, most likely lingering from a recent meal. And yet, amid the symphony of odors, there was a notable absence—the acrid stench of a lie. Either this human was an artisan of deceit, or he spoke truthfully. Yet, there remained a lingering scent, a tantalizing familiarity that eluded Phlogiston's grasp. As a precaution, Phlogiston readied the tip of his mighty tail by slipping its clandestine spot.

"I assure you, illustrious dragon," said Jervis, "I speak the truth."

Phlogiston withdrew his head. "Truth, like a river, may twist and turn with the shifting of stones. Your verity and mine may diverge upon the currents of perception." The dragon paused to draw upon his ancient wisdom. "Let us suppose, tax collector, that I am inclined to accept your words as honest. What then does your king propose?"

"It falls upon me to gauge the wealth amassed within your domain and to estimate the worth of your holdings," replied Jervis."

"And how do you intend to accomplish such a task?"

Jervis cast his torchlight across the expanse of the lair, where golden treasures and sparkling jewels lay strewn like stars in the night sky. "Your wealth is indeed vast. The tax imposed upon you would be considerable, I suspect. I presume you maintain no ledger of your riches."

Phlogiston huffed, and smoke trumpeted from his nostrils.

"I thought as much." Jervis continued, his eyes tracing the heights of the cavern. "Truly, your hoard is magnificent. If I may be so bold as to pose a question?"

"You may ask," said Phlogiston. "However, be warned that your question may be marked with your final breath."

"Why do dragons covet treasures so? It's not as if you travel to the market to buy food and supplies. You have no need for garments or tools. What purpose does such wealth serve to a creature such as yourself?"

"Ah, the riddle of ages," mused Phlogiston. "Many would deem it sheer avarice, while others might conjecture it serves as a gauntlet, inviting challengers to test one's might. Yet for me, it stands as a testament to my triumphs. Each plunder and foe vanquished finds its place within these halls. Here lies the chronicle of my conquests, etched in gold and gemstones within this dormant volcano. Each and every victory is etched in my mind."

"Well, it is indeed a sight to behold," conceded Jervis, his eyes scanning the complex expanse of treasure. "Yet surely, even the keenest eye could not discern the entirety of such a hoard? The wealth is scattered, a chaos to my eyes."

"To you, perhaps," retorted Phlogiston, his gaze unwavering. "But to me, each trinket holds its place as ordained by fate."

"If so, then tell me, what of this?" Jervis posed, placing his torch in a sconce before approaching a towering statue crafted from gleaming gold, depicting a woman armed with a bow. The figure was surrounded by an array of artifacts and riches.

"That," answered Phlogiston with a rumble, "is a likeness of the goddess Florentia, wrought in purest gold. It was claimed upon my victory over the elven city of Olf Serin."

Jervis pressed on, traversing the winding path amid the treasures. "And this?" he queried, halting beside a sword with a jewel-encrusted hilt.

"The sword of Lord Derhan, ruler of Sheydor," Phlogiston recounted. "He bested a throng of goblins before I finally defeated him. As skilled as he was, his steel was no match for the fury of my flames."

Jervis nodded thoughtfully, his gaze sweeping over the treasures that bore witness to Phlogiston's storied past.

Jervis cast a wary glance to his left and right, then proceeded along a new path until he halted beside a battered suit of scale mail armor. Despite evident repairs, the armor bore the scars of fierce battle, a silent testament to its previous wearer's demise.

"And this... intriguing relic?" inquired Jervis, his curiosity piqued.

"Ah, one of my greatest triumphs: The Battle of The Spiraling Tower. The armor belonged to Tyromane the Frost King, a formidable mage whose spells of ice and snow were quite a challenge for my fire. But, as you can see, the superior fighter came out victorious."

"I've heard tales of that battle," Jervis said as he examined the beaten armor. "It's said that King Tyromane had long since been dead before your arrival."

"Nonsense. I confronted him atop the tower's

summit, where he wrought his frozen enchantments. What lies do you seek to sow, tax collector?"

"Not lies, merely tales," Jervis defended, his gaze still transfixed on the armor and all its pieces. "You see, legend has it that the king met his end from a sickness, and to keep fear instilled in the hearts of the kingdom's enemies, a surrogate was employed to maintain the illusion that the king still lived."

"Fabrications," scoffed Phlogiston. "He wielded the ice spells. I was almost defeated. It was the Frost King."

"He did indeed conjure those spells." The tax collector turned to face Phlogiston. "But he did so with this."

With a flourish, Jervis presented a foot-long stick marked with inscriptions and garnished with metallic bands.

A wizard's wand!

Phlogiston summoned his fire, poised to unleash devastation upon the mortal before him. Yet, with a swiftness born of desperation, Jervis flicked his wrist, conjuring a blast of ice and frost in the shape of a mighty sphere aimed squarely at Phlogiston's chest.

The magical ice ball exploded on the dragon, causing his inner fire to extinguish. But before Phlogiston could switch to a different attack, Jervis sent a flurry of ice balls his way.

The magical ice erupted upon the dragon, extinguishing his inner flame in an instant. Before Phlogiston could muster another assault, Jervis unleashed a barrage of icy projectiles, each finding its mark upon the dragon's claws, legs, and wings, rendering him immobile. As Phlogiston lunged forward, his mighty jaws agape, he found himself tumbling awkwardly to the ground, his intended prey now bearing a smirk devoid of fear.

Phlogiston struggled to move but found the only thing that remained unfazed by the ice was the tip of his tail, still tucked in its special place.

With a calculated calmness, Jervis addressed the subdued dragon, his voice carrying the weight of revelation. "Behold," he declared, brandishing the now-broken wand. "This very wand, concealed within the false king's armor, deceived even your mighty flames."

He held aloft the shattered remnants of the wand, its once-potent magic now fractured and spent. "After the king's demise and your assault upon the castle, his body, armor, and wand vanished without a trace. Many assumed them consumed by your fiery breath. Yet, as you see, mail such as this does not yield to mere flame. Some speculated that you devoured the false king, as is your custom, then made off with his treasures and the enchanted armor, the wand still concealed within its steel."

"So, you are but a common thief," Phlogiston accused.

"No," said Jervis. "I am an exceptional thief. As was my father before me. And it was he who regaled me with tales of your exploits, including the Battle of the Spiraling Tower. I knew if I could somehow get into your lair and find the Frost King's armor, the wand would still be secured inside. Fortunately, I was right. As I usually am."

"The wand is now but a shattered relic," said Phlogiston, "and these feeble ice spells shall soon lose their grasp. You shan't reach the passage in time, for I shall reduce you to ash, as I have countless others."

Jervis cast a rueful glance at the twisted wand in his grasp. "I was fortunate to unleash what magic I could, lacking mastery as I do." With a dismissive gesture, he cast the broken wand to the ground and began retracing his steps.

"Yet now, I must attend to my true purpose here." Jervis made his way back to the sword, the object of his initial inquiry. With a firm grip, he claimed the weapon, along with the pavis shield that leaned nearby.

"You see, Lord Derhan was my great-grandfather," Jervis revealed. "When you killed him, and his sword and shield were lost, our realm fell into disarray and is now a sprawling land of poverty, thieves, and chaos. When I return with these, and as the rightful heir to rule our land, I'll unite the people and make us the prosperous and respected country we once were. Sheydor shall rise anew."

"A touching tale," Phlogiston remarked, a hint of skepticism in his tone. "But is it true?"

"Not a word. But to the desperate citizens of Sheydor, it will soon be a miraculous fact, a beacon of hope, if you will.

"As I near freedom from these spells, your end draws near," Phlogiston warned, his patience waning. "Little else shall be achieved this day."

"You underestimate me, foolish dragon," Jervis said, his movements deliberate as he set down the sword and unveiled a cloak of embossed red velvet from his satchel. "Do you know what this is?"

"Allow me to guess. A cloak of invisibility."

"Hardly. Much too difficult to acquire, and invisibility spells don't always work with dragons. No, this is something else, something far more cunning."

Jervis donned the cloak, its rich fabric cascading over his form like a shroud of secrecy. Yet, to Phlogiston's surprise, no enchantment seemed to take hold. Undeterred, Jervis stooped to retrieve the sword, his smirk remaining a thorn in the dragon's side.

Phlogiston assumed the cloak's spell had failed, but Jervis's grin persisted. The dragon tested his limbs; they moved just inches, but that was a start.

"Time dwindles, *tax collector*."

Jervis chuckled at the jab. "Well, I am a collector, of sorts, albeit of a different sort. As the head of the thieves guild, I've amassed quite a fortune and a trove of rare artifacts, including this cloak."

"Which seems to have failed you."

"Has it, though?" Jervis smiled and gave a wink.

With a deft motion, Jervis snapped his finger and said, "Twenty." In an instant, a score of men materialized out of the shadows, each bearing the same cloak, sword, and shield as Jervis himself. Phlogiston strained against his bindings, attempting to discern the truth of this newfound illusion.

"What is this trickery?" Phlogiston demanded. His frustration mounted as he struggled against the spells that held him captive. Despite his efforts, he could conjure naught but a feeble warmth within his chest.

"Do you like it?" said Jervis. "This is a cloak of multiplicity. It cost me a small fortune to obtain, but it was well worth it."

Phlogiston surveyed the duplicates, noting with astonishment that each moved with a will of its own, independent of the others. But before he could fully comprehend the extent of Jervis's machinations, the thief snapped his fingers once more.

"Fifty." Jervis declared, and with another flourish, even more duplicates emerged, scattering throughout the lair like phantoms of mischief. Some offered teasing waves to the dragon, while others roamed aimlessly or rifled through the troves of treasure, each a testament to Jervis's mastery of deceit.

"One hundred."

In an instant, the lair teemed with scores of his duplicates. Phlogiston, disoriented amid the sea of replicas, sought the true thief but found himself ensnared in confusion.

"Looking for me?"

The dragon looked down and standing in his shadow was Jervis. Phlogiston quickly chomped down on the careless human only to find he had bitten the golden statue of Florentia. Enraged, he spat the statue out, launching it across the lair and onto a pile of gold where a pair of duplicates stood. They sidestepped the statue and shook their fists at Phlogiston.

"Come forward, coward," Phlogiston yelled. "Take up that sword and shield and face me as a warrior."

"First," came Jervis's disembodied voice, "I am no warrior. I'm a collector. And the future ruler of Sheydor. And second, I am no fool. As for now, I bid thee farewell."

Phlogiston watched the duplicates as they taunted and teased him. A few were at the entrance to the north passage beckoning him to follow. Some waved their swords in a provoking manner, while others yelled insults, daring the dragon to chase them.

Then, Phlogiston felt something hit his tail.

"Got you."

He flicked his tail, the only thing not affected by

the ice spells. There was a scream and Jervis—the real one—came flying out of the hidden south tunnel entrance.

Just then, the ice spells gave way, and Phlogiston turned on the tumbling thief, grabbed him with one of his massive claws, and tore the cloak away with the other.

Immediately, the Jervis duplicates disappeared, leaving the stunned thief alone in Phlogiston's grasp.

"What happened?" Jervis asked. "How did you—"

"My tail," said Phlogiston. "When I smelled you, there was a scent I couldn't quite place. So, as a precaution, I slipped my tail into an old lava tube to block the south entrance, which appears very few—mainly thieves —know about."

Jervis squirmed in the dragon's clutches, he now reeked of fear.

"But now … now I know where I recognize that scent. It's the same as your father's when he came to rob me not too long ago. But do you know what I smell now?"

Jervis stopped struggling and gave a resigning, "What?"

Phlogiston smiled as he ignited his inner fire.

"I smell lunch."

KEITH J. Hoskins is a short story author, award-winning poet, and founding member of the Bel Air Creative Writers Society. He has seven short stories in seven anthologies. He has released a collection of his short stories in his own anthology: Beyond the Portal, *and a trilogy of novellas in:* Forgotten. *Keith is currently working on his first novel:* Kray and the Coveted Seer, *a fantasy novel set in a magical world. Keith's main genres of interest are fantasy, science fiction, and thrillers.*

Born on January 5, 1968, Keith has always had a love of fiction from an early age. He attributes this to his mother who introduced him to TV shows like Star Trek and The Twilight Zone, as well as authors such as Ray Bradbury, Author C. Clarke, and Stephen King.

Though initially drawn to fantasy and science fiction, Keith has found that he has a talent for writing short stories, especially those with bizarre or twisted endings.

When he's not fighting off dragons or piloting a spaceship through an asteroid belt, Keith is most likely spending quality time at home in Aberdeen, Maryland with his wife Donna, his son Bailey, and their mischievous schnauzer Harley.

https://www.facebook.com/kjhoskins

ACKNOWLEDGMENTS

Our love for dragons in their various forms inspired this anthology. Having grown up on "Dragon Riders", it is very exciting to see so many diverse varieties appear in these stories. Thank you to all the authors!

Inkd Publishing would like to thank A. Balsamo for enthusiastically agreeing to edit this anthology.

Producing anthologies offers writers a chance to expose their creative work, and readers an opportunity to find new favorites. We rely on our Kickstarter supporters for helping to fund these publications.

Please join us in thanking the following backers for helping to make this anthology possible.

Billye Herndon, Chase McGlinchey, Ronald L Weston, Sarah Rogers, Erin Heiniger, Colleen Feeney, Zack Fissel, Kris Salter, Chip Houser, Amanda Eschmeyer, Nicholas Samuel Stember, Sohrab Rezvan, Samuel Eastwood, Craig Hackl, Lorna Hansmann, Anthony Cioffi, Michael Barbour, Ruth Ann Orlansky, Timothy Hansmann, Mary Jo Rabe, J9 Vaughn, Craig Rebmann, Connor Lehmann, Holly Turner, Bob Hansmann, Claus Appel, Kathy, Robert Baruch, KLGaffney, Kim Baldwin, Carla Bermudez, Crystal_Lilly, Grace, Louiz, TonyTone, Samantha Adams, Charles Mulloy, Alexandra Corrsin, Meshi S, and Razie Rayne

TUCKERIZATION

Samantha Adams offered her middle name La'akeanonalani, or La'akea for short in A Foolhardy Rescue by Kevin A Davis

Thank you for your support!

We'd like to thank L.N. Hunter for tuckering his story, *Reactor*, with Benson Strickland's name.

ALSO BY INKD PUB

Hidden Villains

Hidden Villains: Arise

Noncorporeal

Behind the Shadows

Hidden Villains: Betrayed

Detectives, Sleuths, & Nosy Neighbors

Noncorporeal II

Behind the Shadows II

Impulse

Yay! all queer

Please visit us at InkdPub.com or Facebook.

www.ingramcontent.com/pod-product-compliance
Ingram Content Group UK Ltd.
Pitfield, Milton Keynes, MK11 3LW, UK
UKHW030925050225
454656UK00001B/10

9 798230 192107